"WHAT'S THIS? DO I HEAR A LITTLE SONGBIRD?"

At the sound of a man's voice, Sadie jumped up, causing her foot to slip so it slid partially into the water. The only thing that stopped her from falling headfirst into the stream was her quick reflexes. Putting out her hand, she grabbed onto an overhanging branch and steadied herself, trying to regain her balance.

"Are you all right?"

Sadie turned around and found herself face-to-face with a young man. "Oh!" She almost stepped backward again, but this time, he reached out to stop her, gently grabbing her by the elbow.

"Careful now there! You'll be a wet songbird in a second if you're not more careful."

One look at the man and she knew that he, too, was Amish. His plain dress and the straw hat he wore made that obvious. His thick brown hair, curly at the edges, poked out from beneath the hat's brim and his big hazel eyes stared down on her.

"You frightened me," she gasped as she removed her arm from his grasp.

"My apologies," he said as he moved away from her, allowing her to relax a bit. "I didn't mean to startle you." When he smiled, his teeth were white and his face was pleasantly kind. "You can imagine my surprise to stumble upon such a sight. I've walked this way many times on my way back from my cousins' *haus* to Echo Creek and this is the first time I've ever seen another soul out here." He tilted his head. "And such a pretty one at that, not to mention your beautiful voice."

Also by Sarah Price

Belle: An Amish Retelling of Beauty and the Beast

Ella: An Amish Retelling of Cinderella

Published by Kensington Publishing Corporation

SADIE

An Amish Retelling of Snow White

SARAH PRICE

ZEBRA BOOKS
KENSINGTON PUBLISHING CORP.
http://www.kensingtonbooks.com

ZEBRA BOOKS are published by

Kensington Publishing Corp.
119 West 40th Street
New York, NY 10018

All Kensington titles, imprints, and distributed lines are available at special quantity discounts for bulk purchases for sales promotion, premiums, fund-raising, educational, or institutional use.

Special book excerpts or customized printings can also be created to fit specific needs. For details, write or phone the office of the Kensington Sales Manager: Attn.: Sales Department. Kensington Publishing Corp., 119 West 40th Street, New York, NY 10018. Phone: 1-800-221-2647.

First Printing: October 2018
ISBN-13: 978-1-4201-4508-3
ISBN-10: 1-4201-4508-8

eISBN-13: 978-1-4201-4509-0
eISBN-10: 1-4201-4509-6

10 9 8 7 6 5 4 3 2 1

Printed in the United States of America

Prologue

Outside the sitting room window, the snow fell like fluffy wisps of cotton, covering the fields in a blanket of white. The dusty lane that led to the farmhouse slowly disappeared as Sarah Whitaker stared out the frosty panes of glass, one hand on her enlarged belly and the other holding small yellow squares of fabric. She knew that she should be focusing on the quilted baby blanket and not on the weather. It was *almost* finished. But the beauty of the winter's first snowfall kept her mesmerized instead.

Perhaps it was the pregnancy that made her so emotional. Or maybe it was the good fortune that had befallen her during the past twelve months. Regardless, she felt the sting of happy tears in her eyes, and she lifted one hand to wipe them away with her fingers.

"Sarah?"

At the sound of her name, she turned from the window and smiled as her husband walked toward her. He was a large man, taller than most of the Amish in Echo Creek. And his dark beard was finally filling in. Gone was the patchiness of his newly grown beard, replaced with a nice, full set of thick whiskers that covered his strong jawline.

He crossed the room, passing through the small kitchen and into the open sitting room, which still smelled like fresh paint and newly varnished wood. Kneeling before her, he reached for her hand and searched her face.

Sarah shivered at his touch.

"You cold?" he asked, his bright blue eyes filled with concern.

"*Nee*," she whispered, and she gave his hand a gentle squeeze. "The fire's keeping the room warm enough, but *danke*, Jacob."

He didn't look convinced. "I can fetch more wood."

Sarah laughed softly. "I'm fine. I promise."

Such a gut *husband,* she thought. How had she ever managed to win his heart and hand? During her *rum-schpringe*, many of the young women in Echo Creek had been eager to ride home in Jacob Whitaker's buggy. Some-how, however, Sarah had been the one to catch his eye, mayhaps at worship service just prior to her turning sixteen, for, at only the second youth singing she had attended, he had laid claim to her.

It was during one of the breaks, when the songs were put on hold so the young people could get a cool drink of lemonade, that Jacob had sent his older brother, John, to where Sarah was standing with her friends in the far corner of the barn. A nervous John shuffled his feet as he approached them, then quietly asked Sarah if she'd con-sider riding home with Jacob in his buggy.

That was just the way things were done in Echo Creek.

And, with a blush on her cheeks and her eyes focused on the hay beneath her bare feet, Sarah had said yes.

"How's the baby?" Jacob asked. He hesitated before he reached out and placed his large hand on her stomach.

Sarah covered his hand with her own. There were so many things about Jacob that she loved. The tender way in which he handled her was just one of them. He treated her like a precious figurine, always so gentle. It was almost as if he felt she might break under his strong touch. And he was a strong man at that. Most Amish farmers were.

"She's doing just fine," Sarah teased.

He raised an eyebrow. "She?"

Sarah nodded her head. "*Ja*, she."

Jacob tried to hide his smile. She could see that by the way the corners of his lips twitched. "Might be nice to start off with a boy, don't you think?"

"There'll be plenty of time for boys, Jacob," Sarah said in a soft voice. "But I long so much for a *dochder*, someone who can help me raise our sons and keep me company when I bake bread and can vegetables. A little girl who I can teach to sew and quilt." She glanced down at the nearly finished baby blanket.

He leaned forward and lifted her hand to kiss it. But as he did so, the fabric shifted, and Sarah felt the pinch of the sewing needle. "Ouch!" Instinctively, she dropped the blanket and brought her hand toward her mouth so she could suck on the top of her thumb where the needle had pierced her skin.

A look of horror crossed his face. "Did I do that?"

But Sarah merely shook her head. "It's one of the many dangers a woman faces when she quilts a blanket, I'm afraid," she teased. "Bound to happen again, too, so don't you fret none, Jacob."

Jacob, however, barely heard a word she said. Or, if he had heard, he hadn't been listening. Instead, he hurried across the room and made his way to the kitchen sink. With amusement, Sarah followed him with her eyes, then watched as he took a clean dishcloth from the drawer, ran water over it, and hurried back to her side.

"You're bleeding," he said as he pulled her hand away from her mouth. Pressing the cloth to her finger, he shook his head. "I'm so clumsy sometimes," he lamented under his breath.

Sarah responded by placing her free hand under his chin, then gently guiding him so she could look in his eyes. "*Nee*, Jacob. You are the kindest of men. And I can only hope that our *dochder* is just like you."

Despite the worried look on his face, he gave her a soft smile.

"She'll have your dark hair and lively blue eyes," Sarah continued in a wistful manner as she slowly turned to gaze out the window. "And pretty porcelain skin the color of freshly fallen snow."

At this comment, Jacob chuckled and his concern over having hurt his wife slowly disappeared. "Then you'd best give me some sons soon after. We wouldn't want your little princess to have to help much when it comes to harvesting the fields."

Sarah shook her head. "Oh no! No field work for her. We can't have her porcelain skin getting all tanned and freckled, can we now?"

This time, Jacob laughed. "A spoiled Amish girl? I don't think that would sit well with many people in Echo Creek. Nor will it help her land her own husband one day."

"*Nee*, not spoiled!" Sarah made a face at him and shook her head. "That would never do, Jacob Whitaker!" Her expression softened. "*Nee*, our *dochder* will be hardworking, all right, but she'll help me in the house while your many sons help you in the fields."

Jacob glanced down at her hand. "Looks like it stopped bleeding." His eyes traveled to the window that Sarah was still gazing through. "And the snow's sure falling harder." He gave a reluctant sigh. "Reckon I best be settling the livestock down for the evening, then."

He leaned over and placed a soft kiss upon her forehead. Sarah shut her eyes, savoring the moment. When he pulled away, she took a deep breath and prayed her thankfulness to

God for having seen fit to grant her a place in Jacob's heart. She also prayed her gratitude to God for allowing her to conceive so soon after her and Jacob's spring wedding. As she laid both palms on her swollen belly, she could hardly believe how God's goodness had blessed them both in these ten short months. And lastly, she prayed her hope to God for the health of her unborn child.

"One *dochder*," she whispered when she finally opened her eyes. "Just one, God. And then a whole houseful of boys for Jacob."

Oh yes. Sarah could envision her daughter, a smaller and more petite version of Jacob. Yes, she'd have dark hair like his and fair skin, as white and unblemished as freshly fallen snow. Sarah glanced at her thumb and noticed a small bead of dried red blood on the spot where the needle had pierced her skin. The color reminded her of Jacob's red lips, which, when he smiled, lit up her heart. Yes, her *dochder* would surely have those, too.

Outside the window, Sarah watched Jacob's tall, lean figure, hunched over to protect himself from the blowing wind, as he made his way across the front yard and headed toward the dairy barn. The snow was falling faster now, just as Jacob had predicted a few minutes earlier.

Without a radio or television, the Amish had no way of knowing how much snow was expected. But Sarah didn't care. There was enough food in the pantry to last them for days, if not weeks. They had no need to leave the small farm outside of Echo Creek, and with the baby not due for another six weeks, Sarah had no fears or worries.

As long as she had Jacob, she knew she would always be taken care of, and so would their child, regardless of whether it was a son or a daughter. Of that, Sarah was sure and certain.

Chapter One

There was nothing in the world that made Sadie happier than being outside among the dairy cows. How she loved to sit on the large, flat rock near the stream, listening to the herd as the animals grazed in her father's pasture, chewing on the last remnants of summer's sweet grass or stepping into the stream to take a long drink of the cool water.

Overhead, the sky was clear, and it seemed as if the birds were singing their praise for the perfect weather. God had surely blessed this day. Sadie watched as they flew from the nearby fields to the edge of the forest, then back to the stream to dip their beaks in the shallow pools by the water's edge.

Sadie pulled her knees up, pressing them against her chest, then wrapped her arms around them. Her dark blue dress covered her legs but her toes poked out from beneath the tattered hem. She wiggled them, loving the way the smooth rock felt against the bottom of her bare feet.

In a few weeks it would be autumn, and, with that, the colder weather would soon descend on Echo Creek. She'd have to wear a wool sweater and shoes whenever she escaped the farmhouse to sit among the fields and spend time with the animals. She loved being there, listening to the water as it babbled along its journey, hearing the birds sing and watching the black-and-white cows graze among the last of summer's wildflowers.

A sigh escaped her ruby red lips and she let her arms drop from her knees. Leaning back, her palms pressed against the smooth rock, supporting her weight. Sadie shut her eyes and lifted her chin to the setting sun.

The rays fell upon her pale skin and she could feel the last remnants of their warmth as they danced across her face. She smiled to herself. Oh, how she enjoyed being outside, especially since it was on rare occasions that she managed to escape the many indoor chores of the farmhouse. Too often, she was stuck inside. There was always something that needed to be done besides the daily cleaning and cooking. Why, just the other day, she had spent all afternoon canning the last vegetables from their garden in preparation for the long winter ahead. And now that the days were getting shorter, there would be even less opportunity to spend time in the midst of nature.

That thought saddened her.

Winter was her least favorite season of the year, and not just because of the change in weather. Spending more time inside the house meant more time with her stepmother, Rachel. And, even though she loved her father dearly, sitting with him and her stepmother after the supper meal was her least favorite thing to do.

It wasn't that Sadie didn't love her stepmother the way she did her father. She did. However, ever since Sadie's father had married Rachel, the evenings had become the absolute worst time of the day.

Rachel seemed to enjoy nothing more than taking all of Jacob's attention. If Jacob asked Sadie a question, Rachel was always quick to answer for her, before changing the topic to one that interested *her*. And if Sadie did manage to sneak in an answer, Rachel always found a way to challenge or dismiss her.

Why, if Sadie claimed that the sky was blue, Rachel would find a way to turn even *that* around. It was almost as if Rachel intentionally tried to monopolize Jacob, and Sadie often wondered if Rachel felt threatened by the close father-daughter bond that she shared with her father.

Perhaps that was one of the reasons why Rachel seemed so intent on having her own babies.

Just three years prior, when she was thirty-three years old and Sadie just fifteen, Rachel had married Jacob. It had been an odd match, especially since Rachel wasn't from their small community of Echo Creek but from a neighboring sect several miles away.

Sadie vividly remembered when her father had told her that he would be taking a new wife.

"A mother for you," he had said, "and a wife to give me company when you are old enough to leave here and start your own family."

Sadie hadn't been upset. Instead, she had taken comfort in the thought that a young woman would give her father new life. It had been many years since her mother had passed away and it was time for Jacob to begin living again.

So, Sadie had welcomed Rachel with open arms.

But Jacob had been wrong. Rachel wasn't much of a mother to her. Perhaps it was because Sadie was already a young woman herself, being already fifteen and too old for Rachel to have much influence on her upbringing. But she certainly impacted Sadie's life in other ways.

In the beginning, she had been kind to Sadie and never spoke a harsh word to her. Instead, she tried her hardest to be Sadie's friend. She wanted them to do everything together: laundry, cleaning, cooking, even gardening, which was Sadie's favorite chore of all. It was the one chore that she looked forward to because she could commune with nature for hours on end. While she weeded, she loved to watch the bunnies as they tried to make their way under the fence to nibble a sweet lettuce leaf, or the chipmunk families that would dart between the rows of carrots and celery. Sadie knew all the little families by sight and even had funny names for some of them.

But there wasn't a day that passed when Rachel didn't mention one and only one thing: having her own children.

Rachel Whitaker was determined to give Jacob a large family. "Every man wants lots of *kinner*," she had said to Sadie one morning when she had shared her delight that she had skipped her monthly course. "I cannot wait to give him that gift which he truly desires," she announced while placing the palm of her hand on her stomach.

Sadie knew that Rachel wanted nothing more than to give Jacob a son. After all, who would inherit the farm if Jacob didn't have a son to pass it down to? It was most likely that Sadie would soon find a man worthy of her love. And, like most young Amish men, he would already have his future planned. It was unlikely that he would be willing to take over Jacob's farm.

However, God hadn't seen fit to give Rachel that gift. Not yet, anyway. Now that she was nearing thirty-seven, Rachel was becoming more and more despondent with each passing month.

And *that* made life all but unbearable for Sadie Whitaker.

"Sadie!"

She looked up when she heard her father calling her name. "Over here, Daed!"

Within a few minutes, her father made his way over the hill and, upon seeing her, smiled. "Why, there you are!" he said with a wink. "I should've known you would be here."

He knelt beside her, his knees cracking as he did so, and shielded his eyes as he stared across the stream. For three years, it had been just the two of them. When Sadie was twelve years old, her mother had died during childbirth.

She'd suffered four miscarriages in the years since Sadie's birth and the midwife had warned Sarah not to try for any more children. But, like her successor, she, too, was determined to give Jacob a healthy son. Her fifth, and final, pregnancy had ended with a stillborn boy, and Sarah passed away early the next morning.

Heartbroken, Jacob and Sadie spent the next three years trying to live as normal a life as possible. They developed a strong bond, perhaps stronger than that of most fathers and daughters. The first year hadn't been easy. But, with the help of their community, they seemed to get through the worst of it and eventually found a nice rhythm to things. Sadie would take care of the household chores while her father did the majority of the farmwork. The only time he used hired hands was during hay baling, which took place two to three times a year.

"What have you seen today?" her father asked as he glanced across the stream.

Sadie gave him a broad smile and began to count off on her fingers as she listed the creatures she had observed. "Two chipmunks, a field mouse, four sparrows, lots of nuthatches . . ." She paused and pointed to one that was splashing in a shallow eddy of water. "And a wild hare. Came close enough that I could almost have touched it."

Jacob laughed, his eyes twinkling. "I imagine you could have. Those woodland animals have never shown any fear toward you, my dear child."

She liked hearing her father laugh. It reminded her of the three years that they'd spent alone together before Rachel entered their lives. It wasn't that Rachel was an unpleasant woman. No, that wasn't it at all. But, in Sadie's opinion, her stepmother was far too needy of Jacob's time and attention.

And her father was very willing to give it to her, even though it came with a hefty price.

"Were you looking for me for a reason, Daed?" Sadie asked, her large blue eyes staring up at him.

He nodded and reached up, stroking his salt-and-pepper beard. "*Ja*, your *maem* needs your help with supper."

Typical, Sadie thought, her heart feeling heavy for her father. It was always this way. As if it wasn't bad enough that Jacob had no sons to help with the farmwork, Rachel was forever sending him on silly errands. Rather than ring the large dinner bell outside the back door, she had sent Jacob to fetch her. Sadie often wondered if her stepmother did that just to establish her control over Jacob.

Obediently, Sadie got to her feet and brushed off the front of her dress. "Well then, I reckon I best get going."

As they walked back across the field toward the farm, Sadie amused her father by telling him about the sparrow's nest she had stumbled across. Although it was vacant, for the baby birds were long gone now that it was approaching autumn, there remained a bunch of feathers within, which Sadie had gathered together to make into bookmarks. She reached into her apron pocket and handed one to him. A gift.

"I'll use that to mark my place in the Bible," he said. And Sadie knew that he meant it.

As they neared the farm, Jacob gave her an encouraging smile before he turned toward the barn and Sadie headed toward the house.

"Maem?" she called out to her stepmother as she entered the kitchen. Before Rachel could respond, Sadie caught sight of her stepmother standing inside the bathroom, peering into the mirror and fixing her hair. "Daed said you needed my help with supper, *ja*?"

"Just a minute, Sadie."

Leaning against the counter, Sadie watched Rachel with mild curiosity. It wasn't the first time she had caught her studying her reflection.

Rachel took more time caring for her appearance than Sadie thought was necessary. Her self-absorption seemed almost too prideful and sometimes made Sadie uncomfortable. Sadie continued to study Rachel, with her fair face and almond-shaped eyes, the color of a summer shadow on an aging tree trunk. She parted her dark hair in the center and pulled it back in the typical Amish fashion, which made her appear more youthful than other women her age, especially since she had never gained weight from birthing many babies.

But yet, as of late, Rachel appeared a bit piqued and thick around the waist. It made Sadie wonder if, finally, her stepmother was pregnant.

"Feeling well today?" Sadie asked when Rachel finally emerged from the bathroom.

Despite her pale cheeks and tired eyes, Rachel managed a smile. "*Ja*, well enough, I reckon." She pressed her hand against her stomach. "Bit queasy, though."

Was that her way of telling Sadie that, indeed, she was expecting? Sadie knew better than to ask outright. Amish women didn't openly discuss such things, except with their husbands. "Oh. I see." Sadie searched Rachel's face for a hint, hoping she might give something away. Perhaps an indication that her queasy stomach might be resolved in a few months rather than a few hours.

But Rachel remained unreadable.

"Mayhaps I can prepare supper then?" Sadie offered. "You could sit and relax a spell since you're not feeling well."

The corners of Rachel's mouth twitched, almost as if she wanted to frown at Sadie's kind offer. "*Nee*, I can do it. I'm not *that* poorly that I can't fix my family supper."

Stung by the rejection, Sadie lowered her eyes. It wasn't the first time Rachel had refused Sadie's kindness. Whenever Sadie offered to do something extra for Rachel, something to relieve her burdens, her stepmother seemed to take offense. She much preferred being in control and always directed Sadie on how to help. Working alongside each other was one thing, but having Sadie do things her way was quite another.

"But you can go to the cellar and fetch some potatoes." Always a command and never accompanied by a *please* or *thank you*. "You know how your *daed* loves mashed potatoes for supper."

Sadie nodded and headed toward the cellar door, where they kept the root vegetables and canning. She felt dismayed, already knowing how the rest of the evening would most likely play out. Rachel would fret over not feeling well, Sadie would do most of the work under the direction of her stepmother who would take credit for it—and her father would sit at the table, listening intently as Rachel monopolized the conversation.

Oh, how Sadie longed for the morning to arrive. Tomorrow Rachel would be visiting with the bishop's wife so Sadie would have time to escape the house and explore the forest just beyond her father's pastures. More time alone spent among nature was what she hoped for most. In the meantime, she remained the dutiful daughter and hurried into the darkness of the cellar to fetch those potatoes. After all, her father loved his mashed potatoes.

Chapter Two

Wednesdays were usually less busy for the Whitaker women. Laundry was always done on Mondays and Fridays, cleaning on Tuesdays and Thursdays, and gardening on Wednesdays and Saturdays.

But with autumn almost upon Echo Creek, the gardens were all but finished producing for the year. With the exception of a few pumpkins and acorn squash, the plants were brown and dry, their leaves withered already.

After the noon meal, Rachel gathered her shawl and packed up a butter cake to take to the bishop's wife, who lived in Echo Creek proper. It was a long walk to town, and Sadie was glad for that. Now, she was free to explore without criticism. All too often, Rachel would pass judgment on Sadie when she wandered off to the hayloft to see if the new litter of kittens had been born yet or to check on her favorite cow to see if she was feeling better. Or even worse, Rachel would forbid her to bring an injured wild creature into the house so she could tend to it during the night. Sometimes, she would make Sadie sleep in the barn if she wanted to nurse a baby bird back to health or bottle-feed a kitten whose mother had rejected it at birth.

The Whitakers' farm was one of the last ones on the

southern road leading out of Echo Creek. Just beyond their farm was a forest on one side of the lane and patches of pasture on the other. A few miles farther down, there was another small Amish community with its own bishop, preachers, and deacon. Occasionally, the youth might attend the singings and volleyball games at Echo Creek, but other than that, Sadie hardly knew any of those people.

Her interest wasn't in the pastureland or the small Amish community to the southwest. Instead, she enjoyed wandering through the forest on the days when she knew she could escape the house for more than an hour at a time. And, with Rachel gone visiting, today was the perfect opportunity to do just that.

Over the years, she had wandered the woods near her father's farm so frequently, she had worn paths through the small clusters of trees. Sadie knew exactly where the best rocks to sit upon were. The rocks where she could clearly hear the squirrels chatter in the trees overhead and see the bunnies as they poked their heads out of the rabbits' nests. And she knew the watering hole, fed by the creek on her father's property, where the deer came to gather and quench their thirst.

On hot days, she would sit on the edge of the small pond and dip her bare feet into the water. Because of the way the creek fed into it, the water was always fresh and crystal clear. Sometimes she, too, would kneel down and drink from it while she kept an eye out for toads among the grassy reeds. Today, however, she simply sat and leaned back, staring up at the treetops. The leaves were just starting to turn, hints of red, yellow, and orange emerging on the summer greenery. She didn't venture too far from the pond, knowing that the woods were much denser just beyond it. Not being as familiar with that area, she rarely traveled farther than her eyes could see into the forest.

Getting lost in the woods was not something she wanted to chance.

Behind her, she heard a crinkle of leaves and the snap of a twig.

She turned her head and squinted against the bit of sunlight that was filtering through the trees. With a hand lifted to shield her eyes, she could just make out the form of a six-point buck as it made its way to the watering hole.

She sat quietly, mesmerized by the deer. It hesitated for a moment when it sensed her presence, perhaps determining whether she was friend or foe. When it stepped through the brush and approached the water's edge, Sadie was relieved that the deer sensed she posed no threat. Sadie held her breath, captivated by the magnificence of the creature. From its chocolate brown eyes to its cream-colored fur, the buck was a sight to behold. When it dipped its head to the water, taking long sips, Sadie felt as if she were in the presence of God.

For a few minutes, the deer alternated between drinking and lifting its head to look around. Whenever it looked at Sadie, she felt that same sense of comfort. Her entire body felt warm, delighted in the knowledge that she was witnessing a magical moment that few people, with their hurried lives, would ever experience.

Finally, the deer finished drinking and began to walk away.

When it disappeared down the path from which it had come, Sadie stood up and walked over to the water's edge and stood at the exact spot it had just left. She knelt there, not bothered that her knees were in the moist dirt. She didn't care; she could wash her dress on Friday. All that mattered was for her to spend a moment in the same spot where the deer had just stood. She wanted to experience, firsthand, what it had seen and felt. It was almost as if she wanted to prolong the feeling of God's presence.

Leaning over, she peered at her reflection in the water. Only a few ripples remained, which created a wavy image of herself. She bent over farther and stared harder, trying to see if she could spot a few tadpoles. But the water was deeper at this part of the stream than she had thought and there were none to be seen. She sighed, knowing she needed to head back home soon, then let her fingers graze the surface. The cool water caressed her skin and she shut her eyes, imagining that she, too, was a deer. *Oh,* she thought, *how God takes care of his creatures.*

Softly, she began to sing a hymn that her mother had taught her so many years ago:

> *My God, I thank thee, who hast made*
> *The earth so bright;*
> *So full of splendor and of joy,*
> *Beauty and light;*
> *So many glorious things are here,*
> *Noble and right.*

"What's this? Do I hear a little songbird?"

At the sound of a man's voice, Sadie startled and jumped up, causing her foot to slip so it slid partially into the water. The only thing that stopped her from falling headfirst into the stream was her quick reflexes. Putting out her hand, she grabbed onto an overhanging branch and steadied herself, trying to regain her balance.

"Are you all right?"

Sadie turned around and found herself face-to-face with a young man. "Oh!" She almost stepped backward again, but this time, he reached out to stop her, gently grabbing her by the elbow.

"Careful now there! You'll be a wet songbird in a second if you don't mind your step."

One look at the man and she knew that he, too, was Amish. His plain dress and the straw hat he wore made that obvious. His thick brown hair, curly at the edges, poked out from beneath the hat's brim and his big hazel eyes stared down on her.

"You frightened me," she gasped as she removed her arm from his grasp.

"My apologies," he said as he moved away from her, allowing her to relax a bit. "I didn't mean to startle you." When he smiled, his teeth were white and his face was pleasantly kind. "You can imagine my surprise to stumble upon such a sight. I've walked this way many times on my way back from my cousins' *haus* to Echo Creek and this is the first time I've ever seen another soul out here." He tilted his head. "And such a pretty one at that, not to mention your beautiful voice."

Sadie lowered her eyes, feeling a flush of heat cross her cheeks. No one had ever complimented her on her singing before. At least not like that. Sure, she had been told that she had a lovely voice, but only by her father when she would sing hymns on Sunday morning while doing some sewing. Never from a complete stranger.

The man shoved his hands into his front pockets. "Which leads me to ask what you *are* doing out here? Don't you know that the forest is thick and dark just that way? And not the safest place for a *maedel* such as yourself to be wandering alone." He pointed over his shoulder toward the worn footpath he had traveled on, the same path the deer had used.

Sadie felt foolish, having been caught staring into the water. She needed to explain. "There was a deer. A buck." Her eyes traveled over his shoulder. "Surely you must have seen him?"

"I did not."

Sadie frowned. Only a few minutes had passed since the deer had left. How could he not have seen the large buck? "It was so beautiful, standing here, drinking from the stream. I wanted to feel what it felt."

When the man smiled, she couldn't help but notice how handsome he was. There were tiny laugh lines around his eyes, and his face seemed so warm and welcoming. "So, instead of feeling what the deer felt, you almost experienced how a wet fish feels when it swims downstream."

Again, she felt a flush caress her cheeks. "And then there was that."

He laughed at her reply. It was a joyous laugh, one that warmed her heart at once. If she'd suspected that the man meant her no harm, she knew it to be true for certain now.

"A songbird. A little fish. You are certainly full of tricks, aren't you?"

Sadie managed to return his smile.

And then he sobered. "But you should be careful. You could get lost in the woods, or worse yet, it's hunting season, and someone could mistake you for an animal," he said as he nodded toward the edge of the dark forest.

"I never go that way," she answered quickly. "My *daed*'s farm is just through the woods toward Echo Creek. I like to come here so I can sit and watch the critters."

"A fine hobby, I must say." He glanced up at the sky. "The forest is about as close to heaven as I have ever witnessed. God's hand can be seen in every tree, every plant, and, of course, every animal. Surely the beauty of nature speaks volumes about the majesty and goodness of God."

Sadie caught her breath. She couldn't have agreed more.

"Now, if you live toward Echo Creek, mayhaps you might walk with me. I'm headed that way now." He paused and tilted his head. "And I'd feel much more at ease, escorting you home and knowing you are safe."

His request caught her off guard. Unable to answer, Sadie merely nodded her head in agreement and walked beside him. It wasn't until they reached the worn trail that led away from the water that he spoke again.

"I don't believe I caught your name," he said.

"Sadie," she responded.

"From Echo Creek."

"*Ja*, that's right. And you?"

"Frederick." He glanced at her. "From the small Amish community south of Echo Creek."

"You mean Bishop Stutzman's district?"

He nodded.

While she had never visited it, she knew that it was a small cluster of Amish farms located south of Echo Creek without a town center. Sometimes the farmers would travel to Echo Creek to purchase supplies or visit extended family. But, from what little she knew about them, they mostly kept to themselves.

"I don't believe I've seen you before," she said, immediately wishing she had thought before speaking. "I mean at the youth gatherings."

He gave a slight shrug of his shoulders. "*Ja*, I don't normally venture to Echo Creek for those. Too busy on my *daed*'s farm. We raise cattle for beef sales at Liberty Falls."

"Oh!" She placed her hand over her heart. "How sad that must be for you when they're taken to auction."

Frederick's expression became solemn. "I admit, that's my least favorite part of raising cattle. But I know that they had a *gut* life with us, were treated with kindness, and served a greater purpose than just grazing our pastures."

That was one way to look at it, she thought. Still, she knew she could never be happy raising cattle for that purpose, knowing that one day they would be sent to slaughter. Why, even though her father raised dairy cows, he was always telling her not to get too attached to the herd for fear her emotions would get the better of her. But Sadie didn't heed his concerns and even named every cow. All forty-three of them!

As if reading her mind, Frederick sighed. "One day, when I inherit the farm, I intend to do something a bit different."

Intrigued, Sadie looked at him. "And what's that?"

He made a funny face and squinted at her, a strange

expression crossing his lips. "I'm not sure I should tell you. What if you share my idea with your *daed* and he steals my future business?"

Abruptly, Sadie stopped walking. "I would never do that!"

Frederick laughed. "I'm teasing you, Sadie."

For the second time, she felt her cheeks grow warm.

"Anyway, my idea is to invest in educational farming."

Sadie caught her breath. "I don't know what that is, but it sure sounds impressive."

Once again, he laughed at her reaction. "It's something new. A lot of the *Englischers* are doing it. Having a farm where young people can visit and learn about the daily life of a farmer." As they approached the edge of the woods, he made a broad, sweeping gesture. "There's so much land here, Sadie. And, from what I hear, many of the young people from Ohio and Pennsylvania can't afford to buy land in their area. Our little Amish community could grow and welcome so many new families. We could be as big as Echo Creek." He paused. "With a town center and lots of farms without any influence from outsiders."

Sadie knew he was talking about the *Englische*. "That sounds heavenly."

"*Ja*, indeed. My *daed* has five hundred acres. It's a large parcel of land. We could help other young Amish men learn how to farm out here and do profit sharing, raising crops and focusing on dairy, instead of beef. And then those men could save their money and one day buy their own farms. There's enough land for everyone here. But they need a helping hand to get started."

"Oh, that's a right *gut* idea, Frederick."

He nodded, a look of appreciation on his face. "*Danke*, Sadie. I think so, too." He leaned over and nudged her with his arm. "It will be a great help to others, and no cattle will ever be sold to market for slaughter, at least not from my land."

Once they approached the road that led to her house, Sadie pointed toward the mailbox at the end of her father's driveway. "That's our farm."

He nodded and continued walking beside her. "You weren't kidding about living next to the forest," he said as his eyes scanned the large pasture. "I take it those are your dairy cows, then?"

"*Ja*, dairy. And Daed plants corn in the back fields."

"A true farmer's *dochder*," he quipped.

At the mailbox, Sadie paused, then lifted the flap and peeked inside to see if the postman had delivered anything. When she found the box empty, she wasn't surprised, for it was a rare occasion that they received mail. She knew she was stalling for time, wanting to spend a few more minutes in Frederick's company. She had enjoyed her un-expected visit with this stranger, and she didn't know how to tell him without seeming too forward. She bit her lower lip and took a small breath. "Well, *danke*, Frederick, for escorting me to my farm."

He gave her a little bow and she smiled. "My pleasure, little songbird. Now that I've seen you safely home, I shall continue on my way."

Sadie started down the driveway, stopping just once to look over her shoulder. It was only then that she realized she hadn't learned Frederick's last name and he didn't know hers. *Such a shame,* she thought, *that he never attends youth gatherings*. She would have liked to get to know him better.

Chapter Three

The next morning, as soon as Sadie stepped into the kitchen, she knew that something was very wrong.

It was already seven o'clock and the coffee hadn't been brewed yet. Rachel *always* had the coffee brewing by sunrise and, more often than not, had already taken a nice hot mug out to the barn for Jacob before Sadie had even woken.

But not today.

Instead, Rachel stood at the sink, her hands pressed firmly against the counter as she stared out the window with a blank expression on her face. Rachel was so engrossed in her thoughts, she didn't appear to notice when Sadie entered the room.

And, when Sadie greeted her, Rachel failed to respond.

"Is everything all right?" Sadie asked as she slowly approached Rachel from behind and placed a hand on her shoulder. Rachel spun around, as if startled, and that's when Sadie saw tears streaming down her stepmother's face. "Rachel?"

"I'm not pregnant." Her voice quivered. "Again."

"I'm so sorry," Sadie said softly. She stepped forward and tried to embrace Rachel, but her stepmother pulled away and turned her attention back to the dishes in the sink.

"In God's time, though, it will happen," Sadie muttered, trying to offer what consolation she could. Yet, in her own mind, she couldn't help but think, *If he wills it.* Every night she prayed that her stepmother would be with child, for Sadie knew how desperately Rachel wanted a baby. "Maybe you shouldn't think so much about it."

"That's easy for you to say!" Rachel snapped as she dropped a coffee mug into the sink and stormed away, glaring at Sadie. "Just look at you! So young and pretty. Why, you'll land a husband in the blink of an eye!"

Sadie's eyes widened. What on earth had *she* done to deserve Rachel's wrath? Oh help, Sadie thought. It seemed each time Rachel's monthly course came, she fell into a deep depression that lasted for days. And each time it happened, her reaction was worse than the last. Clearly this time Rachel was dealing with her disappointment by lashing out at Sadie.

"*You* didn't have to take care of a disabled parent for ten years. *You* didn't miss out on courting the young men! Why, I should've had ten *kinner* by now!" she yelled. But then, just as suddenly as her anger had appeared, it disappeared, and Rachel covered her face with her hands. Her shoulders shook as she sobbed. "I so wanted to please Jacob."

Sadie suddenly felt guilty, and her hurt was replaced with compassion for the woman standing before her. She stepped forward and pulled Rachel into her arms and comforted her, then said a silent prayer. She wanted nothing more than for God to take care of her stepmother. To ease the pain of her disappointment at not having her own family and to grant her peace of mind in whatever way God felt was righteous and fit.

Sadie was sure that God had a plan for everyone. The Bible said so. It was one of the first things young Amish children learned in their religious schooling. But she just wished she knew *what* his plan for Rachel was. Three years without one pregnancy would tax any woman's nerves.

"Let me fetch *Daed*," Sadie offered in a soft voice. "He'll know what to do."

Quickly, Sadie let go of her stepmother and moved toward the front door, a rush of emotions flooding her. When she stepped outside she felt relieved to be away from Rachel, even though she couldn't help feeling extreme sorrow over her stepmother's infertility. If anyone knew how badly Rachel wanted a baby, it was Sadie.

"Daed?" She walked into the barn and tried to find her father among the cows.

When she called out his name a second time, he popped up in the far aisle, his crumpled straw hat smashed onto his head, plastering his hair to his forehead.

"Over here, Sadie." He gave her a big grin. "If you've come to offer your help, I'd gladly accept it today. The cold morning air makes my fingers stiff and uncooperative."

Sadie hurried toward him, stepping over a pile of cow manure that was in her path. Standing next to the cow her father was milking, she peered over its haunches. Her father was seated on a short stool, already bent over, his fingers deftly pulling on the cow's udder. Like many of the Amish in Echo Creek, he had never bought into installing an automated milking system. With such a large herd to milk by hand, it was almost impossible for him to get ahead. Why, once he finished with the morning milking, he only had a few hours left in the day to tend to the fields before he had to start all over again with the evening milking. She made a mental note to help him more often, and especially today, after he comforted his wife.

"I'm sorry, Daed, but you best come inside. Rachel's in a bad state."

Immediately, he stood up, bumping into his stool and nearly tipping over the milk pail. His eyes appeared tired as he searched her face for assurance. "Bad state?"

Averting her eyes, Sadie gave a slight shake of her head. "She's upset. You know, about . . ." She let her voice trail off, feeling uncomfortable about sharing such intimate news. "Well, she's just needing you, Daed."

He nodded, then slowly began to walk out of the dairy barn, Sadie close on his heels.

Inside, Jacob found his wife crumpled in a ladder-back chair in the living room, sobbing into her hands. Clearly, her emotions had deteriorated in the time it had taken for Sadie to fetch her father.

Seeing her stepmother so broken was almost too much for Sadie to bear, and she had to fight the urge to shed her own tears. Life had not been easy for Rachel, what with tending to her ailing parents and missing out on her *rum-schpringe*. Never being able to attend youth gatherings and singings, or even the friendly volleyball games and picnics that were such a big part of the young people's social life. If only God would see fit to ease Rachel's burden and give her a child.

"Rachel?" Jacob knelt beside her and reached for her hands. He gently pulled them away from her face and spoke softly. "*Wie gehts?*"

Tears streamed down her cheeks. Her eyes were red and puffy, and there were fine lines around her mouth. For the first time, Sadie noticed that Rachel's youthful glow had disappeared, and it wasn't just because she was crying.

"It's . . . it's just that . . ." Rachel let out a sob and shook her head. "I'm not pregnant."

"Rachel," he said in a soothing voice as he rubbed her arm. "It's just not your time."

"It's *never* my time." More tears fell from her eyes. "It'll never be my time."

Jacob pulled Rachel to her feet and took her into his arms. For a long while, she cried on his shoulder. Sadie hurried to the hall bath and fetched a tissue, handing it to her father so he could wipe away Rachel's tears.

"Shh," he said softly. "It'll be all right."

Shaking her head, she whispered, "*Nee*, it's not all right.

I want nothing more than to give you a child." She sniffled. "A son."

His large, calloused hands rubbed her back, and he whispered into her ear, "Now, now, Rachel. It's not the end of the world. You *are* older."

Immediately, Sadie saw her stepmother's body freeze. Her expression changed from sorrow to something else. Something that Sadie had never seen before. There was a coldness to her stepmother's face; her mouth tightened and the tiny lines around her lips appeared deeper.

"Older?" she repeated as if the word dripped poison from her tongue.

Jacob hadn't seen the transformation. "*Ja*, older. It's not like you are young like our Sadie is." He paused, embracing her tighter and kissing the side of her head near where her prayer *kapp* covered her ear. "Maybe you just can't have a *boppli*," Jacob said as he comforted his wife. "It isn't meant to be."

Rachel pulled back from her husband, then swatted his hand away from her shoulder. "Not meant to be?" she asked in an incredulous tone. Her eyes studied his face as if his words were a jest.

"*Ja*, that's what I said, Rachel," he replied. "You aren't as young as you once were, after all."

Inwardly, Sadie cringed. With her stepmother's obsession about her youthful looks, Sadie knew that her father's words were sure to sting. They were the last thing Rachel wanted to hear. As soon as those words crossed his lips a dark cloud of despair passed over Rachel's face. Sadie wondered that her father didn't notice it, too.

"Not as young as I once was," Rachel repeated in a quiet, even voice that was edged with resentment and disbelief.

"And that's okay, Rachel," Jacob offered by way of comfort, starting to realize that Rachel did not take kindly to the reminder of her advancing years.

"Abraham's wife was eighty years old before she had her first child," Sadie offered, trying to give Rachel hope.

As soon as the words left her lips, Sadie knew she had made a grave error. Rachel pushed Jacob away and stood abruptly, knocking over the chairs as she did so. "Why, it's not as if I'm eighty years old!" she yelled out as she took a few steps backward.

Jacob laughed and tried to reach for her, but Rachel backed farther away.

"I'm not even forty!" She glared at Sadie. "From the sounds of it, even *you* don't believe God will let me carry my own *boppli*!"

Immediately, Sadie rushed forward. "*Nee*, Rachel. That's not what I meant—"

Rachel held up her hands, keeping Sadie at bay. "Just because *you* are so young and have young men escorting you home, you think you are better than me?"

Jacob's shoulders slumped and he appeared wearier than ever. "That's not what she said, Rachel."

"It's what she meant!" Rachel spun around, turning her back on both of them.

In the three years that Rachel had been married to Jacob, Sadie had never seen her stepmother demonstrate such erratic behavior. The way Rachel was raging frightened Sadie even more than her deep sorrow did.

"Truly it's not," Sadie begged. "I simply meant that there's always hope."

"Go away!" Rachel waved her hand over her shoulder. "Just leave me alone, Sadie. You, too, Jacob."

But Jacob wasn't about to leave. Sadie knew that her father cared too much for his wife. He'd never been one to handle tears and heartbreak very well, and his nature was far too kind to simply walk away without trying to help.

"Rachel, please. You cannot believe that my Sadie was trying to insult you."

Sadie started to back away, suspecting that Rachel's

emotions were far too out of control for any such kind words to quell her sudden temper.

Spinning around, Rachel faced Jacob, her eyes narrowed, and an ugly scowl crossed her face. "You always did favor *her* over me anyway!"

Sadie's mouth opened, shocked at the venom that dripped from her stepmother's tongue. Her eyes fell upon her father and she saw that he, too, appeared taken aback.

"Rachel," he said in a wavering voice. "She's my *dochder*!"

As he spoke that one word, "*dochder*," Rachel grimaced. It was as if she found the word distasteful, and her reaction sent a shiver up Sadie's spine. Who was this angry, hateful woman who sat before them? For a moment, Sadie wondered if they should fetch the doctor, or even the bishop.

"She may be your '*dochder*,' Jacob," Rachel spat out, "but I am your *fraa*!"

Jacob took a step toward his wife and reached his hand for hers. "Rachel, please—"

But she slapped it away, a gesture that caused Sadie to cover her mouth and gasp out loud. Rachel stretched out her arm and pointed toward the door. "Leave me be! Both of you!"

Sadie's heart ached for the pained look she saw upon her father's face. How could Rachel say such horrible things to Jacob? How could she strike him with her hand? It was beyond unchristian, behaving in such a manner to anyone, never mind to her husband. God had appointed the husband as the head of the household. Children obeyed parents. Wives obeyed husbands. And everyone obeyed the church. That was the order of things in the Amish faith.

Rachel, however, had just stepped over that boundary.

With his shoulders hunched even farther and an expression of hurt etched on his face, Jacob avoided Sadie's eyes as he left the room, pausing at the door as if waiting for something.

Or someone, Sadie realized.

Upon realizing this, she hurried to join her father and followed him outside.

"Daed?"

He lifted his hand over his shoulder and shook it at her. It was a clear indication that he didn't wish to talk about the scene that had just unfolded before their very eyes.

"But, Daed," Sadie pleaded, "she's not well."

He walked toward the barn, the gravel driveway making a crunching noise under his heavy work boots, and ignored Sadie's words.

She picked up her pace, trying to keep up with him. "Daed, you can't just pretend that didn't happen."

Deep down, she suspected that was exactly what he wanted to, and would, do. So typical among her people: when unpleasant things happened, a wall of silence went up around them. But Sadie knew she couldn't ignore what she had just witnessed and always suspected—that her stepmother was jealous of her husband's relationship with his own daughter.

"*Nee*, Sadie. We will speak no more about this."

He passed through the doorway that led into the dairy barn. Sadie started to follow him, but when he stopped walking, his back still facing her, she stopped as well.

"I'll finish the chores in here. Mayhaps you can tend to the horse and mules."

He didn't wait for her to respond. Instead, he disappeared into the dairy barn, leaving a bewildered Sadie standing outside as the sky began to darken, hinting at an approaching storm.

Chapter Four

Sadie finished hanging the wet laundry on the clothesline. Despite the cold temperature, she had awoken extra early this Monday morning to tackle her chores, hoping she could finish before the noon meal. If she got everything done, there would be just enough daylight left for her to escape to the woods before she had to be back to help her father with the evening milking.

The previous day, Rachel's sorrow had not dissipated. Instead, she'd spent most of the afternoon lying in her bed, alternating between crying and barking orders at Sadie. Thank heavens it was a Sunday and a day of rest. At least Sadie had been able to escape the house for a bit and take solace in the outdoors.

This was worse than the other times Rachel had learned she was not carrying a baby. Not only was she sad and despondent but she seemed especially bitter as well.

And she was taking it out on Sadie.

"Those sheets aren't clean enough!"

Sadie was startled, then froze in place, her hand on the wooden clothespin. She refused to turn around, not wanting to give Rachel the satisfaction of having startled her.

"You need to bleach them. Take them down and wash them again!" Rachel yelled out from the front porch.

Sadie wasn't about to argue. Instead, she unpinned the sheet, popping the clothespin into her apron pocket.

"All of them!"

Sighing, Sadie did as Rachel commanded. She knew that obedience to one's parents was one of God's commandments, but Rachel was making it a hard rule to follow, indeed. Sadie knew that those bedsheets were as white as freshly fallen snow, but she also knew that there was no sense in arguing with Rachel.

"And the kitchen floor . . . It's filthy. I want that scrubbed today."

Another sigh escaped Sadie's lips. She had just scoured it with borax two days before. Surely it hadn't gotten "filthy" in just forty-eight hours.

Clearly, a walk in the woods was not going to happen today.

After removing all the sheets, Sadie hoisted the laundry basket onto her hip and slowly made her way back to the house. When she got to the kitchen, she ran the hot water in the diesel-powered washer that sat in the far corner. She could feel the scorn from her stepmother's eyes as she peered over her shoulder from time to time while making dough for a pie crust. She was relentless, watching Sadie's every move, and Sadie couldn't help but feel that no matter how many times she washed the sheets, they would never be clean enough.

By the time Sadie began to rinse them, Rachel had started preparing the late-afternoon meal. She could hear her stepmother talking to herself in a low voice as she moved about the kitchen peeling and rinsing the carrots and cutting the chicken with a meat cleaver. If Sadie didn't know better, she would have thought Rachel was preparing a great feast, for all the pot banging and dish clanking that was going on, rather than making chicken and dumplings.

An hour later, Sadie had finally wrung out the last of the bedsheets and hung them back on the clothesline to dry. She suspected that Rachel had retired to her bedroom while the chicken stew cooked in the oven. She was thankful for the quiet time without Rachel's eyes watching her every move. Uncertain as to whether Rachel was napping, Sadie made sure to be extra careful when she entered the house. She gently closed the screen door so there would be no noise and tiptoed into the kitchen to begin washing the floor. She certainly had no desire to accidentally wake Rachel if she was sleeping. Just as she was about to fill the bucket with hot water, she heard the sound of the hinges on the bathroom door creak. Rachel wasn't in the bedroom, after all. Sadie put the bucket down and quietly made her way along the hall, stopping just shy of the partially open door. In the dim lighting of the hallway, she could just make out Rachel leaning toward the mirror to study her reflection.

Sadie watched, her back pressed against the wall so Rachel wouldn't see her shadow as Rachel scrutinized every angle of her face. She gently grabbed her skin with the tips of her fingers and pulled. First the corners of her eyes, then her upper lip and chin. Finally, Rachel pulled the skin on her neck, stretching her flesh upward as if to tighten her skin.

"I'm not old," Rachel mumbled to herself, unaware that she was being watched. She turned her head from side to side, still gazing at her image. "And I'm still as beautiful as always. More so than that young girl!"

Stunned, Sadie pressed her lips together and tiptoed back to the kitchen. *Such vanity,* she thought, astounded by her stepmother's self-admiration. Prideful behavior was frowned upon by the Amish and rarely reared its head. To see it on display so close up was shocking, indeed.

It wasn't what a person *looked* like that mattered, but what the person held in his or her heart. God did not judge people on their outward appearances but by their actions toward others as well as their commitment to his word.

And yet Rachel appeared to be overly concerned with her looks as well as her age. Sadie was suddenly reminded of Psalm 119:37, a Bible verse she had memorized in school. "Turn away my eyes from looking at vanity, And revive me in Your ways."

Vanity has no place in this world, Sadie thought, disturbed by this revelation.

All her life, Sadie had been taught that vanity was a sin. Indeed, that was a core belief of the plain Amish way of life. Oh, Sadie knew that there had to be some level of attraction between men and women before they started courting and eventually married. But she also knew that a young man would never court a woman if he felt that she was not kind and righteous, a true believer in God and Jesus. And it was equally important that both individuals followed God's commandments.

Only then would a couple consider whether they were well suited for a lifetime commitment. Looks were the least of the qualities considered.

"Did I just see you re-hanging the laundry?"

At the sound of her father's voice, there was a small gasp from the bathroom and then the door was latched shut. Sadie turned around. She must not have hidden her emotions, for the look on his face quickly morphed into one of concern.

Jacob reached out and touched her arm. "Why are you standing in the dark hallway? Are you feeling poorly, Sadie?"

She wanted to deny it and force a smile. There was no point in telling her father about what she had just witnessed. Jacob thought highly of Rachel; after all, she *was* his wife. Although Sadie often wondered if he truly loved her, at least in the way he had loved his first wife. Still, Sadie would never intentionally speak disparagingly about Rachel to him, even if she was telling the truth.

"I'm . . . fine. I was just checking on Rachel to see if she was feeling any better."

He made a face as if he didn't quite believe her. "What happened with the laundry, then? I know I saw you hang those same sheets earlier this morning. Why are they back on the clothesline?"

Sadie knew she couldn't lie to her father. She hesitated, though, hoping to find the right words to respond in truth without speaking ill of her stepmother.

"Rachel didn't think they were clean enough, so she asked me to rewash them," she offered at last.

Jacob took a deep breath and exhaled slowly. He reached up, removed his hat, and wiped his brow with the back of his sleeve. A ring of sweat pressed down his hair where the hat had rested. "That's not right, Sadie. Those sheets looked perfectly fine. Why, they practically sparkled in the morning sunlight."

Sadie held her tongue.

"She must be truly hurting," he muttered, more to himself than to Sadie, while looking down the hallway to the closed bathroom door with concern etched on his face. "I don't understand why it's so important to her. If it's meant to be, it's meant to be." He plopped his hat back upon his head. "Why, last night, I told her that she's not young anymore, not like you are, Sadie. She just might be too old to have a *boppli*."

No doubt that *was* the reason for her strange and hurtful comments, Sadie thought.

"Still," Jacob sighed, "that's no reason to take it out on you. Let me go talk to her."

"*Nee*, Daed," Sadie said as she grabbed his arm and led

him toward the kitchen. She knew that if her father spoke to Rachel, it would unleash even more bitterness. "I don't think that's a right *gut* idea. If she's hurting inside, she needs time to heal. I didn't mind washing the sheets again. Honest."

But Jacob wasn't easily convinced. "You're a truly righteous woman, Sadie. And my heart warms that you're protecting her." He stopped talking and lifted his eyes upward as if reflecting upon something. "But, just as I can't have her doubting God's will like that, I won't tolerate my *dochder* being browbeaten. It ain't right and I can't condone it under my own roof."

"Daed, I don't think—"

But he didn't listen to her. Instead, without saying another word, he sat down at the kitchen table.

Sadie made her way to the stove and grabbed for an oven mitt so she could check on the stew. When she opened the oven door, the aroma of roasted vegetables and savory chicken filled the kitchen.

"Rachel," her father called out, and Sadie could feel the rapid beating of her heart. When there was no response, her father pushed back his chair and stood. "I best check on her, then," he stated as he left the room to seek Rachel out.

A few moments later, there were muffled sounds coming from the other room. While she couldn't hear the words that were spoken, she could tell by the sound of her father's voice that he was, indeed, chastising Rachel.

Cringing, Sadie shut her eyes and said a quick prayer. She didn't want her stepmother to suffer further, but she also didn't want to be subjected to any more of Rachel's misdirected wrath. Her stepmother was already making her life more difficult. How would she respond to Jacob's reprimanding her?

It wasn't long before Jacob and Rachel entered the

kitchen together. Rachel's eyes appeared red and her cheeks were puffy. Had she been crying again?

Jacob stood behind Rachel, his arms crossed over his chest and a stern expression on his face.

Rachel, however, looked dull and emotionless as she faced Sadie. "Your *daed* says I've been unfair to you," Rachel said, her voice flat and unfeeling. "If that is so, then I apologize."

Dipping her head, Sadie stared at the linoleum floor. A silence ensued, and she realized that both her father and stepmother were awaiting her response. She swallowed hard and sought the right words.

"Rachel, I know you've been feeling poorly." Sadie bit her lower lip. Her compassion for Rachel was genuine, even though she had heard the hollowness in the woman's apology. "I truly understand and pray for you to find comfort."

Rachel made a noise, barely audible, that made Sadie glance up. When her eyes met Rachel's, she noticed a darkness that cast a shadow of doubt in her mind. For the only word Sadie could find to describe what she saw was "loathing." It was all too clear now. Her stepmother loathed her. And, for the life of her, Sadie could not understand why.

Jacob, however, had not witnessed this. Upon hearing his wife profess her regret, he had uncrossed his arms, clearly pleased with the exchange between the two women, and missed the ominous look of disdain in Rachel's eyes.

"Now, let there be no more strife under my roof. There's enough of that in the world. Besides, the Bible is quite clear about the root of strife. For it is written, 'What is causing the quarrels and fights among you? Don't they come from the evil desires at war within you?'" He waited until Rachel turned around and met his stern gaze. "And no more sorrow from you. That only means you are questioning God's will. Only *he* decides our fate, not us. It is not our place to dispute or doubt his decisions."

Satisfied, Jacob plopped his hat back on his head, and after glancing at Sadie, he passed Rachel and walked across the room to the back door, then headed toward the barn to finish his chores before supper.

Sadie stared after him. She realized that she had never heard him speak so harshly to Rachel, or anyone for that matter. Then again, no one had ever given him reason to rebuke them.

Yet he spoke true wisdom, demonstrating understanding of both Scripture and the Ordnung. The man was the head of the household and it was his word that led the family. And, as head of the Whitaker household, Jacob had made his point clear in his rebuke to Rachel: he would not tolerate strife between his wife and daughter.

When Sadie turned to face Rachel, the wisdom of her father's words seemed to vanish into thin air. Rather than act humbled and chastised, her stepmother glared at her with a cold, hard stare that spoke more than words ever possibly could.

Sadie shuddered, an eerie feeling washing over her. She couldn't help but wonder what evil desires resided in her stepmother's heart. What driving force was at the root of her anger? If anything, it was evident to Sadie that Jacob's reproach had angered Rachel even more. And it was clear to Sadie that, regardless of her apology, Rachel had only spoken because Jacob had demanded it, not because she meant it. She might have honored her husband's wishes, but it was all too obvious that she still harbored ill feelings toward Sadie.

"I . . . I best go finish the rest of my chores," Sadie mumbled, lowering her gaze, then stepped to the side of Rachel to pass. But she knew that Rachel's eyes remained upon her as she grabbed the bucket and began scouring the floor. She would do what she could to avoid her stepmother as much as possible. Surely this, too, would pass once Rachel grasped the truth of Jacob's words. In the meantime, Sadie took no comfort from the empty apology or the hateful expression that crossed her stepmother's face as she started to grind the cornmeal and crack the eggs for the dumplings.

Chapter Five

On Sunday, nothing could have stunned Sadie more than hearing the bishop announce that her friend Belle was to marry Adam Hershberger, the Amish recluse who lived on the outskirts of town. And, even more surprising, the wedding was to take place in just under twelve days. Not only was it rare to have such a quick ceremony but it wasn't even wedding season.

When the bishop made the announcement after the three-hour worship service, a soft murmuring rippled throughout the congregation. Like many of the others, Sadie turned to look at Belle, trying to read her expression. But when they made eye contact, there was little emotion on her friend's face. Belle sat with her back rigid and her hands folded in her lap. She lowered her eyes and began to pray with the others.

Sadie wanted to go to her friend as soon as the service had ended and the church members were beginning to disperse. But everyone seemed to be staring in the young woman's direction. As if to avoid the curious looks, Belle immediately busied herself among the other women who were setting out the common meal.

Deciding she would talk with Belle later, when they

could have more privacy, Sadie wandered across the room
to where her other dear friend, Ella, was standing.

"Can you believe it?" Ella whispered with her blue eyes
wide and her expression full of distress. "Belle and Adam?"

Not only couldn't Sadie believe it, she also didn't understand it. If there was one person Sadie would never have
guessed Belle would marry, it was Adam Hershberger.
"She hardly knows Adam!" Sadie muttered in a low voice.

Ella leaned her head in closer. "Does anyone?"

It was true. No one knew Adam Hershberger. He rarely
left his farm, let alone came to worship. His disfigured
face made him the subject of malicious stories that were
whispered behind covered lips.

Sadie didn't blame him for not worshipping with the
rest of the community. Not with the idle gossip that circu-
lated about his appearance. Sadie remembered hearing
about the fire that had disfigured Adam when he was but
a small boy.

Besides, he lived on the far outskirts of town, toward
Liberty Falls. From what Sadie heard from other people in
Echo Creek, he rarely came to town except to buy supplies
a few times a year.

And now he was to marry Belle?

Sadie looked over to where Belle was now standing with
her older sisters. Going by the animated expressions on
their faces, Sadie guessed that Verna and Susie were giving
Belle an earful. It seemed that Ella and Sadie weren't the
only ones blindsided by the bishop's announcement.

As soon as they could, Sadie and Ella made their way
to Belle's side.

"What on earth, Belle?" Ella said softly. "Adam?"

"I . . . I had to do it," Belle whispered back. Her pale
face and frightened eyes revealed her true feelings. It was
plain to see that she did not favor this marriage any more
than her friends did. "If I marry Adam, he won't make my
family leave the farm. And after there's a son . . ."

Sadie bit her lower lip and widened her eyes. She had forgotten that Adam had bought Belle's father's farm when the family had almost lost it to the bank. "A son?" she asked, wondering what that had to do with anything.

Belle looked forlorn and averted her eyes. Sadie could read the underlying sadness in them and it broke her heart.

"If I bear him a son he will give the farm back to my *daed*," Belle explained. "Otherwise, my family will be homeless. And I can't have that on my conscience. Not if there's something I can do to prevent it."

Sadie knew that Belle's family was poor and struggled to make ends meet. She had heard that her friend's family might have to move if they didn't come up with payment soon. But marrying Adam Hershberger to save the family farm was a sacrifice far beyond any daughter's duty.

"Oh help!" Nervously Ella scanned the room. "My *maem* will have quite a lot to say about this turn of events. I'll never hear the end of it, I'm sure and certain."

"Perhaps I should leave," Belle said.

"Let's go walk a spell," Sadie offered. There were too many people standing around, whispering and staring at Belle. Sadie felt compassion for her friend, who looked terribly uncomfortable under their pointed scrutiny. There was no sense in adding to the town's weekly dose of gossip. Putting her hand on Belle's arm, she gently guided her toward the door. "Fresh air might do us all some good."

Quietly, they slipped through the door and made their way down the lane.

After they had put some distance between themselves and the Riehls' farmhouse, Sadie was the first to speak. "Please, Belle, you must reconsider. You don't love that man."

Ella quickly added her own thoughts. "Love him? Why, you don't even know him!"

But Belle stood her ground. "I've promised to marry

him and I cannot back out." She paused. "*Nee*, I *will not* back out."

"But he's . . ."

Turning to Ella, Belle frowned. "Disfigured? Is that what you thought to say?"

"Oh, Belle!" Ella's expression changed from concern to sorrow. "Would you think so little of me? *Nee*, I was going to say that he's such a recluse, and bad-tempered, too."

"I'm sorry, Ella. I should've known you wouldn't say something so horrid."

Her friend acknowledged the apology with a soft smile. "*Ja*, I know that he prefers a solitary life, but that doesn't mean he's a bad person. And bad-tempered? *Mayhaps* that's because so many people are so cruel to him."

"I find this very sad," Sadie said. "Getting married for convenience, rather than love? That's not for me. Why, I can just look at my own *daed* and how he married so quickly after my *maem* passed away."

Ella concurred. "Mine, too."

Belle frowned. "But both of your *daeds* were happy when they remarried, *ja*?"

Sadie shrugged. "My *daed* isn't *un*happy. But she sure does rule the house. It's not a partnership like he had with Maem. And she sure is hard on me at times."

She wasn't going to gossip about her stepmother, so she didn't mention the past week, which had been filled with constant criticism and berating. Even if she did choose to tell her friends how Rachel was treating her, Sadie knew this was not the appropriate time to discuss such things. Her issues with Rachel were nothing compared to Belle's current state of affairs.

Belle gave her friends a forced smile that was meant to reassure them. "I think I'll just walk home now," she announced. There was a faraway look in her eyes which her friends had never seen before. "Might you tell my family when you go back inside?"

Ella and Sadie watched as Belle walked down the driveway, her head hanging and her shoulders slumped over in defeat.

"Such a heavy burden she carries," Sadie said with a sigh. "I just can't imagine marrying a man I didn't love."

Ella shook her head. "Me neither."

The sound of crunching gravel announced the approach of someone. Sadie glanced over her shoulder and saw Anna Rose Grimm walking toward them. Her eyes traveled the long driveway and watched as Belle disappeared down the lane.

"Such shocking news," Anna Rose said. "It's all everyone's talking about."

"I can only imagine," Sadie replied. Oh, how the townspeople of Echo Creek loved to gossip.

Anna Rose stood next to Sadie. She was older than Sadie and, like Ella, blond-headed. With her pale skin and her propensity for wearing pink dresses, she always looked like a little fairy. Her older cousin, Elizabeth, was the teacher at the local schoolhouse, and sometimes Anna Rose helped her with teaching the lessons. She was kind and patient in that way.

"Are you coming back tonight for the singing?"

Sadie shrugged. Her heart felt heavy and she wasn't in the mood for attending a singing anymore. In general, she didn't like them much anyway. Too many of the young men clamored for her undivided attention. Not one singing passed when Sadie wasn't asked to walk home with someone or ride in some fellow's buggy. And she always politely declined.

She felt embarrassed by the interest the young men showed in her. It wasn't that she didn't like them. She just didn't like them *that* way. And she knew better than to lead on a man she had no intention of marrying.

"I'm not much in the mood, Anna Rose." No, attending

a singing that evening was the *last* thing Sadie wanted to do after hearing today's distressing news.

Someone called Ella's name from the Riehls' house. She sighed. "Best get going, then."

"Tonight?" Anna Rose prompted Ella.

But Ella shook her head. "I doubt I'll be able to go," she said as she walked away.

That didn't surprise Sadie. Ella's stepmother rarely let Ella do anything. Everyone knew that it was because Linda Troyer wanted her own daughters, Drusilla and Anna, to get all the attention—which they usually did. But it was never for the reasons Linda wanted.

Anna Rose looked at Sadie. "Please come," she pleaded again.

Without Ella, there was no way Sadie was going to attend. "I don't know, Anna Rose—"

Anna Rose exhaled and made a face. "I know several young women who would love to have so many men ask them to ride home in their buggies."

Sadie frowned, suspecting that Anna Rose was referring to Drusilla and Anna. "Then those young women would be rather vain," Sadie responded.

Anna Rose laughed. "True. Very true." She placed her hand on Sadie's arm. "Say you'll come, then. It won't be any fun if you aren't there." She paused. "Perhaps this will help. My cousin will be attending and *he* can bring us home. Then you will have a valid excuse for disappointing so many of the boys looking to escort you home."

"Mayhaps," Sadie reluctantly responded.

"Please!"

Seeing the look of desperation on Anna Rose's face, Sadie finally relented. "Okay then. I'll go. But don't leave me alone with those Troyer girls. You know I can't stand their willingness to share their opinions with anyone who will listen."

Anna Rose laughed. "You and everyone else in Echo Creek. No wonder no one's gone calling on them yet."

Sadie shook her head. "Not so, Anna Rose. I've seen Drusilla at our neighbor's farm on more than one occasion. Seems she's struck up quite a friendship with Jenny Miller's older *bruder*, Timothy."

Opening her mouth, Anna Rose let a small gasp escape. "You don't say!"

"I do say, but only because you must be the only person in Echo Creek who doesn't already know it." Sadie wasn't one to carelessly spread gossip. Common knowledge, however, did not fall into that category.

"I wonder if they'll marry this season."

Sadie gave a slight shrug, knowing that speculating about such things *did* fall in the category of gossip.

Chapter Six

As soon as Sadie arrived at the singing, she knew she had made a terrible mistake. Not only were Drusilla and Anna holding court with the other young women, but Belle's sisters, Verna and Susie, were there, too.

Those four were the most eligible young women in Echo Creek, and the only reason Sadie knew that was because each of them made certain everyone recognized it.

"What's wrong, Sadie?" Anna Rose asked. They had arrived together, having met up in town so they could walk to the Riehls' farm, the same place the worship service had been held earlier that same day. In the brisk autumn air, Sadie had felt unexpectedly optimistic about going to the singing, but now that they were there, she was having second thoughts and wished she hadn't come at all.

"Just not feeling altogether social, I reckon," she said, giving a little shrug. She tried to force a smile, but it felt strained. "Truth is that I keep thinking about Belle's predicament."

Leaning forward so no one could overhear her, Anna Rose whispered, "I know. It's all so very strange!"

"Strange?" Sadie could think of many other words besides "strange" that would better describe Belle's wedding announcement. The word "tragic" immediately came to mind, and her spirits sank even lower. "It'll be different now that she won't be attending singings with us anymore."

"And living so far from town."

Sadie hadn't thought of that. With Belle marrying Adam, they would rarely get to see their friend. "Adam does live far from the town proper, doesn't he?"

A sigh slipped through Anna Rose's lips. "I suppose she has her reasons, Sadie, and that she has made peace with her decision. No sense in us feeling sorry for her. We don't know the whole story and might never learn much more about it. But God has plans for all of us." She waited until Sadie looked at her before she smiled. "And I'm sure he has a *wunderbarr* plan for Belle, even if none of us can figure out what it might be at the moment."

Somehow, Anna Rose's words made Sadie feel a bit better. Her heart still felt heavy, but she knew that God would take care of Belle, just as he always took care of all his children.

Trying to take her mind off Belle, Sadie scanned the crowded first-floor room of the Riehls' house. The youth singings were held on every other Sunday at the same house where morning worship took place. On the off-Sundays, when they didn't worship, there were no singings, either. Sometimes members of the youth groups, usually the more adventuresome ones, traveled to neighboring towns to attend their singings. Likewise, other youth groups sometimes came to the Echo Creek singings during their off-Sundays.

Today, however, it was especially crowded.

"I feel like an outsider," Sadie whispered. "There's an awful lot of young folk here whom I don't know. Why, I don't think I've met half the people in this room," she added while wondering again why she had agreed to come.

Anna Rose also surveyed the room, but she appeared

to be searching for someone particular. "I reckon you're right. I only recognize a few people from Liberty Falls."

"That's an awful long way to travel for a youth singing."

"Oh, just an hour or so by buggy, if they live on the east side, don't you think?"

Sadie shrugged. She had never been to Liberty Falls. In fact, when it came right down to it, she had never left the vicinity of Echo Creek. At least not that she could remember. "I reckon. Still a long way."

A group of young men walked by and Sadie frowned when she caught them looking at her and Anna Rose in a leering way. It made her doubly uncomfortable because she had never seen them before.

"Clearly those Liberty Falls fellows don't have the same manners as our young men do," Sadie observed drily.

Distracted, Anna Rose suddenly lit up and lifted her hand in the air. "Oh, look, Sadie! There's my cousin," she said while waving at a group of young men that were gathered on the other side of the room. Sadie glanced in the direction her friend was waving, but the room was so crowded, she couldn't figure out who her friend was talking about.

"Sadie Whitaker!"

Upon hearing her name, she turned around. "Rhoda!" She embraced the young woman, a friend of hers from Liberty Creek. "I didn't know you would be here tonight."

Rhoda smiled, her pale face lit up by the curly red hair that framed it. "And why not? It isn't often that our youth groups have a singing together. How are things here in Echo Creek?"

Sadie hadn't seen Rhoda since the springtime, when she had traveled to Echo Creek with some friends to spend a day visiting with Ella, Belle, and Anna Rose. But that time, Sadie had known that Rhoda was coming, for she had written a letter the week prior. This time, Rhoda had surprised her.

"Quite well. And how are things in Liberty Creek?" She paused, remembering something from their visit several months ago. "How's your *grossmammi*? She was feeling poorly the last time you visited."

Rhoda's smile left her face, and for a moment, Sadie feared the worst. "She's not doing much better, I'm afraid. She's bedridden now. But I spend time with her every week."

Sadie wasn't surprised. While Sadie considered Rhoda a friend, she wasn't as familiar with her as she was with Ella, Belle, and Anna Rose. But it had always been apparent that Rhoda was thoughtful and kind. "She's not gone to live with you, then?"

Shaking her head, Rhoda sighed. "Every week I ask her. But she's still very stubborn, my *grossmammi*. She won't give up her little *haus* in the woods." Somehow, she managed to smile. "God's taking care of her, I'm sure." She glanced over Sadie's shoulder. "Oh, I see Elizabeth. I best go say hello before the singing starts."

Watching Rhoda hurry off toward Elizabeth, Sadie couldn't help but think that Rhoda and her grandmother were fortunate to have each other. Sadie had never known her own grandparents. But if she had, she knew that she would've been as attentive to them as Rhoda was to *her* grandmother.

That was one of the things that Sadie loved about the Amish community. Aging parents weren't sent away to old-age facilities; they were happily taken care of by their children and grandchildren at home. However, sometimes an older person, especially if they weren't living in the *grossdaddi haus* on one of their children's farms, refused. Clearly Rhoda's grandmother fell into that category.

"So deep in thought, little songbird."

Sadie was startled by the sound of the familiar voice near her ear. She couldn't quite place it but knew she had heard it before. She spun around, even more surprised to see Frederick standing by her side. How could she not have noticed him sneaking up on her? "It's you!"

He laughed. "Indeed it is." Then, he pointed at her. "And it's you," he teased back.

Immediately she felt her cheeks redden.

She hadn't given much thought to the handsome stranger who had caught her singing in the woods by the stream a few days earlier. It wasn't that he hadn't intrigued her, for he most certainly had! But she hadn't expected she would ever see him again. And it had never crossed her mind that he'd show up at a youth gathering.

"I simply meant that . . ." What had she meant? The back of her neck began to feel warm. "I mean, well, I—"

He saved her from further awkwardness. "—You're surprised to see me here?"

A wave of relief washed over her. "*Ja*, that's exactly what I meant."

With his hat tipped back on his head, Frederick rocked back and forth on his heels, his eyes scanning the room. "Understandable, since I rarely go to singings in my own church district, let alone another one. However, I heard that some of Echo Creek's young women are magnificent singers." His eyes met hers. "How could I resist?"

Sadie couldn't help but smile. "I imagine you couldn't." When his eyes widened, she quickly added, "Hearing the singers, of course."

Something lit up on his face—a look of amusement. She hadn't meant to sound flirtatious or playful, but it was hard not to tease him back. And it was clear that he was enjoying their lively banter.

"There you are, Frederick!" Anna Rose appeared beside them, then linked her arm through Sadie's. "This is my friend, Sadie Whitaker. She's the one I'm hoping you can take home."

Frederick raised an eyebrow. "*This* is Sadie Whitaker?"

Anna Rose frowned. "I don't know of any other."

He pursed his lips and gave Sadie serious study. "Can she sing?"

"What?" Anna Rose appeared shocked, but Sadie knew that Frederick was just teasing.

"I'll agree to let her ride home in my buggy, but only if her voice is as pretty as she is."

Her smile faded and Sadie felt the heat rise to her cheeks for the second time that night. She averted her eyes. Did he really think she was pretty?

Anna Rose recognized the jest and gave his arm a smack. "Oh, you! Always fooling and teasing." She rolled her eyes and turned her attention back to Sadie. "Clearly you must realize that this is my cousin, Frederick Keim. And you might also realize that he's rather witty, or he at least *thinks* he is."

Frederick leaned over and, in a whisper loud enough for Sadie to hear, said to Anna Rose, "Remember when I told you I heard a little songbird sitting by the stream when I was on my way to town the other day?"

Anna Rose gave him a quizzical look.

He nodded his head in Sadie's direction. "We've already met."

Within seconds, Anna Rose put two and two together. Her eyes grew larger and her lips made a small O shape. It took her a second to collect herself. "I see." The corners of her mouth lifted into a teasing smile. "*Now* I understand why you wanted to come to the singing."

Feeling uncomfortable with all the attention, Sadie stood on her tiptoes and glanced across the room. "They're getting ready to start," she announced, suddenly grateful that Frederick would have to take a seat on one of the long wooden benches on the men's side of the room.

When the music started, the first few songs were hymns everyone was familiar with from worship. The only difference was that they were sung faster, instead of at the slow-paced rhythm the congregation used during service.

Sadie tried to focus on singing, but she found it difficult. On more than one occasion, she snuck a peek across the room to where Frederick was sitting on a pine bench with the other men. And, on more than one occasion, she caught him sneaking a look in her direction, too.

Sadie felt as if butterflies were fluttering around inside her stomach. So much so that she found it difficult to concentrate on the music as she anticipated the long buggy ride home with Frederick.

After an hour, the group took a break, so Anna Rose and Sadie made their way to the table by the fireplace that was laden with refreshments. There were all sorts of goodies, including home-baked desserts and fresh-squeezed lemonade. When they had each finished a glass of lemonade and a shortbread cookie that was dusted with powdered sugar, Anna Rose excused herself to use the restroom. Standing alone, Sadie clasped her hands behind her back and rocked a little on her heels. She hummed a tune from the last song as she waited for her friend to return.

"Would you be near ready to leave?" a husky voice whispered. The hot breath on her ear made little goose bumps appear on her neck.

Startled, Sadie gave a little jump and quickly turned around. She wasn't surprised to see Frederick standing there. "You like doing that to me, don't you?" she said in a serious tone of voice, but she smiled when she spoke the words.

"Undoubtedly." He gave her a friendly grin. "It's clearly become my calling card. Now, about my question . . ."

"The singing isn't over yet, though." She scanned the room, looking for Anna Rose. Her friend was nowhere to be found. "And Anna Rose is—"

"—Going home with Ben Trautman."

Sadie froze. Her breath came in short bursts and her nerves were suddenly on edge. It was one thing to have walked home with Frederick the other day, but to ride home *alone* in his buggy? And she couldn't help but wonder how Frederick had known that Anna Rose was riding home with Ben Trautman, one of the older youths who, Sadie had thought, was courting Jenny Mae.

"I . . . I . . ." she stammered as she hesitated, looking around for Anna Rose again. She was glad when she finally spotted her. Frederick had been right, because Anna Rose was, indeed, standing beside both Ben and Jenny Mae. Sadie wondered if, perhaps, Frederick had arranged for Ben and Jenny Mae to take Anna Rose home.

Seeing the surprise on her face, Frederick winked at her. "So. Are you ready to go?"

Before Sadie could answer, Frederick placed his hand gently on her arm and began directing her toward the door. No one seemed to notice them leaving, just as Frederick hadn't noticed her hesitation.

Timidly, yet with a strange sensation of excitement coursing through her veins, Sadie followed him outside into the dark night for her very first buggy ride home with a young man.

Chapter Seven

Once seated inside Frederick's buggy, Sadie shivered from the cold. With the days becoming shorter and night falling sooner, the evenings were often in the low 40s. Tonight was no exception.

The buggy jiggled from Frederick's weight as he stepped into the driver's side and settled down in the seat beside her. He glanced at her and frowned. "Cold, then?" Without waiting for her to respond, he reached into the back seat and retrieved a blue wool blanket. "Can't let my little songbird freeze," he quipped. "Wouldn't want you migrating south on me."

My little songbird.

His words both excited her and made her feel nervous. She didn't know him well enough to have formed a strong opinion about him, but it sure seemed as if he had formed one about her. Oh! She hoped he was as wonderful as he seemed, for she realized that she would be mighty disappointed if she were to learn otherwise.

"*Danke.*" She took it and placed it over her lap. For a moment, she paused, wondering if she should offer him the edge of the blanket for his own use, but she felt that might appear too forward. She knew that couples often held hands under a blanket, but she wasn't ready to take a step like *that*.

As if reading her mind, he chuckled. "*Nee*, Sadie. I'm not cold."

"Oh!" She was glad that the buggy was dark so he didn't see the rush of color that heated her cheeks. "I thought . . . I mean, I was just . . ."

He interrupted her with a gracious, "—being very thoughtful. But truly, I'm fine."

She sighed, once again grateful that he'd come to her rescue as she struggled for the right words. Frederick Keim certainly seemed to have a knack for saving her.

After the buggy lurched forward and began rolling down the Riehls' driveway toward the main road, she relaxed. She couldn't remember the last time she'd ridden in a horse and buggy other than her father's. Most days, she merely stayed on the farm, and even though they lived to the south of the town center, Sadie usually went on foot everywhere she could. She didn't mind, either, because she always enjoyed the peace and quiet as she walked, whether traveling to town or to visit her friends. And she especially enjoyed watching the birds and animals as she traveled through the fields along the woods.

Tonight, however, she delighted in the rhythmic noises the horse's hooves made on the macadam as it trotted down the road. The vibrations and hum of the wheels as they gently rolled along nearly made her nod off. She blinked her eyes and took in the soft light from the dashboard's buttons and the glow from the battery-operated lights, which created a romantic mood. She was enjoying it so much, she was grateful that Frederick hadn't jumped right into conversation.

Several minutes passed before Sadie realized they were not headed toward her father's farm.

"Oh help! You're going the wrong way." She leaned forward, her eyes scanning the dark road as she tried to pick out a landmark, so she could make sense of where they were. Out near Ella's house, she reckoned.

"Not to be a contrarian," Frederick said, "but I'm going the right way, Sadie."

She shifted her body to face him. "But my *haus* is back that way," she said as she turned her head and looked out the little back window.

He stifled a laugh. "And this road leads to it, but only after it goes around the farms behind Echo Creek."

"Why, that makes no sense. You're going out of your way."

This time, he laughed out loud. From the faint light, she could see the amusement etched across his face. "Have you never gone home from a singing with anyone, Sadie Whitaker?" Before she could answer, he held up one hand, the other holding both reins. "*Nee*, don't answer that. I'd be faced with the sin of jealousy."

"I have not," she admitted softly.

He leaned over, and his arm brushed against hers. "Ah, *danke* for saving me from surely having to confess to the church," he said before returning his attention to the road and steering the horse and buggy. "So. Since this is your first time, let me explain how it works."

She tried not to smile at the teasing tone in his voice.

"First, the young man plots a long, winding road to take the young woman home." He raised an eyebrow and snuck a sideways glance in her direction. "One could argue that the longer the ride, the more interested the young man, you see."

"Why's that?"

His eyes widened in amusement. "Must you truly ask?"

"I must," she teased back.

"So that he can spend more time with his girl."

His girl. Oh, how those words made her heart flutter.

"Then," he continued, "he stops the buggy just shy of the young woman's *haus* so they can continue talking."

"Is that so?" She tried not to smile. "But shouldn't they have had ample time to talk during this extra-long ride?"

"Absolutely not!" He shook his head in an exaggerated manner. "If the conversation during the ride was interesting and engaging, why would they ever want it to end?"

She was enjoying this flirtatious game Frederick was playing with her. "What more could they talk about?"

"Life. God. Aspirations. Those are important things, you know."

Settling into the seat, Sadie pulled the blanket up until it covered her chest. "Seems to me that we already discussed those things the other day. Why, I seem to recall covering all those topics when we first met."

He slowed down the horse until it stopped in the middle of the deserted road.

"What are you doing?"

Frederick faced her. "I reckon you're right! Why, I best turn the buggy around and take you straight home, then. We've nothing more to talk about!"

For a moment, she thought he was serious. But then, when she saw the hint of a smile on his lips, she couldn't help herself and burst out laughing. He joined her, then clicked his tongue, urging the horse forward again.

"You're very witty." Sadie had never met anyone who teased in such a manner. She liked it.

Frederick shrugged. "I am who I am, I suppose. That's just how God made me." He paused, tilting his head as if a thought had just occurred to him. "Mayhaps more people should find humor in situations. Too many people are so serious all the time. I don't think God minds a few laughs and jests every once in a while."

"Ah, now we're talking about God," she quipped. "I thought that was supposed to be reserved for the end of our ride."

He smiled at her. "True that."

Sadie gave a small sigh. "However, since you've brought God up now, there's no sense waiting until later." She heard him give a soft giggle. "And I agree. People should do what they must, but do it with a happy heart."

"And a song?"

"But of course! Singing is a tribute to God, don't you think?"

"If one does it well," he replied.

"Maybe God is tone-deaf."

At this, Frederick slapped his thigh and chuckled. The sound of his laughter warmed her heart.

For the next hour, Frederick drove the buggy, keeping the horse at a slow walk rather than a trot. They leisurely traveled down the back roads behind Echo Creek and talked while Sadie occasionally paused to point out the glow of a light from a farmhouse in the distance. Frederick asked questions about the families that lived along the way, interested in learning more about the people of Echo Creek.

As they approached her father's farm, true to his word, Frederick slowed down the horse until it stopped walking altogether.

"Since we've covered all your crucial topics," Sadie started, "what do we talk about now?"

He kept his foot on the brake and leaned back, turning his body just enough so that he faced her. "Whatever you want, Sadie Whitaker."

"Hmm." She tried to think of something fun and light to say, but nothing came to mind. Instead, she had a question for him. "It might not be about life, God, or the future, but I was wondering one thing."

He reached out and pulled the blanket up so that it covered her shoulders. "And what's that, little songbird?"

"How is that you know the streets of Echo Creek so

well, but not the people? And why have I never seen you in town before?"

He let his hand fall onto his knee. "Ah. Good question." He seemed to take his time formulating the answer. "I don't come to Echo Creek often, as you so cleverly observed. Growing up, I was usually in school when my *daed* drove into town for supplies. And at that, it was only but once a month due to the conditions of the roads and the distance."

"Oh?"

He nodded. "*Ja*, they aren't well-tended and they do tend to wind quite a bit. That's why I almost always walk here. I can cut across fields and through the forest where there are no roads. Believe it or not, it's much faster."

She couldn't imagine that walking would be faster than taking a horse and buggy.

"Just a few years back, I started making the trip for my *daed*. But almost always on Mondays. I buy supplies for my *maem* as well as my cousins when they can't make the journey."

"That's an awful lot for one person to carry, Frederick."

He shrugged. "If it's a lot, I will take the buggy. Sometimes I stay with Anna Rose's family overnight so the horse can rest."

"Will you do that tonight?"

He nodded. "*Ja*. It's too hard to travel these roads at night, that's for sure and certain. And I can buy supplies first thing in the morning when Troyers' opens for business."

After hearing his reasoning, everything made sense. If he usually traveled to Echo Creek on Mondays, that would explain why she'd never met him before. She was always washing clothes and cleaning the house with Rachel on Mondays.

"But how are you so familiar with the roads then?"

"When I spend the night and while the horse rests, I

like to go and explore on foot. But Anna Rose lives to the north of town so I'm mostly familiar with that area."

That made sense.

With the conversation winding down, Sadie wasn't certain what she was supposed to do. Was she supposed to wait for Frederick to let her out of the buggy? Would he walk her up the driveway? Would he ask to escort her home from the next singing?

When he made no move to get out of the buggy, Sadie decided that she was supposed to simply bid him good night. He was so quiet, she wondered if she had done something wrong. Perhaps he was having second thoughts about escorting her home at all.

Suddenly anxious, she lowered the blanket and reached for the handle on the sliding door. "I best get going," she said softly.

He reached out and touched her other hand. "*Nee*, Sadie. Just sit for a moment. Sometimes silence can be as powerful as words, don't you think?"

She *did* think that, but she also felt uncomfortable not knowing what was expected of her. Slowly, she released the door handle, but noticed that Frederick made no move to remove his hand from hers. It felt odd, the way the warmth of his fingers made her skin tingle.

"Do you ever just look up at the stars, Sadie?"

She raised her eyes and realized that he was staring out the front window, his head tilted as he gazed upward.

"God made those stars," he told her in a solemn voice, "just as he made us. When I was younger, I always thought that the stars were God's angels watching over everyone."

"Do you still believe that?"

He inhaled and slowly let out his breath. "I don't know, Sadie. It sure would be nice if it were true." He turned his head toward her. "But then again, isn't it enough to have God watching over us?"

She felt his grip tighten on her hand, a gentle squeeze.

"Reckon I best walk you in now, *ja*? Just let me tie the horse to that tree limb first."

She watched him as he got out of the buggy, being mindful to quickly shut the door so he didn't let the cold air in. With the light from the headlights, she saw him take a lead rope and attach it to the horse's halter. Once he'd secured the horse to a low-hanging tree limb, he walked to her side of the buggy and opened the door.

"Let's wrap the blanket around your shoulders." He didn't wait for her to do it. Instead, he did it himself. "Can't have my little songbird catching a cold now."

She smiled to herself. She loved the way he called her his little songbird. Surely that meant he was interested in seeing her again.

They walked down the driveway in silence, the only sound being their footsteps on the loose gravel. Frederick kept his hands in his coat pockets, removing them when they reached the front steps. He took her arm and helped her onto the front porch.

"*Danke*, Sadie."

She stood before him, staring into his face. She wasn't certain why he would thank her. She hadn't done anything for him. "*Danke?* For what, Frederick?"

Thrusting his hands back into his pockets, he took a step backward. There was a calm look about his face as he stared at her, his eyes studying her as if trying to memorize each and every feature. "For being such enjoyable company tonight."

Sadie was about to say *You're welcome*, but he turned away before the words could form on her lips. Slowly, he started walking down the driveway.

A feeling of warmth washed over her. She had never imagined that she could feel such joy, especially when it came to a person she had only just met.

As she stepped inside the house, she looked over her shoulder and saw him jogging down the rest of the driveway toward the lights of his buggy. Sadie closed the door, then leaned her back against it. She shut her eyes and listened to the fading sound of his buggy as it turned onto the road and disappeared into the night.

She lifted her hand to untie her black bonnet, only then realizing that Frederick had left the blue blanket still wrapped around her shoulders. Pulling it tight around her, Sadie smiled to herself as she climbed the stairs to her bedroom. More than the blanket would keep her warm tonight, she thought as the memory of Frederick's company burned in her heart.

Chapter Eight

On Wednesday, walking through town, Sadie took her time getting to Troyers' store. The past few days had been terrible. Rachel remained cranky and quick-tempered, taking out most of her frustration on Sadie. No matter how hard Sadie tried, it seemed *nothing* she did was good enough to satisfy her stepmother.

Earlier that morning, her father had asked her to go on a few errands for him. Sadie half suspected that he wanted to give her a break from Rachel's constant berating. Regardless, she could hardly contain her relief when her father requested her help.

The first place she visited was Troyers' General Store. The bell over the door jingled when she entered, and as soon as she stepped inside, she scanned the store to see if Ella was working that day.

Linda Troyer glanced up from a notepad she was writing figures in as Sadie approached the counter.

"*Gut martiye*, Sadie!"

"Morning, Linda." Sadie smiled at Ella's stepmother and waited for the older woman to finish what she was doing.

Shutting the cover, Linda set down the pencil. "What can I help you with today?"

Sadie withdrew the list her father had given her. "Daed sent me for some things." She handed it to Linda.

The older woman glanced at the slip of paper. "I'll check in the back to see if we have these. What's happened? Another cow break through the fence?"

"I reckon. Happens from time to time."

Linda disappeared through a doorway behind the counter and Sadie wandered over to one of the aisles. She looked at the sewing section, her eyes appraising some bolts of pale yellow and green fabric that she knew would be wonderful for a summer quilt.

"Sadie!"

She turned around in time to see Ella hurrying toward her.

"Maem said you were here." Ella grabbed her hands and pulled her over to an empty aisle. "Have you been to see Belle?"

Sadie shook her head. It was Wednesday, and she hadn't left the house all week. "Not since Sunday last. At worship. Why? Has something happened?"

Ella's blue eyes filled with tears. "*Nee*, but I can still hardly believe that Belle's to marry Adam Hershberger! She barely knows him, much less cares for him."

"Oh, the poor girl." Sadie could hardly imagine anything worse. "I'd never marry someone I didn't love, never mind barely knew."

Ella nodded her head in agreement and a mournful look clouded her eyes. "You know," she said, "the wedding's just a week from tomorrow."

Sadie paled. With all the turmoil in her own life, she hadn't given much thought to her friend Belle's plight. A wave of shame washed over her. How could she have forgotten about Belle? "She must be a nervous wreck. I'd run away rather than be forced to marry!" she stated in a low voice so Ella's stepmother couldn't overhear. "Even for my family!"

Ella nodded. "I agree."

Upon hearing Linda's approaching footsteps, Sadie whispered, "You will be going to the wedding, *ja*?"

"Of course!"

"I wish I had time to go visit her," Sadie said, "but Rachel's not been feeling well."

"And Linda always keeps me so busy with chores," Ella added before their conversation ended abruptly.

"Here's two rolls of that wire for repairing the breaks in the fence and a new wire cutter," Linda told her as she placed the items on the counter. She glanced at Ella and her expression seemed to darken. Ella lowered her eyes and said a quick goodbye to Sadie before she retreated into the stockroom from which she had come.

Linda turned her attention back to Sadie and smiled. "Now, anything else that you'll need today, Sadie?"

Outside the store, Sadie shifted the bag of items her father had requested in her arms, then made her way down the front steps. She couldn't wrap her mind around the conversation she had just had with Ella. And Belle? She was far too special a young woman to live life in a loveless marriage.

"Sadie!"

Startled from her thoughts, Sadie looked up in time to see Frederick driving by in his buggy. For a moment, she thought something must be terribly wrong. What would he be doing back in Echo Creek? Why, it had only been three days since the weekend.

Frederick pulled back on the reins to stop the buggy. "That bag looks heavy," he said with a bright smile lighting up his face. "Let me give you a ride home."

For a moment, she thought about refusing his offer. Too

many people might see her get into his buggy, and she didn't want anyone having cause to gossip. The last thing she needed was the community thinking they were courting. Despite their two meetings, she reminded herself that two outings did not a marriage make. She needed to get to know Frederick better, at least before tongues started wagging.

However, the bag *was* heavy, she reasoned. And what better way to get to know him than by accepting his invitation?

"*Danke*, Frederick. I normally don't mind walking," she said, "but I'd be much obliged to accept." She walked over to the buggy, then handed Frederick the bag through the open door before climbing up and sitting beside him. "It's a bit warm out, isn't it?"

Frederick waited until she was settled before he released the brake and slapped the reins, urging the horse to walk on. "*Ja*, it is. Looks like autumn isn't arriving anytime soon."

"It was sure cold the other night."

He laughed. "Quite true."

She noticed that he held the reins taut in his hands, as if holding back the horse so that it walked, rather than trotted, down the road. "You're becoming a regular in Echo Creek," she pointed out, curious to know why he was back so soon but too afraid to ask. She didn't want to appear too forward, especially if he was here for a personal reason.

"I am that!" he answered, then smiled and Sadie knew that he was teasing her. "I had to visit my cousins who live south of Echo Creek—"

"The Grimm brothers?"

He nodded. "*Ja*, those fellows. Maem asked me to bring them some canned food. Too heavy to carry that, so since I was close by, I thought I'd ride up to Echo Creek."

Sadie frowned. She had never been to the forest where

the Grimm brothers lived, but she knew that it was a far distance from Echo Creek. "Were you visiting with Anna Rose then?"

Frederick shook his head.

"Elizabeth? She's teaching today, you know."

He nodded. "*Ja*, I know that."

Sadie couldn't help but wonder why he would have made the detour to Echo Creek, especially since he had just been there earlier that week. Suddenly, she worried that she was putting him out of his way.

"I enjoyed the singing at the Riehls' the other night," Frederick said at last, breaking the silence and interrupting Sadie's thoughts. "It was a nice change of pace. We don't have such a large youth group as yours."

"Oh?" Sadie turned to look at him. During their drive home the other night, they had talked about so many things, but, embarrassed, Sadie suddenly realized that she hadn't inquired about his church district. "Your town must be very small, indeed, then."

He tilted his head as if contemplating what she had just said. "*Nee*, not so small. Certainly, it's the size of Echo Creek, but we've fewer young folk than you do, I reckon. And when we go visiting, we usually head to Blue Springs."

"Blue Springs?" She'd never heard of that town before.

"*Ja*, Blue Springs. It's farther south from us, but the road is easier to travel, especially at night."

That made sense. Sadie nestled into the seat and stared out the window. They passed the schoolhouse and she could see inside the windows along the side of the building, recognizing Elizabeth, Anna Rose's cousin—and therefore Frederick's, too—as she stood in front of the class, talking to her students.

As Frederick drove farther, she looked at the clothes-line that was hanging from a nearby house. On the line were white sheets and several blue quilts, which reminded her of something.

"Oh!" Turning to face Frederick, she noticed he had been watching her out of the corner of his eye. His attention made her heart race. "I almost forgot to tell you that you left your blanket with me the other night. Mayhaps I can run inside to fetch it when you drop me off."

But he shook his head. "*Nee*, Sadie. You keep that."

Sadie raised her eyebrows in confusion. "Keep it? With winter coming up? Surely you will need it in the buggy to help stay warm."

"I'd much prefer to know that it's keeping *you* warm this winter, Sadie."

The heat rose to her neck and she knew that her cheeks were flushing red.

For a few minutes, they remained silent until, in the distance, Sadie spotted the mailbox of her father's farm.

"Well, *danke* again for the ride," she said as they neared it.

Frederick cleared his throat as if he wanted to say something more. But then, as if on second thought, he changed his mind. "My pleasure, Sadie Whitaker."

As the buggy made its way down the driveway, Sadie could see Rachel sitting upon one of the rocking chairs on the front porch, a blue blanket covering her knees.

Frederick's blanket.

Sadie's blanket.

A wave of anger washed over her. Why would her stepmother have gone into her bedroom? And an even better question was why would Rachel take something that didn't belong to her?

But then, Sadie's irritation turned into fear as she watched Rachel's eyes follow the buggy as it approached the house. Her expression seemed to be growing darker with each passing moment. Sadie found herself shrinking inside the buggy, wondering what Rachel would say about her accepting a ride from Frederick. She was certain that Rachel would demand to know where the mysterious blue blanket had come from.

"You can stop here," Sadie said in a small voice. She only hoped that Frederick hadn't noticed the blanket covering Rachel's legs and put two and two together. "My stepmother hasn't been feeling well. I don't want to disturb her."

Sadie was relieved when Frederick slowed down the horse and buggy and stopped halfway down the driveway. He turned and faced her.

"It was right *gut* to see you, Sadie," he said as she reached for the door handle and started to get out of the buggy.

Sadie could barely reply. Her nerves were taut with tension. She reached for the bag and felt Frederick's hand touch hers. Looking up, she couldn't help but lose herself in the moment, in the dark eyes that stared back at her with such tenderness.

"I hope to see you again soon," he said softly.

She felt her cheeks grow hot. Surely, she was blushing. "*Danke*, Frederick," she whispered, hoisting the bag onto her hip and backing away from the buggy. She raised her free hand and waved. Frederick leaned out the open window and tipped his hat, then continued down the road, traveling south.

Away from Echo Creek, she thought.

It dawned on Sadie that, perhaps, Frederick Keim had traveled all that way from his little Amish community just to see her. The thought made her insides grow warm and she felt gloriously happy. Did this mean that he intended to come call on her?

The sound of a door shutting interrupted her happy thoughts. She turned in time to notice that the rocking chair was still moving, but empty now. Sadie walked up the front steps, wondering why Rachel had disappeared so abruptly. But then she stopped, because the second thing she noticed was the blue blanket, the one that Frederick had given to her, lying in a crumpled heap on the floorboards.

With a sigh, Sadie reached down and lifted the blanket off the dirty floor and hung it on the back of the rocking chair. She was so disturbed she decided to go to the barn, instead of the house. She would give her father the bag of items from town and see if he needed any help with the livestock. Anything to avoid being alone with Rachel.

Chapter Nine

All through the following week, Sadie would catch Rachel watching her.

At first, Sadie wondered if she was imagining it. Perhaps she was just being paranoid? But sure as rain, every time Sadie looked over at her, Rachel had her eyes narrowed and trained on her, taking stock of her every move. The only time she seemed to be kind to Sadie was at mealtime when Jacob was present. Oh, how she wished her father could witness Rachel's behavior firsthand.

Rachel never said anything out loud, but the sour expression on her face clearly stated her displeasure. In fact, the intensity with which Rachel scrutinized her from sunup to sunset became so uncomfortable, Sadie found herself grateful when Belle's wedding day arrived. Despite her concern about her friend's willingness to wed a man she barely knew and obviously didn't love, Sadie welcomed the opportunity to be away for the entire day and, hopefully, well into the night.

She needed a break from Rachel, and Belle's wedding afforded her the perfect excuse. And even though Rachel would be attending the service and reception along with

Jacob, she would surely be on her best behavior. Sadie wouldn't have to worry about being criticized in front of her father or the congregation. *At least I'll have one day of peace,* she thought that morning as she prepared white butter cookies to bring to the wedding reception.

During the service, Sadie and Ella stood together, at one point clenching their hands as they watched their dear friend marry Adam Hershberger. The wide brim of his black hat covered most of his face, hiding the scars that disfigured the left side and added to his disrepute.

As soon as the ceremony was over, Adam turned his back to their guests and walked to the rear exit of the house, leaving his new bride standing alone. Anna Rose and Sadie stepped forward to give Belle their blessing, along with other members of their congregation, then joined the other women to help set out the tables of food.

"I can't believe he left right after the ceremony!"

Sadie couldn't, either, but she wasn't about to say such a thing. Whether they liked it or not, Adam was now Belle's husband.

"I wonder if everyone will stay for a singing afterward," Drusilla said.

Sadie shrugged her shoulders, not caring either way. There was nothing that could bring joy to this day as far as she was concerned. Nothing except the love of God, who had blessed this marriage for whatever reasons He might have. Sadie just wished she knew what those reasons were. But it wasn't her place to question the will of God.

"Well, if there is a singing, I want *him* to drive me home," Drusilla added, gesturing with her head toward the other side of the room where the young men were gathered.

Ella, Anna Rose, and Sadie followed her gaze.

"Oh!" Anna Rose exclaimed when she realized who, exactly, Drusilla was referring to. "That's my cousin Frederick!" She turned to Sadie. "I didn't know he was invited."

"Do *you* know him?" Drusilla asked Sadie, her question more pointed than casual.

Sadie swallowed, feeling exposed under the other girl's scrutiny. "I met him at the singing the other week." For some reason, she didn't want to share with Drusilla that she had, in fact, met Frederick even earlier, while sitting by the stream. She justified the omission since, in truth, she *had* officially met Frederick when Anna Rose had introduced them at the singing.

"I didn't see him at the singing." Drusilla sounded disappointed.

Anna Rose ignored Drusilla's comment but made sure to let her know that he was interested in Sadie. "And he drove Sadie home afterward," she told her matter-of-factly.

Anna Rose's announcement caused Drusilla to snap her head in Sadie's direction. Sadie knew better than to make eye contact with her. Everyone in Echo Creek knew that Sadie had never ridden home from a singing with *any* young man, not even young men that she might consider just friends. Surely this little tidbit of news would soon have tongues wagging.

"I see," Drusilla said, her tone dry and unforgiving.

But something about Drusilla's previous comment struck a chord with Sadie. "He frequents your *maem*'s store, Drusilla. On Mondays, usually. Surely you've seen him there before?"

Drusilla made a face of disapproval. "On Mondays? I try to avoid the store on Mondays. It's too busy. One can hardly think straight!"

Sadie fought the urge to roll her eyes. Ella wasn't one to complain, but most people in Echo Creek knew that her stepsisters avoided work at all costs. Or at least, avoided it when it didn't benefit them. Clearly, Mondays fell into that category.

Their conversation was suddenly interrupted when

Rachel neared, a smile on her face, which caught Sadie off guard. She hadn't seen her stepmother look so happy and cheerful since she'd learned she wasn't pregnant. Perhaps she's beginning to feel more like her old self, Sadie thought with a glimmer of hope.

"Sadie, come with me. I want to introduce you to someone," Rachel told her as she turned back around and started to walk away.

Curious, Sadie left her friends and followed her stepmother toward the middle of the room, where Jacob was talking to an older man. Sadie could hear snippets of conversations as she followed Rachel. People were talking in hushed voices while glancing at Belle, and Sadie didn't have to guess as to what they were talking about: Adam's departure from his own wedding reception.

"Have you met John Rabor?" Rachel asked when they reached Jacob and the elderly man.

Sadie looked at the old man and smiled, then shook her head, perplexed as to why Rachel had come to fetch her at all. She had heard of John Rabor, who lived south of Echo Creek, almost three miles from the Whitakers' farm. Normally he attended worship service at the smaller neighboring church district, but on a few special occasions, he traveled the distance to worship in Echo Creek. Sadie had never met him.

Now, standing before him, she only saw an older man with thinning gray hair and a long, wiry beard. Clearly, he was married, and if Sadie had to guess, she figured he was well into his forties.

The old man studied Sadie with such intensity that, for a moment, she couldn't help but wonder if this was how livestock might feel when put to auction. He pressed his lips together and made a noise that sounded a bit like approval.

"You like farming, then?" he asked, his voice gruff and direct.

The question caught her off guard. What on earth was Rachel up to?

"I do," Sadie responded warily. "Although I'm more often to be found helping Rachel in the *haus*."

Another noise. "That's *gut*," he mumbled.

Sadie glanced at her father and noticed that he was watching the exchange, his expression bored and uninterested.

Rachel, however, appeared oblivious to her husband's lack of interest and Sadie's confusion. "John Rabor lives near the forest, you know."

Sadie had not known that and, frankly, didn't much care. But she feigned interest. "Oh?"

"He's quite the hunter."

Somehow Sadie hid her aversion to that announcement. She knew that the food she ate came from the farm: the vegetables from the garden, the eggs from the chickens, and the meat from a neighboring farm that raised Hereford cows. But that didn't mean that she liked it.

As for hunting, she deplored the thought of anyone shooting a wild animal, be it a deer, pheasant, or wild hare.

"I just took down a nice buck this week," John said, his muddy-colored eyes staring at Sadie from behind round wire-rimmed glasses. "I'll bring some meat to you."

Nothing could have turned Sadie's stomach more. "I'm not much of a venison eater," she confessed and glanced over her shoulder toward where her friends were still standing. She tried to think of a polite way to escape, but before she could feign an excuse, she was interrupted.

"Oh, such nonsense." Rachel gave a nervous little laugh. "That would be *wunderbarr*, wouldn't it, Jacob?"

"*Ja*, right *gut*."

"I haven't had venison in ages," Rachel said.

Sadie frowned. The thought of eating meat from a beautiful deer repulsed her. But she knew it would be rude to say so. So instead of speaking her mind, she merely forced a weak smile.

The old man turned toward Jacob. "In fact, I shot that deer right near your farm."

Immediately, the smile vanished from Sadie's face and she started to feel nauseous.

"A nice six-pointer," he continued, oblivious to the change in Sadie's demeanor. "Why, it was standing quiet as could be near that little stream. Just minding its business and drinking some water. One shot in the neck and it went down right in the very spot it was standing. One of the easiest kills I've had in a long while. Didn't have to track it none this time."

Sadie felt light-headed and faint. She could clearly envision the majestic buck she'd had the privilege of watching just two weeks ago. Another wave of nausea washed over her, and she knew that the color had all but drained from her face.

"If you'll excuse me," she said in a hushed voice, "I need some fresh air." She didn't wait for anyone to say anything before she quickly slipped away.

Outside, Sadie stood on the front stoop, leaning against the beadboard of the house. She shut her eyes and took deep breaths, willing herself not to cry over the buck. Surely it had to be the same one. And her heart broke even further at the thought that it might have trusted the presence of John Rabor, because *she* had caused it no harm when *she* had observed it.

Oh, the cruelty of man, she thought bitterly. When there was so much food readily available, why did men like John Rabor insist on killing such beautiful creatures? There wasn't an abundance of deer in the area and now, to her dismay, there was one less.

"We meet again," a voice whispered behind her.

Startled, Sadie turned around and saw Frederick standing in the open doorway. The color rose to her cheeks and she took a small step backward. "You frightened me."

He pressed his hand against his chest. "For that, I apologize. I didn't intend to catch you off guard." But no sooner had the words left his lips than she noticed a little sparkle in his eyes that told her otherwise.

"I wasn't aware that you knew Belle or Adam Hershberger." At first, Sadie hadn't thought that Frederick would be attending the service and ceremony, as he lived outside their district. But over three hundred people had filled the small house, so she hadn't been that surprised to see him across the room earlier. Secretly, she'd wished that he might talk with her. And now, her wish had been answered. He looked most attractive in his Sunday best, and she was certain that Drusilla would feel the same. Frederick gave a little shrug of his shoulder. "Anna Rose mentioned there was a wedding today. I've met Belle's *daed* once or twice, and when I stopped in to visit him last week, he invited me. He tried to sell my own *daed* a grill that he made."

"Did he buy it?"

"The grill?" Frederick shook his head. "*Nee*, he did not. We already have one, although it's not as fancy as what Melvin created."

Sadie knew *that* had been part of the problem with Melvin Beiler. No one wanted to buy his inventions, not just because they already owned similar devices but because most Amish people avoided fancy things. That was one of the reasons Melvin hadn't been able to keep up with the mortgage payments and Belle had been forced to marry Adam.

She sighed and glanced around the room, looking for Belle.

"I'd like to ask you a question, Sadie."

She returned her attention to Frederick, wondering what he could possibly want to ask her.

He leaned down and lowered his voice. "I've concluded that this is a most unconventional wedding."

Though Sadie couldn't agree more, her curiosity was piqued. "That's not really a question," she observed, "but I am curious as to why you would say that."

His eyes sparkled. "The groom left, and the bride remains."

She was glad he hadn't brought up the fact that Belle hardly knew Adam and wasn't in love with him. "So what's your question then?"

"Because it is an unconventional wedding, I thought I, too, would do something out of the ordinary."

"Oh?"

With a very serious expression, he nodded. "Indeed."

"And what is that?" she asked, genuinely curious.

"I would like your permission to take you home, and, from the looks of things, perhaps sooner rather than later."

He had, once again, caught her off guard.

Most weddings went on for hours, well into the evening. However, she suspected that this would not be the case today. While the tables seemed plentiful—Sadie couldn't help but wonder where all the food had come from—there was a heaviness in the air that suffocated the typical joy of most wedding celebrations.

"Why sooner rather than later?" she heard herself ask, realizing too late that she hadn't answered his question.

He gestured toward where Belle sat alone at the *eck* table; the place beside her, where her groom was supposed to sit, remained empty. She also noticed that the young unmarried adults, who were supposed to be partnered up, were not following custom. No one was certain what to do or how to behave.

It was, indeed, unconventional.

"I imagine once everyone is finished eating, they will

quietly leave," Frederick said in a soft voice. "So, I thought we might go up and say a kind word to Belle, then slip out the back door. No one would be the wiser and . . ." His voice trailed off, his sentence unfinished.

"And what?" Sadie asked.

He took a deep breath and studied her face, his gaze soft and gentle. "To be truthful, I would not have come except that I wanted to see you again. So, given the current mood in the room, I'd much prefer taking a nice, leisurely buggy ride rather than staying here among so many morose people on what should've been a day of enormous joy."

His words touched her. It was true that the guests seemed to be milling about, uncertain of what traditions to follow when so many had already been broken. But the food looked wonderful and Sadie had intended to offer her help cleaning up.

"I haven't eaten yet," she said. "Have you?"

Frederick's lips twitched, and he smiled in a secretive sort of way. "I have not," he admitted. "But Anna Rose made two plates and put them in a basket for us. We can have a picnic."

Sadie caught her breath. *Us?* Had he been so convinced that she would agree to sneak out with him? And yet, one look at those sparkling blue eyes convinced Sadie that there was no possible response but to say yes. Frederick might be clever and shrewd, but he was not at all malicious. Of that, she was sure and certain. No, he was being a perfect gentleman and his intentions seemed pure.

"A picnic sounds like a fine way to spend the rest of the afternoon," Sadie said with a lighthearted feeling she hadn't experienced in a great while.

Chapter Ten

Sadie felt wonderfully carefree as Frederick helped her step into his buggy. Sure enough, as she glanced around, she caught sight of a wicker basket and a red plaid blanket sitting on the back seat. Clearly Frederick had planned this excursion, and that thought alone made her feel warm inside, despite the cool weather.

He climbed into the other side of the buggy and sat beside her. "Ready?" he asked as he released the foot brake and reached for the reins.

Nodding, Sadie leaned back against the seat, feeling the buggy jolt forward. The wheels crunched over the gravel driveway, and when they turned onto the road, there was a creaking noise as one of them hit the rub iron, the piece of metal on the side of the buggy that helped keep it from overturning.

"So . . ." Frederick started. but didn't finish the sentence.

"So?"

"So where is a nice place to go sit a spell? As you know, I'm not very familiar with Echo Creek. This part, anyway."

Sadie pursed her lips and thought about it for a bit. The only place she could think of was the swimming hole on the edge of town. The creek that fed it was the same one that meandered behind town and led to her own father's farm.

She pointed toward a narrow dirt lane. "Turn there if you can, but be careful. I've never seen a buggy travel on the track before."

Frederick leaned forward as if assessing the lane. "Looks wide enough. Is there a turnaround?"

"*Ja*, near the swimming hole."

"Perfect," he said cheerfully. "Once again, we shall head toward the water."

The buggy rolled down the lane and, except for a few small rocks in the path, it barely jostled at all. Upon reaching the clearing, Frederick pulled back on the reins and pressed the foot brake.

Without being asked, Sadie climbed out and held the horse by the bridle until Frederick could secure the tether to the low branch of a nearby tree.

"There!" He wiped his hands on his pants as he finished up. "This is a *wunderbarr* spot, Sadie Whitaker. Do you come here often?"

"*Nee*, not often. It's too far from my own *haus*. But sometimes Belle, Ella, and I come here in the summer when we visit Ella. Her *haus* is just on the other side of the road."

"It does get rather busy during the autumn on a farm, doesn't it?" He shoved his hands in his pockets and looked around. His eyes fell upon a large flat rock. "Ah, there's the perfect spot. Let me fetch the basket and blanket."

She watched as he jogged back to the buggy, half of his body disappearing through the open door. When he reemerged, he had the blanket over his arm and was carrying the basket with his other hand.

Eyeing him suspiciously, Sadie couldn't help but ask, "Do you always come prepared to picnic?"

Laughing, he walked past her and set down the basket

on the flat part of the rock. Sadie joined him, and then they each took one end of the blanket and spread it out on the ground. "*Nee*, I do not, Sadie. Except when I'm hopeful of meeting up with a particular young woman."

"Does that happen often?"

"*This* is the first time."

Sadie didn't know how to react to his words. She looked over at the water, feeling flustered, nervous, and happy all at once.

Frederick knelt on the blanket and lifted the lid of the wicker basket. "Let's see what Anna Rose packed in here for us."

"I feel a little guilty for not having stayed at the wedding reception," Sadie confessed. "Poor Belle."

At her words, Frederick looked up at her. "Why poor Belle?"

His question startled her. Hadn't he been present when Adam left right after the ceremony? Perhaps he had arrived after the bishop had ordained the marriage with his final blessing? But then she remembered that he had been the one who had pointed out that the wedding was rather unusual. "Unconventional" had been his exact word.

"Why, you know that her new husband left just moments after the ceremony ended!"

He took a deep breath. "I suppose I don't blame him."

Sadie gasped.

"Now hear me out," Frederick said quickly, raising his hand as if to stop her from judging him and his words. "From what little I know about him, Adam Hershberger has not been treated kindly by the good people of Echo Creek. I suppose he could have opted for a small, private wedding, but it appears that he did not. I'd imagine that was because of your friend, Belle. Doesn't every young woman want to have a large wedding with her family and friends around her? And"—he paused as he lifted a plate from the basket—"from the looks of it, Adam provided quite a feast."

When Frederick set down the plate, Sadie was surprised by the variety of food that Anna Rose had packed for them: fried chicken, mashed potatoes, glazed carrots, fresh biscuits, green beans, and sliced ham.

"It seems to me," Frederick continued, "that Belle's new husband went to great lengths to take care of his new wife, even if he chose to not stay and enjoy the wedding feast. Mayhaps he simply didn't want to be the focus of whispered discussions."

Sadie hadn't thought of it that way. "You certainly are looking at both sides of the question."

While she had never been one to participate in the spreading of rumors, she knew that she had not stopped others from doing so. She said a silent prayer to God, asking him to forgive her for not having stood up to the wagging tongues of people in Echo Creek.

And then she said a silent prayer thanking God for having put Frederick into her life. He had just taught her a very valuable lesson. Surely, she had needed that reminder.

While she was focused on her thoughts Frederick continued unpacking their little feast. "Mmm, apple pie for dessert."

Sadie froze. "Oh no!"

He paused. "Something wrong?"

"I'm allergic to apples."

Quickly, he slid the plate of pie back into the basket. "So. No apple pie for us today."

"I'm not that allergic that you can't enjoy it."

He gave a little shrug. "How could I possibly enjoy something, knowing it's harmful to you? That would take away the joy in it for me."

She laughed. "I suppose that's one way to look at it."

After they bowed their heads for a silent prayer of thanks, they began eating their fried chicken and biscuits.

"How long have you known Adam?" Sadie asked before taking a bite of chicken.

"I don't really."

Startled by his response, Sadie coughed and had to take a sip of water to clear her throat.

"You okay?"

She nodded and set down the bottle of water. "You showed up at his wedding without ever having met him?" Such an idea surprised her.

Frederick shook his head from side to side. "Well, maybe that's not true entirely."

"So you *do* know him?"

"I suppose you could say that. I met Adam several times at the livestock auction in Liberty Falls. He seemed like a congenial fellow."

Sadie gawked at him. "You met Adam at an auction? Why, I heard he was so reclusive he never left his farm but a few times a year to get supplies in town."

"*Ja.*" He reached for a spoonful of his mashed potatoes. "I sat next to him at the last auction. Daed and I were looking for a new bull for our herd. Seems that Adam was, too." He took a bite of mashed potatoes and a forkful of carrots. "We got to talking and all. Once you get past the scars on his face, he's a right *gut* fellow." He paused. "In an odd sort of way."

Sadie was more than curious. "What do you mean?"

"Well, it seems to me that Jesus taught us quite a bit about not judging people. We're all his children, *ja*?"

She nodded.

"And while Adam might not be comfortable to look at on the outside, there are many attractive people who wear their ugliness on the inside." He took a deep breath. "We're all sinners, Sadie." He held up his hand in an exaggerated way. "*Ja*, even you and me, shocking as *that* might be to consider."

She laughed.

"In my short life, I've learned that outer appearances mean nothing. It's what's in here"—he placed his hand over his heart—"that matters the most."

For a split second, Sadie thought about Rachel. For so many years, Sadie had thought she was a beautiful woman. But when she began noticing how much time Rachel spent caring for her appearance, and harboring jealousy toward others for their youthfulness, Sadie realized that her stepmother cared more about her looks than about what bloomed in her heart. Now, with Rachel being so erratic and moody of late, Sadie realized that what her stepmother carried in her heart did not match the reflection that intrigued her so much in the mirror.

"Is it possible," Sadie began to ask slowly, "for a person to mask their true self for a long time?"

Frederick picked up a drumstick. "I sure reckon so. Why! Look at all the people in the Bible who did just that. Judas Iscariot is a perfect example. He walked with Jesus, but he was still quick to betray him for bits of silver."

"Thirty pieces."

His eyes widened. "Excuse me?"

Sadie tried not to smile at the surprised expression that covered his face. "Thirty pieces of silver." And then she quoted from the Book of Matthew:

"Then one of the twelve, who was called Judas Iscariot, went to the chief priests and said, 'What will you give me if I deliver him to you?' And they paid him thirty pieces of silver. And from that moment he sought an opportunity to betray him."

Frederick chuckled. "My, my. A woman after my own heart. Not only does she sing like a beautiful little songbird, she knows her Scripture, too."

She sat up straighter.

Frederick narrowed his eyes in a mischievous sort of

way. "Did you know that Joseph was sold to Egypt as a slave for twenty pieces of silver?"

Sadie hid her smile. "And did you know that Eve sold mankind for one bite of an apple?"

"Ah!" Frederick slapped his hand on his knee. "Got you on that one."

"How so?"

Frederick cleared his throat dramatically before he, too, began quoting Scripture:

"The woman said to the serpent, 'We may eat fruit from the trees in the garden, but God did say, "You must not eat fruit from the tree that is in the middle of the garden, and you must not touch it, or you will die."'"

Laughing, Sadie covered her mouth. "Ach! You're right. It never said an apple. Why, it could have been any fruit, couldn't it?"

He took another bite of his chicken. "How do you know so much about the Bible?"

She raised an eyebrow and pursed her lips. "How do *you* know so much about the Bible?"

He shrugged. "I enjoy reading Scripture in my spare time. And, when I was younger, my *maem* and I always played a game repeating Bible verses to each other." He paused and looked at Sadie. "I think my *maem* will like you very much."

Will. He hadn't said "would" like you but "will" like you. Did he intend to introduce her to his parents? She could hardly imagine how that would be possible, as they lived too far away to make a one-day trip.

Feeling shy upon this statement, Sadie focused on her plate. However, she found that she no longer had much of an appetite. She didn't want to make any presumptions about Frederick Keim and his intentions, but she couldn't help imagining becoming his *fraa*. Oh, how much she enjoyed his company! She'd never imagined feeling this way, at least not with any of the other young men she knew from Echo Creek.

But she didn't know much about the rituals of courting and wasn't sure how everything worked. Without having siblings and with Rachel's limited experience, Sadie felt as if she were drowning in a sea of uncertainty. Most of her friends, being a bit younger, hadn't really courted, either, so Sadie couldn't even turn to *them* for guidance.

"Sadie."

Upon hearing Frederick say her name, she looked up to find him staring at her, his green eyes holding hers. "I haven't done this before, either."

Had he read her mind? She pressed her lips together and was quiet.

"It's okay. You don't have to say anything. But I can see your fears in your eyes." He gave her a soft smile. "The eye is the lamp of the body."

"I think Jesus meant that we should keep our eye on God."

"Good point. But still, our eyes speak volumes about what we are feeling inside. And I know that I feel as if God led me to that stream the day we first met. Had I traveled another route, and if you hadn't been singing, I never would have known you were there." He took a deep breath. "God led me to you, Sadie Whitaker," he repeated. "And I'm glad that he did."

She bit her lower lip. "Me, too, Frederick."

"So."

"So."

His lips twitched, and she knew that he was trying to hide his smile. "I reckon it's okay with you if"—he paused for a moment—"well, if I keep calling on you, Sadie?"

She felt goose bumps on her arms. Oh, the irony that on this very day, one of her oldest and dearest friends had married a man she did not know or love while she, Sadie

Whitaker, was in the company of a man who had just asked permission to court her, the very final step before a proposal. While her heart broke for Belle, everything in her rejoiced for herself.

"You may keep calling on me," she whispered, hoping that her voice didn't give away her true feelings. "Frederick Keim."

Chapter Eleven

Ever since Belle's wedding, the days felt extra long to Sadie.

Of course, in reality the days were shortening as the sun rose later in the morning and set earlier in the evening. And yet, Sadie felt as if each one dragged on with a somberness that matched her state of mind.

The only good news was that Rachel's mood had softened toward her—just enough to be bearable. While their relationship hadn't returned to the previous level of congeniality, Sadie felt that Rachel was making an attempt to be more pleasant and less demanding.

For that, Sadie was grateful.

Now that it was Sunday, Sadie was anxious to see her friends and was eagerly anticipating the youth gathering. She hadn't had any contact with Ella or Belle or even Anna Rose since Belle's wedding. Instead, she had been cooped up in the house helping Rachel with the many chores that needed to be completed before the winter set in. They had spent two whole days canning and sorting the root vegetables in the cellar and another few days washing the heavier winter quilts and blankets. Sadie was going stir crazy and knew that a little socialization with her friends would definitely improve her mood.

Besides, Sadie hoped that Frederick would also attend. He had asked her to go courting, though she still wasn't exactly sure what that entailed. Certainly, it would mean that he would be taking her home from the singing this Sunday, should he attend, and Sadie was looking forward to the possibility that she might spend some more time with him at the gathering.

But after the noon meal on Sunday, Rachel told Sadie that she wouldn't be attending the youth gathering that evening.

"Why not?" Sadie asked. It wasn't too often that Rachel told Sadie she couldn't visit with her friends. In fact, under normal circumstances, Rachel encouraged her step-daughter to do more things outside the house. But, clearly, these weren't normal circumstances, because on this night, Rachel remained adamant.

"If you must know," she said while peeling potatoes over the counter and letting the scraps fall into a round metal pan that she used for composting, "we've a guest coming to supper. And I want you here."

A guest? In the three years since Rachel had married Jacob, the only guests that had ever come for supper on a Sunday were the bishop and his wife. But Sadie knew that, because it was an off-Sunday, their bishop had traveled to Liberty Falls to preach at another Amish community's worship service.

"Must I stay?" Sadie looked at her father, who sat in his chair reading the Bible. "*Daed?*" she pleaded.

"Rachel says so," was the only comment he made before he turned his attention back to the Bible he was reading.

And that ended any discussion about attending the youth gathering. Her father could have overruled Rachel, but clearly, he didn't want to tempt fate. His wife's mood had improved recently, and he wasn't about to go against her wishes now that things were becoming more bearable at home.

Disappointed, Sadie slumped into a chair and stared out the window. She knew better than to challenge her father; however, whoever was coming for supper was certainly no one of interest to her. Surely it must be one of the elders in the community. From the way Rachel had cleaned the house the previous day, Sadie should have suspected that something was afoot.

When the clock on the wall chimed four times, two hours had passed since Rachel had told Sadie she was to stay home. During that time, Sadie had helped set the table, then retreated to a chair by the fire to read a devotional. While Jacob napped in his recliner in the sitting area of the kitchen, Rachel bustled about, preparing side dishes for the late afternoon meal: chow chow, pickled beets, and, of course, the potato salad that she had made just an hour or so earlier. For once, Rachel hadn't asked Sadie to help with the cooking. Instead, she seemed eager to do everything herself. That, too, was unusual.

It was almost ten after four when the sound of a horse and buggy could be heard coming down the lane toward the house. Rachel made a noise of delight and took off her apron, hanging it up on the hook on the back of the kitchen door. Sadie put down the devotional and stood up to look out the window. She was anxious to see what mystery guest was so important that she had to miss the youth gathering. But all she could make out was the horse and buggy, still too far down the driveway to discern who was at the reins.

Out of the corner of her eye, Sadie could see her stepmother as she slipped into the first-floor bathroom and checked her reflection in the mirror above the sink. Only when she was satisfied did she emerge and walk toward her husband, who had nodded off in his recliner.

"Jacob."

That was all Rachel needed to say to rouse him from his catnap. He jumped up from the chair and stretched his legs, then made his way to the front door.

Sadie, more curious than ever, peeked out into the foyer. But before her eyes could focus in the dim lighting, she heard a gruff voice greet Rachel and knew exactly who had come to visit: John Rabor.

Sadie shut her eyes and cringed. Why on earth would *that* man be having supper at their house?

Sadie could hardly think straight. Rachel had insisted that she stay home from the youth gathering because *he* was their guest for supper? She felt something akin to anger at her stepmother but did her best to swallow it. The last thing she wanted was to cause a scene. But she was still livid. How terribly selfish and unfair of Rachel to make Sadie miss out on the gathering to spend time with old man Rabor.

"Sadie," Rachel called out. The sugary tone of her voice made Sadie hesitate. Why was her stepmother being so nice and why was she trying to impress this man? "Come greet John Rabor."

Confused, Sadie did as she was told. Why on earth would Rachel have felt compelled to invite this man to their home? It wasn't as though he was a neighbor or distant relative! Or even a member of their small congregation. Try as she might, Sadie couldn't think of any reason that made sense at all.

John leered at Sadie as she approached. It was so uncomfortable, the way he made her feel; she imagined she was hunted prey. The thought chilled her, and she could barely respond when he greeted her. His face, so weathered and ancient-looking, showed little emotion. Even his eyes, dull and dark, appeared devoid of emotion.

But she managed to find the wherewithal to speak. "Good day to you, too, John."

He grunted in response. "Brought you that venison from the buck," he told her before dropping a package wrapped in newspaper on the counter. It landed with a sickening thud and Sadie shivered, her stomach feeling queasy at the thought that *her* buck could have been killed and butchered by this callous old man.

"Reckon you can't cook it today anyhow, being Sunday." With that, he turned his attention to Jacob.

Sadie frowned, wondering at his comment. She knew that some of the strictest Amish communities forbade cooking on Sundays. Was John Rabor one of *those* Amish? If so, she wondered what he had thought when he'd entered the Whitakers' kitchen and smelled meatloaf cooking in the oven.

Rachel nudged her. "While the men talk, come help me with dishing out the food, Sadie."

Miserable, Sadie followed Rachel into the kitchen and did as her stepmother instructed.

She was still baffled by this turn of events. Even when they sat down for the meal, and John was seated beside her—not Jacob—she still didn't have a clue as to why he'd been invited to their home to share in the midday meal. From what little she knew about the man, he wasn't a frequent visitor to the Echo Creek community.

Somehow, he had connected with Rachel, possibly at Belle and Adam's wedding, and had made quite an impression on her. Sadie couldn't read her father to see what, if anything, he thought of this John Rabor.

After prayer, John didn't utter another word to her. In fact, he completely ignored her, his attention and focus directed on Jacob alone. Rachel seemed to be hanging on every word he said, but she did not interrupt him. Not even to ask if he would like seconds.

Quietly, Sadie stewed. She could have been at the youth gathering, not here with John Rabor, who, clearly, had no interest in *her* presence whatsoever. She had nothing in common with this stranger who had no respect for God's creatures.

She remained completely silent until dessert was served.

"So, Sadie, John needs some help with his *kinner* during the last week of hunting season," Rachel announced after she set down a freshly baked pumpkin pie in the center of the table. "I told him that you would be willing to help."

Sadie's eyes shot to her father, but he avoided her pleading look. *Kinner?* Why on earth would Rachel have made such a commitment without discussing it with her first? "I . . . I thought John lives toward Blue Springs. Surely that is too far—"

Rachel interrupted her. "Three miles isn't too far. You'll take your *daed*'s buggy. You start tomorrow."

Sadie had suddenly lost her appetite for dessert.

John, however, reached over and grabbed the largest piece of pie. "In the mornings," he said as he shoveled a forkful into his mouth, "you'll feed the *kinner* and get the older ones to school. And I'll be expecting a meal when I return from the morning hunt."

His gruff manner and complete lack of gratitude made Sadie feel invisible. Surely his children couldn't be as ill-mannered. In fact, she wasn't certain *anyone* could be as rude as this man seated beside her.

So, this was what Rachel had had up her sleeve. No wonder she had been so perky of late. She had found a way to punish Sadie, after all. She had found a way to get rid of her, at least for the next week.

"I see." She took a deep breath. "How many are there?"

John barely looked up. "How many what?"

"*Kinner.*"

"Nine."

Sadie felt ill.

"Oldest one's twelve. Youngest is two."

Sadie couldn't help but to feel sorry for his deceased wife. Surely, she had been pregnant every year of their marriage!

Rachel smiled across the table at Sadie. "And, of course, I told him that you'll shop for him when you return to Echo Creek. Such a shame that your church district is so far away, with no stores nearby."

With his mouth full of pie, John motioned at Rachel with his fork. "So I said to the church leaders. It's high time someone opened a store in our district, but the leaders are adamant that merchants bring tourists and outsiders, and with that, worldliness."

Rachel clucked her tongue. "Whoever heard of such nonsense?"

He scoffed, and a piece of pumpkin pie dropped from his mouth onto the tablecloth. He brushed it aside and it fell to the floor. "They'd rather we live off the land, and for the things we cannot grow, we are forced to drive to Blue Springs or Echo Creek once a month or so. It's an inconvenience, to say the least."

Sadie grimaced at the noise John made as he chewed, his mouth open and his beard full of graham cracker crumbs. "It's a wonder you don't move," Sadie mumbled.

"Move?" John dropped his fork and faced her. "Oh, the simplistic world of the young!" he stated, mocking her. "Just pick up and move, *ja*? It's that easy?" He shook his head, laughing at her in a way that made her skin crawl. "Don't be fillin' my young ones' heads with such ridiculous thoughts."

Sadie pressed her lips together. She wasn't used to being spoken to with such disrespect. "If you don't like living there, I fail to see why the idea of moving is ridiculous.

Surely some families enjoy the quaintness and seclusion in your community and others do not. In fact, I understand there is much land to be had for new farms for those who seek seclusion."

But John merely shook his head, dismissing her comments as he returned his attention to Jacob and his pie.

Stewing, Sadie leaned back in her chair. She knew this kind of man. Pompous and arrogant. A firm believer that women were there to serve them and had nothing to offer beyond a hot meal and a clean house full of *bopplin.*

The only good thing, she thought, about traveling to John Rabor's farm was that she might run into Frederick along the way. That idea warmed her and occupied her thoughts for the duration of John's unexpected visit. His departure, which came shortly after the meal ended, could not come soon enough to suit her. Only then did Sadie excuse herself, leaving the kitchen for her stepmother to clean.

"I've to awaken early, it appears," she said drily. Without waiting for a response, she retreated to the comfort and seclusion of her bedroom.

Wrapping herself in the blue blanket that Frederick had given her, she fell asleep with thoughts of him dancing in her head.

Chapter Twelve

As far as Sadie was concerned, John Rabor's house was nothing more than a shack. She arrived at his farm long before the sun rose, but was greeted with anger nonetheless. John flung open the door before she even walked up the front steps.

"The deer will be long gone!" he snapped. "Why didn't you come earlier?"

Taken aback by his harsh welcome, Sadie stammered, trying to find the words to quell his temper. "It's not even six o'clock yet and I had a long ride in the buggy."

"Six o'clock!" He made a noise and waved his hand at her in a dismissive manner. "I should've been out there an hour ago!" He turned his back to her and stomped into the kitchen. "What do you expect me to feed my family if I don't get enough meat for the winter?"

Some hunter, she thought bitterly. His welcome left her with a sour taste in her mouth. After all, she hadn't wanted to come at all. She was doing him a favor, and his lack of gratitude irritated her. Before she could stop herself, she muttered under her breath, "Mayhaps the deer can't tell time."

He stopped walking, frozen in place as he contemplated

her words. She hadn't meant for him to hear her, but clearly, he had. Embarrassed, she started to apologize. However, to his credit, he didn't reply to her brazen comment.

I'm sorry, God, she prayed, even though a part of her thought God might have understood why she'd made the comment in the first place, *forgive me my impudence.*

"The *kinner* will awaken soon. Feed them, pack their lunches, and get them off to school."

His orders lacked any attempt at demonstrating gratefulness.

"And then?" she asked.

John looked over his shoulder at her, his eyebrows furrowed together in a scowl. "And then what?"

"What would you like me to do after they've gone to school?"

"Goodness, girl. You do know how to manage a household, *ja*?" He gestured toward the kitchen. "Do whatever it is you women are trained to do!" And then, still grumbling under his breath, he grabbed his coat and hat before storming out the door.

While she was thankful he was gone—for she had never met such a miserable sort of man!—she wasn't certain what to tackle first.

The kitchen, so dark and dreary, needed a good cleaning. Sadie stood in the center of the cold room—he hadn't even started a fire to warm it for her!—and slowly turned, staring at the dusty shelves that lined the back wall. They were filled with a mismatched set of pots and pans, chipped plates, and different-sized cups. The old cast-iron wood-burning stove was dirty, and the wall behind it was covered in a layer of grease.

"I'm not cleaning this," she mumbled to herself, then, upon hearing her words, felt guilty for her uncharitable remark.

Sadie knew better. She also knew that she could no

sooner *not* clean the kitchen than she could turn and walk out of the house, leaving John Rabor's children unattended. She sighed, remembering her friend Belle's words: a promise is a promise. At least Sadie only had to deal with John and his nine *kinner* for five days, not a lifetime.

Sighing, she walked over to the counters. She began to open the crooked cabinet doors, searching for cleaning supplies.

There werc none to be found.

Settling on a bucket of hot water with a bit of rough hand soap, Sadie took a rag and started cleaning the back wall behind the stove. Dark greasy soot slowly melted away. She had to change the water five times before she managed to get it clean.

And then she began to scrub the kitchen counter and cabinets. While they were not nearly as bad as the stove wall, she still went through four buckets of hot, soapy water.

By the time the sun started to lighten the sky, the kitchen was mostly clean, except for the brown linoleum floor. Progress, she thought as she stared at the fruits of her labor. Even John Rabor would notice that his kitchen was no longer akin to a pigsty.

"Who are you?"

A sleepy voice from the staircase startled her. She spun around and saw a young boy, no more than twelve, staring up at her.

"Sadie Whitaker."

He glanced around the room. His eyes were close together and his face was as dirty as the kitchen had been. "Where's Daed?"

"Hunting." Sadie gestured toward the set table. "You best get cleaned up and ready for school. Then you can have breakfast. And awaken your *bruders* and *schwesters*."

The boy's eyes narrowed. "You're not the boss of me."

So that's how it's to be, Sadie thought. She cleared her

throat, suddenly realizing how long a week it was going to be. "Mayhaps not. But if you want some pancakes, I reckon you might want to do as I've asked."

His eyes widened at the word "pancakes" and, without saying another word, he hurried back upstairs. Within minutes, the kitchen was filled with more children than Sadie could count, and she found herself hovering over the stove, making batch after batch of pancakes and scrapple. She wondered when they'd last eaten a proper meal.

Once their bellies were full, the older children's attitude immediately shifted from compliance to defiance. With the three oldest being boys, Sadie knew that she had her hands full. It was all she could do to insist that they carry their plates to the sink before going upstairs to make their beds.

"Aw, that there's women's work!" Owen, the twelve-year-old, scowled.

"*Ja*, women's work," Matthew repeated his older brother's words.

Sadie took a deep breath and counted to ten. She knew that she'd get further with sugar than with spice. "All right then," she said with a sigh. "I can do it, but I just won't have time to make my special cookies. Such a shame. My oatmeal cookies are so chewy and full of sweet yellow raisins."

Owen looked at Matthew and John before shrugging. The three of them carried their plates to the sink, then took the small children by their hands and led them upstairs. Before long, she heard the sounds of busyness and knew that they were, indeed, making their beds as she'd asked.

By the time she'd made sandwiches and packed their lunch pails, then sent them out the door to walk to school, Sadie was already exhausted. Whatever Rachel thought Sadie had done to deserve such punishment, Sadie knew she had already served her time.

It was close to eleven o'clock when John returned from hunting. The two youngest children were napping, one on the sofa and the other upstairs in bed. The cookies were made, the kitchen was as clean as Sadie could get it, and a warm dinner rested on the stove.

He barely noticed the effort as he hung his gun above the door and tossed his hat on the counter.

Sadie could barely wait to leave.

She noticed he didn't even wash his hands before he sat down, waiting for her to serve him his meal.

She clenched her teeth. "I best get going," she said as she set the pot of chicken casserole onto a trivet in the center of the table. "Maem will be waiting for me."

He grunted and, without even a word of gratitude, dug into the pan.

Relieved, Sadie slipped out the door, hurrying to the stable where she had left her father's horse in a vacant stall. As fast as she could, she harnessed the horse and hitched it to the buggy. She wanted to put as much distance between herself and John Rabor's farm as possible.

Without doubt, it would be a very long week and, after it was over, she vowed she would never set foot on his property again.

When she returned home, her father was in the horse stable, mucking the stalls. He stuck the pitchfork into the ground and walked outside to help her unhitch the horse.

"How was it?"

Sadie didn't want to complain to her father. However, she couldn't find the will to cover up how awful her morning had really been.

"I'd prefer if Rachel might discuss such arrangements with me in the future, Daed," she said after telling him about the filthy house, insolent children, and ungrateful man. "I feel uncomfortable in his presence. He's not a kindly man."

Jacob pursed his lips as if considering her request.

"Why did she offer my help anyway?"

"Reckon she thought you needed to get out more, Sadie. 'Sides, helping our community is a right *gut* thing to do. Jesus tells us as much in the Gospel."

She wished that she could argue with her father, but she knew she couldn't. "You're right," she admitted. "But I sure will be glad when this week is over."

Jacob laughed, then took the horse by the bridle and led it into the stable to be unharnessed before putting it into its stall for the night.

For the rest of the week, Sadie awoke extra early so she could drive to John Rabor's farm and take care of his children. Fortunately, she didn't have to spend too much time with him. Unfortunately, she never once ran into Frederick.

By Friday, Sadie was tired, exhausted from the early mornings, long drives, and hard work. Taking care of someone else's children—and house!—was more difficult than she could have imagined. And the lack of gratitude and appreciation shown to her by the children, especially the oldest boys, made her grateful that, come Saturday morning, she'd be able to sleep until six thirty and not have to deal with nine children anymore!

"When are you comin' back?"

Sadie took a dishrag and wiped the jelly-stained hands of the four-year-old boy, Wilmer, who was sitting on the counter. "Today's the last day of hunting season." She tossed the cloth into the sink. "That makes it *my* last day, too, Wilmer." She put her hands under his armpits and lifted him, intending to set him back on the floor so he could scamper off to play while she washed the breakfast dishes.

But Wilmer wrapped his arms around her neck, refusing to let go.

"Come now," she said, reaching for his hands and trying

to disentangle them. "I need to finish my chores before your *daed* returns."

"But this *is* your new home."

She laughed. *Such silliness,* she thought. "*Nee*, Wilmer, it is not. I have my own home in Echo Creek with my own *daed*."

"Do *you* have a *maem*?"

The question caught her off guard. Her irritation at having been tricked into tending to John Rabor's children and John's miserable attitude had made her forget that the children were without a mother. With the youngest child only two years old, the wounds of having lost their mother were most certainly still fresh in all their hearts.

She knelt down and stared directly into Wilmer's cherubic face. "*Nee*, Wilmer. My *maem*'s gone to heaven."

He lit up. "Then she must know my *maem*!"

The fact that the child found joy in such a notion warmed Sadie's soul. "*Ja*, Wilmer, I imagine they are the very best of friends." Realizing that, in all likelihood, she would not see the boy again, Sadie embraced him.

He squeezed her as tight as he could.

"Now," she said as she extracted herself, "mayhaps you could help me finish my chores. I'm sure your *daed* will be right pleased to hear what a big helper you've been to me."

Wilmer gave her a distrustful look. "Daed always says that men don't do women's chores."

"Oh? Is that so?" She stood up and put her hands on her hips. "And what would your *maem* have said?"

Wilmer grinned. "She'd have told me to jump to it and help her, I reckon."

Sadie smiled at him. "I reckon so, too. So, let's make *her* happy then."

He nodded his head and, together, they went outside to take down the laundry, which, by now, was dry and ready to be folded. Sadie felt a tug at her heart, knowing that, like her, little Wilmer had said goodbye to his mother far too early. But perhaps one day he would get a new mother. She only prayed that whoever agreed to marry old John Rabor was kinder and more genuine than her own stepmother.

Chapter Thirteen

The weather continued to change, and with it, so did Rachel's attitude. Surprisingly enough, Sadie found Rachel slowly returning to her old self. Some of the hostility dissipated and what had become a permanent frown disappeared. When Sadie began to do the washing on Monday, not only did Rachel volunteer to help, but she complimented her when she saw that she had gotten the berry stain out of the white tablecloth. And on Tuesday, Sadie came downstairs to the smell of freshly brewed coffee and sizzling bacon and eggs.

By the time Friday rolled around, Rachel greeted Sadie with a cheerful smile and a happy, "Good morning!"

Things were back to normal indeed.

"After breakfast, I'll get started on the laundry," Sadie said, wondering if Rachel would volunteer to help her again. They always washed sheets and towels on Mondays and clothing on Fridays, and from the looks of it, the weather would cooperate.

"And I believe your *daed* wanted some help in the pasture," Rachel said as she handed Sadie a mug of steaming coffee. "The cows broke some fencing last night."

Another good sign. If Rachel knew that Jacob needed

help, she must have spoken to him already. Surely that meant Rachel had been outside, probably taking a thermos of coffee to Jacob while he milked the cows. Perhaps there *was* hope that she had only been temporarily distressed when she realized she wasn't with child. The explanation did not excuse Rachel's behavior, but knowing it was caused by Rachel's disappointment in not being pregnant—and not a deep-rooted resentment toward her stepdaughter—made Sadie feel better about the temporary rancor her stepmother had displayed toward her.

"The cows broke through again?" Sadie took the mug and inhaled the nutty scent of coffee that arose from it.

"*Ja*, that back field near the forest." Rachel started dishing the eggs into a large white bowl with a chip on the edge. "Something about that forest seems to draw those cows." She gave a little laugh. "With the leaves starting to fall, they should know the grass isn't greener on that side, for sure and certain."

Sadie smiled at the joke.

Rachel finished dishing the eggs and, with steam rising from the bowl, she handed it to Sadie. "And, after that's done, it's nice enough outside that mayhaps we should rake the garden soil and spread some manure. It's a *gut* time to fertilize for next year."

Another surprise. Rachel was already thinking ahead to next spring. That was a good sign. "Did you ask Daed for manure, then?" Sadie took the bowl from Rachel and placed it on the table.

"*Nee*, I haven't. But I'm sure he hasn't mucked the dairy yet."

As if on command, Jacob entered the room, stomping his feet on the front step before he removed his hat and coat.

"Feeling brisk out there today," he said as he hung up his jacket on the wooden hook behind the door. Rubbing his hands along his arms to warm up, he glanced at the table and smiled. "Scrambled eggs and scrapple? Well, that looks right *gut*, Rachel."

Sadie knew that her father loved scrapple in the mornings.

Wiping her hands on a dish towel, Rachel graced him with a smile. The compliment clearly sat well with her. "Thought I owed you a nice breakfast."

It was the closest she had come to apologizing for her moodiness, and Sadie suspected it was enough to satisfy her father.

"Well, *danke*, Rachel. That's right thoughtful of you." Jacob's words caught in his throat and, as if to avoid facing either one of them, he turned to wash his hands. It wasn't usual for her father to show such emotion, and Sadie knew that he felt a sense of relief at Rachel's kind gesture. His reaction warmed her heart and helped Sadie find it within herself to forgive her stepmother, too.

Rachel grabbed a plate of sliced bread and set it down on the table. For a moment, she stood there, her hands on her hips as she assessed the spread of food. Then, as if as an afterthought, she hurried over to the refrigerator, opened the door, and withdrew a small plate of jam. "There!" she said as she placed it on the table next to the bread. "I reckon that's enough food to refuel our bodies for the day, don't you think?"

Drying his hands on the dish towel, Jacob glanced at the table. Sadie followed his gaze. With eggs, scrapple, bread, and even a bowl of peaches, canned just a few weeks ago, no one was apt to go hungry.

"Looks right *gut*." Jacob moved away from the seat toward the head of the table. He sat down and waited for his wife and daughter to join him before he bent his head to silently pray.

Only after he took his first bite did Rachel follow suit. "We'll be spreading manure on the garden today, Jacob. I hadn't mentioned that before. I reckon you haven't done the dairy yet?"

He shook his head. "*Nee.* I'll bring over the wheelbarrow when I'm finished mucking it." He winked at Sadie. "If there's one thing that's abundant on a farm, it's natural fertilizer, *ja*?"

No matter how many times he told it, Sadie always smiled at his joke. It was true. Life as a farmer did come with its ups and downs. Weather dictated the success of the crops. Even though an experienced farmer could make decisions to aid his success, such as watching the weather before cutting hay so that it had time to properly dry before baling, there was little that could be done about droughts or a profusion of rain that often ruined crops. But manure was always available in plenty.

"Speaking of it being chilly out," Jacob said, turning toward Sadie, "I'm afraid it looks like it will be cold for your youth gathering tomorrow."

Suddenly, Rachel stiffened, a tightness returning to the edges of her mouth. "What youth gathering?"

Wondering at the reason behind the terseness of her stepmother's tone, Sadie tried to avoid looking at her. "The large autumn picnic where the Liberty Falls youths join us. We always have a volleyball game." She used her fork and cut her scrapple before dipping it into maple syrup. "They beat us last year. Echo Creek hopes to win this time around."

Jacob laughed. "Is that competition still going on? Why, that dates back to when I was a boy!"

"And who won back then?" Sadie asked before taking a bite of her eggs.

"Usually Liberty Falls."

She sighed. For the past few years running, Liberty Falls had *always* won the annual volleyball game.

But her father merely shrugged. "They've a larger community there, so I reckon that's to be expected. More players to choose from. And it's not as rural there, so the boys have more free time on their hands. Not like Echo Creek, where most of the families farm."

It was true. Living on a farm meant that there was always work to be done. Unlike having a regular job in a town such as Liberty Falls where Amish youth might work in stores or doing trade jobs, the Echo Creek young men tended to livestock and crops. Their slow time was during the winter months, and by then, it was too cold to want to play volleyball. It made sense that the Liberty Creek team usually won.

For a few minutes, silence befell the table as everyone ate. Or, as Sadie noticed, she and her father ate. Rachel, however, sat rigidly, a scowl etched on her face.

"Is something amiss, Rachel?" Jacob asked at last.

"*Ja*, something is amiss." She lifted her eyes and stared at him, and Sadie noticed a strange harshness about her expression. "There seems to be an awful lot of mingling going on with these young people."

Jacob reached out his fork and speared another slab of scrapple. "And what's wrong with that?" he asked as he dropped it onto his plate.

Rachel grimaced. "Well, I'll tell you what's wrong with that!" Her eyes flickered in Sadie's direction. "There's work to be done around here. We need to prepare for winter. Why, we haven't even canned any beef or soup. Besides, there's been enough gallivanting, I should think!"

Once again, Jacob laughed, and *that* clearly did not sit well with Rachel, either. Her face contorted at the sound of her husband making fun of her complaint. "'Gallivanting'? Rachel, that's what a *rumschpringe* is all about, *ja*?" He turned and winked at Sadie. "And let's hope that Echo Creek breaks Liberty Falls' winning streak in that volleyball game this year."

Sadie smiled. "That would be nice, but as long as everyone has fun—"

But Rachel wasn't finished and interrupted her. "So you sanction this, Jacob? This commingling of young men from other towns with your *dochder*?"

This time, Sadie cringed. Rachel never had called her *his* daughter. She always referred to Sadie as *their* daughter.

Jacob set down his fork and leaned his arm on the table. He wore a stern expression on his face. "Might I remind you, Rachel," he said firmly, "that I met *you* at an annual charity auction where there was a 'commingling' of young women from other towns."

Her lips pressed together at the rebuke from her husband.

"And the bishop arranged for us to meet again at a community bake sale. That, too, had 'commingling,' as you call it." Jacob tilted his head and leveled his gaze at her. "Surely you remember that, *ja*?"

Rachel turned her head and looked away.

"Youth gatherings are chaperoned, Rachel. And sanctioned by the church leaders. Surely you find no fault in *their* judgment, even though you clearly question Sadie's."

Sadie hadn't thought of that. How on earth could her stepmother have questioned her judgment? Not once had Sadie given her reason to think that she behaved in any other way than the most righteous and godly.

"Besides," her father continued, "how else is Sadie to meet other people?" His frown deepened. "She's of the age to find a nice young Amish man to marry."

Sadie wished that she could shrink in her seat. Her shoulders hunched over and she slid down, just a little. Just as she had never witnessed her stepmother behave so irrationally, she had never heard her father speak in such a way to his wife.

"A nice *young* Amish man?" The way Rachel stressed

the word "young" made it sound as if Jacob had used a bad word. "Why not just meet a nice Amish *man* who can provide for her?"

Jacob raised an eyebrow.

"And *ja*, I do agree that it's high time for Sadie to find such a *gut* Amish man," Rachel continued, a tilt to her chin in defiance of her husband's words. "Soon she'll be a *maedel* and living here forever."

"Rachel!"

"I can assure you that it would be a burden, at least on me."

Jacob glowered. "I suggest you think carefully about your next words. This conversation is not fit to have in front of Sadie."

Suddenly, Rachel's demeanor changed. Her expression softened and Sadie thought she saw the hint of tears in her stepmother's eyes. Tears always melted her father, and Sadie knew that Rachel was more than aware of that.

"Are you crying?" he asked.

Rachel wiped at her cheeks. "How could I not cry? You favor her so much that it stresses me, Jacob. Perhaps *that* is why I cannot have a *boppli* of my own."

At this, Jacob took a long, deep breath and exhaled. "I'm sure that has nothing to do with it."

"A stress-free home environment is very important!"

Sadie couldn't listen to any more of this conversation. She stood up and grabbed her plate and silverware.

Immediately, Rachel's tears vanished and she glared at Sadie, venom returning to her words. "Where do you think you're going?"

Sadie could hardly look at her stepmother. She felt angered by the accusation Rachel had just made. How could Rachel possibly think that her presence was the reason behind her stepmother's inability to have a baby?

"I've laundry to gather," she managed to reply.

"Sit back down!"

But Jacob waved his hand at Rachel. "Let her go. No sense upsetting the girl. She's done nothing to deserve this."

Quickly, Sadie carried her plate to the sink, then hurried upstairs. As she ascended, she could hear Rachel berating Jacob, insisting that it was high time for *her* to enjoy her own family—and, clearly, that did not include Sadie.

In her bedroom, Sadie flung herself onto the bed and covered her head with her pillow, trying to drown out the voices from downstairs. She didn't want to hear another word from that woman, even though Rachel's words would be forever etched in her memory. How her father could tolerate such ugliness was beyond her comprehension. Even more confounding was the fact that her stepmother seemed intent on using Sadie as the scapegoat.

Where had this mean, self-serving side of Rachel been hiding for the past three years?

Chapter Fourteen

On the outskirts of town, Sadie stood next to Ella, looking across the grassy knoll that bordered the creek. At least sixty young men and women stood around, some playing volleyball, others fishing, and still more lingering in smaller groups, talking and gossiping.

As Sadie had told Rachel the previous morning, it was one of the rare occasions when other youth groups from nearby towns joined them. From the looks of it, at least three other towns had joined up with the Echo Creek sect.

Sadie suspected that Frederick's youth group would be joining them, too.

"I like your dress," Ella said when Sadie removed her crocheted shawl.

Despite its being the time of year when the days were rapidly growing shorter and the air increasingly cooler, God had blessed the young people with a gorgeous autumn day for their picnic, no matter her father's prediction the previous day.

Folding the shawl, Sadie hung it over her arm.

"*Danke*, Ella." Sadie looked down and brushed off an imaginary piece of lint. The red dress was new. Sadie had purchased the fabric when the bishop approved the new

color for the young women of Echo Creek to wear. For a
long time, she hadn't wanted to don it, too afraid that
someone might think she was being worldly. But now
that a few other girls were wearing the red color, she felt
a little more confident.

And she wanted to look nice, just in case Frederick *did*
show up.

She hadn't seen him since Belle's wedding and she
worried that he might have changed his mind about her.
She hoped not. In their short time together, Sadie had
learned a lot from Frederick, and for the first time in her life,
she found herself eager to learn more from a young man.

Anna Rose appeared, a smile on her face. "I thought
you'd never get here!"

"There's a lot of new faces today," Ella said, looking
around.

But Anna Rose reserved her biggest smile for Sadie.
"And a few familiar ones." She pointed toward a crowd of
young men who were already practicing their volleys on
the grass near the volleyball net. "Frederick's over there."

Despite the rapid increase in her heart rate, Sadie tried
to appear nonchalant. It would do no good to have anyone
suspect that she might have an interest in getting to know
him better. "Oh? That's nice."

Anna Rose tried to hide her smile, but her blue eyes
twinkled at the secret she shared with Sadie.

After an hour had passed and Frederick had not approached her, Sadie began to fret that she might have
offended him. Perhaps, over the past week, he had reflected upon her comments that revealed she had judged
Adam without even knowing him. Perhaps he regretted
having asked to come court her. After all, she hadn't

seen him since the wedding. Suddenly, fear overtook her thoughts and she began to panic.

Several times, Sadie glanced in the direction where Frederick stood. Not once did he look her way.

"What's wrong, Sadie?"

"Nothing." She tried to smile at Ella, but she knew that it came across as insincere.

Ella frowned at her. "Surely you realize I know you much better than that, Sadie Whitaker. Something is *definitely* bothering you."

Sadie shook her head. She couldn't confide in her friend; her shame was far too great. "It's nothing, Ella," she said, her voice soft and wavering.

She felt a warm hand on her arm and turned to see Anna Rose. "Sadie!" She gave Sadie a mischievous smile. "Come with me to greet my cousin." Without waiting, Anna Rose grabbed her hand and pulled her across the picnic area to where Frederick sat at a table with two other men.

"Frederick!" Anna Rose practically bounced over to him, her face alight and her eyes blazing with joy at seeing her cousin. "I suspected you'd be here today." Her gaze darted in Sadie's direction. "And look who is with me!"

Frederick barely glanced in Sadie's direction. His expression remained stoic and stern as if masking some emotion, one that Sadie couldn't identify.

Anna Rose, too, noticed the difference in the usually jovial Frederick. "*Wie gehts?*" she asked, staring first at Sadie and then Frederick. "Why are you not greeting her?"

He straightened his shoulders and lifted his chin, turning in Sadie's direction at last. There was no emotion in his eyes as he said, "Congratulations, Sadie Whitaker."

"Congratulations?" Sadie winced. "For what?"

"On your engagement."

Anna Rose's eyes widened and Sadie's mouth opened

to protest. For a moment, though, she could not speak, her shock was so great.

"My engagement?" she repeated after she finally regained her composure. "I can assure you that I've no idea what you're speaking about."

Frederick gave her a hard, cold stare. "I understand that you're to wed John Rabor."

She blinked her eyes. What on earth was he talking about? "John Rabor?" She could hardly believe that anyone would think such a partnership was even possible!

But Frederick nodded just once. "It's the talk of our church district."

Sadie moistened her lips. How had such a rumor been started? And why would Frederick, of all people, believe it? She gave a slight shake of her head. "I imagine it would be," she said slowly, "*if* it were true. But I can assure you that it is another instance of the Amish grapevine growing weeds instead of bearing fruit."

She thought she saw him catch his breath. Had he truly thought she would agree for him to come calling and then immediately promise to marry another? Did he think so little of her? And to sincerely believe that she might agree to marry John Rabor, of all people? The thought was preposterous.

But, then again, Sadie had found it hard to believe Belle was to marry Adam. And she had. Perhaps *that* unlikely marriage had prompted Frederick to believe his ears instead of his heart.

She found herself feeling disturbed that anyone would credit such a story, much less spread it. If the unspoken accusation hadn't been so serious, she might have laughed out loud.

Anna Rose, however, did laugh. "Oh, Frederick," she said, her voice light and full of mirth. "I believe *you'll* be confessing to jealousy when your church congregates for October's Council Meeting."

The color rushed to his cheeks and Sadie made herself look away. It gave her no pleasure to see him so uncomfortable. And yet, she felt sad that he thought so little of her.

Anna Rose must have felt the uncomfortable undercurrent that passed between them and quietly excused herself.

Once they were alone, Frederick shuffled his feet and cleared his throat, clearly uncertain how to address his blunder.

Sadie saved him the trouble. "Is that why I haven't seen you all week?"

He swallowed. "I *have* been busy."

"I see."

"And I . . ." He took a quick breath and exhaled it. "I . . . I admit that I listened to gossip."

"Apparently."

He pursed his lips. "One of the boys bragged at school that his *daed* was getting married. And then I heard you were helping at his *haus* with the *kinner* so I—"

Sadie gave him a look of disbelief as she interrupted him. "Oh, Frederick, how could you make such an assumption?"

"I'm so sorry."

And he looked it, too. Sadie took pity on him and placed her hand on his arm. "I'm sure it was upsetting to you to think that I'd betray our special friendship," she said. "I can assure you, however, that betraying you—or anyone else, for that matter—is not something I would do."

He glanced around, as if making certain no one else could overhear. Then, when he saw some young people too close for his comfort, he gently led her farther away from the crowd.

"Sadie," he whispered, "I can only beg your forgiveness. I'm not one to listen to gossip, but when I heard your name associated with John Rabor, I was"—in the momentary pause, he pressed his lips together and took a deep breath—"stricken with grief at the thought. And rather than maintain hope that the gossip was not true only to be disappointed later, I accepted it so that I would not be hurt later on."

She tried to imagine how she would have felt if she had walked in Frederick's shoes. Their relationship had only just begun, and she knew just enough about him to want to learn more. What if she had heard that *he* was to marry another woman? Sadie knew she'd have been overcome with grief.

She managed to give him a small smile. "I understand, Frederick, and I forgive you."

He didn't look as if he believed her.

"Honest," she reassured him. "Truly I do."

He sighed, a long exhaling of breath, as if he had been holding it for far too long.

"My stepmother arranged it, Frederick," Sadie began to explain. "My helping with his *kinner*. It was only for the final week of hunting season. I'm not certain why she volunteered my help, but I could hardly refuse once she did."

Frederick contemplated this before he nodded. "I understand now."

"And as far as I have heard, John Rabor isn't engaged to anyone, so I've no idea why any of his *kinner* would say such a thing." She imagined it was Owen, with his dark eyes and sassy attitude. "Mayhaps to have something of interest to say for once. They truly lead a sad and lonely life, those children of John's." She lifted her gaze to meet Frederick's eyes. "Now, if it's all the same to you, I'd prefer never to mention this again. The week is over, and I'd just as soon forget it."

This time, Frederick smiled, clearly relieved at her words. "I agree to that wholeheartedly."

"*Gut!*" She graced him with a cheerful smile. "I've heard there are *wunderbarr* hiking paths toward the forest. Mayhaps we could go walking a spell and look out for birds. I just love hearing them sing and seeing their bright, colorful feathers."

"That," Frederick said, returning her smile, "sounds like the perfect plan!"

Together, they strolled toward the edge of the woods, Frederick helping her climb over a fallen log that blocked the dirt path leading to the trail. To Sadie's delight, a red cardinal alighted on a nearby branch as they neared.

"Look, Frederick, isn't he beautiful?" But when she turned toward her companion, she saw that he was staring not at the bird but at something else farther down the path: a six-point buck.

Sadie gasped and stepped away from Frederick. "Oh!" Slowly she moved toward the buck, who stood partially hidden in the brush, its large brown eyes watching her. "I pray that you are my buck," she whispered. "I had thought you were killed by the old man."

To both their surprise, the buck remained still, making no attempt to flee.

When Sadie stood on the other side of the brush, she stopped moving and faced the buck.

"Such a glorious creature," she cooed, and then, as slowly as she could manage, she reached out her hand. On the branch overhead, the red cardinal appeared, landing on the narrow part that hung over the deer's antlers. For a moment, she felt as if the forest fell silent and there was no one else nearby. Just her, the cardinal, and the buck.

Slowly and with great caution, Sadie raised her hand and reached toward the buck's face. Her fingers paused just shy of touching its fur. The buck snorted, the warm breath escaping its nostrils and caressing her fingertips.

Smiling to herself, Sadie withdrew her hand and then, as slowly as she had approached the buck, she backed away.

It wasn't until she was back at Frederick's side that the buck lifted its head, sniffed the air, and then turned to amble away, disappearing through the trees and undergrowth.

"Oh, Frederick," she gushed, her cheeks pink with excitement. "Wasn't that special?"

"Special, *ja*," he murmured. But when she glanced at him, she realized that he wasn't watching the place where the deer had vanished, but was staring directly at her, instead. "So very special indeed."

Chapter Fifteen

"Someone's here to see you," Rachel called up the stairs the next morning.

Sadie had been lying down. Even though she hadn't returned home from the youth picnic until almost ten o'clock at night, she was far from tired. Instead, her mind whirled with thoughts of Frederick.

The previous afternoon, after she had cleared the air about the gossip regarding her and John Rabor, Frederick had barely left her side.

To Sadie, it had felt as if no one else was even there at the picnic. True to her word, she had forgiven—and forgotten—the incident about Frederick believing the idle gossip that she was to marry John Rabor. After all, stranger things sometimes happened. She had only to remind herself once again about her friend Belle marrying Adam Hershberger so suddenly.

Toward the evening, some of the young men had started a bonfire. With the flames stretching to the heavens, several young women began to sing. Sadie joined them, lifting up her voice to praise God. She had many things to be thankful for, Frederick being one of them.

When the embers began to die down, Frederick had

whispered to her that he'd like to take her home. She was only too willing to leave the picnic with him.

As Frederick had done after the youth singing two weeks before, he took the longest route, just so they could spend more time together.

And when she finally said goodbye to him on the porch of her father's house, he had held her hand and stared into her face in silence.

No words were needed.

Now, the following morning, when she heard Rachel call upstairs to her with eagerness in her voice, Sadie knew that Frederick must have come calling! He had said that he wouldn't be able to see her until the end of the week. He needed to bale hay with his father and then stack it in the barn for the winter. With so much acreage, he wouldn't finish until Thursday or Friday at the latest.

But today was Sunday. No one worked on Sunday. Surely Frederick had decided that he couldn't wait that long and had come to visit before his week of hard work began.

Sadie jumped up and immediately straightened her prayer *kapp*. She didn't want to appear too excited, so she tried to catch her breath. If Frederick had come calling at the house, her father and stepmother would know of his intentions. And then it was only a matter of time . . .

But she didn't want to jump too far ahead. For now, she needed to focus on the moment. She pinched her cheeks, hoping she didn't look pale from not having slept all night. It would do no good for Frederick to realize how much of an effect he had on her.

Satisfied that enough time had passed so that she wouldn't appear overly anxious, Sadie took a deep breath and exited her room. Slowly she descended the staircase.

But, to Sadie's surprise, when she emerged at the bottom of the stairs and glanced over to the sitting area near the windows, the man seated on the sofa, talking with Jacob, was not Frederick Keim but John Rabor.

Rachel must be mistaken, Sadie thought and stopped on the last step. Why would John be there to see her?

"There you are!" Rachel was the perfect picture of a happy stepmother. She bustled over to where Sadie stood, frozen in place on the bottom step, and gestured toward the sofa. "Go sit and visit a spell while I fetch some water and pretzels for your guest."

Visit? With John Rabor? And why had Rachel referred to him as *her* guest? Sadie had nothing in common with the man and even less to talk about with him. Besides, wasn't he engaged to someone? That was what had started all the gossip.

Hesitantly, she took a few steps toward the sitting area. "Sadie."

That was all John said when he saw her. In fact, he barely looked in her direction as she approached.

Uncertain what to say, she merely sat down in the wooden rocking chair near the sofa.

To her further surprise, her father only acknowledged her presence with an abrupt nod and avoided meeting her eyes.

"As I was saying," John Rabor continued, returning his attention to Jacob, "the increased price of hay more than makes up for the decreased price in milk. You should consider switching next spring and grow more hay while culling your herd."

John's words made Sadie cringe. Cull the herd? Her father only sent his cows to slaughter when they were too old for breeding. He would never send his herd off for slaughter.

But her father appeared to be listening intently to John Rabor's suggestion. He tugged at his beard and nodded. "You make a right *gut* point, John. Given the times, growing hay does make sense. And I don't have to feed hay or clean up after it. Much more economical, *ja*?"

John Rabor made a noise that, if Sadie didn't know better, might have been an attempt at laughing.

Horrified that her father had agreed with John's alarming suggestion, Sadie leaned forward. "Daed," Sadie said in a low voice, "you aren't seriously considering that, are you?"

Jacob ran his hands through his hair, causing the front to stand up just a bit. "There's sense to what John says, Sadie."

John scoffed. "Does your *dochder* run your business, Jacob?" He chortled in an unkind way.

Sadie whispered, "You promised you'd *never* send the cows to slaughter. Not unless it was for our personal need for food at home."

Her father ignored her comment.

Carrying a tray with mugs of hot coffee on it, Rachel walked in between Sadie and the two men. Clearly she had been eavesdropping. "Oh, Sadie, what do you know of such things? Silly girl." She shook her head as if what Sadie had just said was the most ridiculous thing ever. "Times are changing." Rachel looked at her husband. "Isn't that so, Jacob?"

"*Ja*, they are." Despite his former promises to live close to the land and not slaughter his cows, Jacob now seemed resigned to the fact that going against his word was a real possibility. "Corporate farming, especially in the dairy industry, sure does seem to make it next to impossible for small dairy farmers to survive. People no longer care about having healthy milk; they just buy cheap milk from those large farms where cows don't free-graze and are fed hormones. Might be time to rethink some things around here."

Sadie couldn't believe her father had said those words. How many times had he told her that having enough was more than plenty? Only the *Englischers* continually wanted more and more, their insatiable greed causing them to work away from their families and homes.

"We live just fine, Daed," Sadie said, bewildered by this conversation. "You always say so."

John made a face and scowled at her. "Such opinions for a young woman with little experience of the real world," he commented unkindly. His words belittled her as if she knew nothing about farming, even though she had grown up on a farm.

Inwardly, Sadie rolled her eyes. However, she knew better than to actually *do* that. "Other Amish folks need milk just as much as they need hay," she said sharply, unwilling to let a man like John Rabor denigrate her. "Perhaps we should market our dairy products differently. Perhaps we should promote the care given to the dairy cows who graze in pastures instead of living unhappy lives chained up in large, dirty barns as they do with those big *Englische* farms. We could command a higher price for our products rather than trying to compete with the corporate dairy farms."

The expression on her father's face shifted, changing from indifference to curiosity. For a moment, she thought that her father might comment on her suggestion, praising her for such a creative idea.

But John Rabor ruined the moment. He made a face of mockery, staring at Sadie as if she were crazed. "Whoever heard of raising dairy prices when we can hardly sell milk for lower ones?" He shook his head. "Who has been filling your head with such nonsense, Sadie?" He looked at Jacob. "And *this* is why womenfolk belong in the *haus* and must leave the important farmwork to us men."

Stunned that her father didn't jump to her defense, she pressed her lips together and leaned back in the rocking chair. She stopped listening to their conversation, which really was one-sided, with John talking and her father merely nodding his head.

Oh, how she detested that John Rabor! And while she knew that she'd have to pray forgiveness later that evening for thinking horrible things about John, she knew that he was far too vain to even consider doing the same for having actually *spoken* his horrible ideas.

Hurt and bored, Sadie stared out the window. How she wished that it wasn't a Sunday so she could work on a quilt while she sat there during John Rabor's visit. As no one was permitted to work on Sundays, unless it was essential work like caring for livestock or tending to the family, the bishop would surely hear if she took a needle and thread to her latest quilting project. So, instead, Sadie was forced to sit there, listening to John Rabor's bluster about the benefits of giving up dairy farming, unable to politely leave or to make productive use of her time.

Finally, almost thirty minutes later, to Sadie's relief, she saw that John was preparing to leave. She said a silent prayer of thanks to God for the short visit. Still, she felt frustrated that she had been forced to sit there in the first place.

"Sadie," John said, turning to speak directly to her for the first time since she had come downstairs. He peered at her with cold, steely eyes. "I need to cut wood for the winter this week. Not only for myself, but also for my neighbors. Would you . . ."

Sadie cringed, for she knew what was coming. Another request for help.

". . . help with the *kinner* again?"

Before she could speak, Rachel replied, "Of course she will." Rachel turned toward her, a sweet smile plastered to her face. "Right, Sadie?"

Sadie's heart pounded and she felt sweat form on the back of her neck as she realized that all three pairs of eyes were upon her.

I can't. I can't. I simply can't. While the words screamed inside her head, she couldn't form them on her tongue. She couldn't imagine having to spend any more time in the presence of John Rabor or his *kinner*. Nothing would make Sadie feel more miserable. And yet she could tell that she was expected to acquiesce and agree to do just that.

Swallowing, Sadie tried to think of the most graceful way to escape such a fate.

"I . . ."

Rachel's eyes narrowed.

"I . . . I really cannot."

"Sadie!" Rachel glared at her, appalled at her response. "The good Lord tells us to help our neighbors."

Sadie pressed her lips together. "*Nee*, he said to love one another as he loved us."

"Isn't that the same thing?" Rachel snapped.

"*Nee*, it's not. Besides, even if it were, haven't I already helped enough?"

Rachel shut her eyes and took a deep breath, clearly displeased with Sadie's response.

Sadie lifted her chin. "Mayhaps *you* could watch his *kinner* and I'll stay here to tend the *haus*."

Rachel gasped and John stood up, the abruptness of his movement causing him to knock over his almost empty coffee mug. "Such insolence!" He faced Rachel. "And I thought you said—"

Just as quickly, Rachel jumped to her feet. "Let me walk you to the door," she said, interrupting him before he could finish his sentence. She placed her hand on his arm and started guiding him away from the sitting area. As they walked away, Sadie thought she heard Rachel whisper, "Let me talk to her. I'm sure she'll come to her senses."

John grunted in response.

They disappeared outside, leaving Sadie to sit there, wondering what mischief Rachel was up to. Why would Rachel be championing John Rabor of all people? She barely knew the man. She wondered if Rachel had been behind John's visit, and she suspected the answer was yes.

Sadie turned toward her father, eager to ask if he knew why, exactly, John had come visiting, but he had already returned his attention to the Bible. There was no sense in disturbing him, for the matter clearly was of little concern or interest to her father.

Frustrated, Sadie turned her attention toward the window. She knew that her stepmother was scheming something. Whatever it was, Sadie would have to keep up her guard. There was something about the new Rachel she could not trust.

Chapter Sixteen

On Thursday, Sadie managed to gain permission from Rachel to go into town to pick up a few things at the store. The fact that she even needed permission now was frustrating to Sadie. She was eighteen—not a child, but a responsible adult with a good reputation.

For some odd reason, Rachel had merely waved her hand dismissively at her, a silent granting of her consent.

"You can stop at the store and fetch me some flour, sugar, and yeast," Rachel added coldly.

Eager to escape Rachel's wrath, Sadie didn't hesitate to agree.

Sadie hadn't been permitted to leave the house all week and, therefore, hadn't seen Frederick since the youth picnic the previous Saturday. She hoped to run into Anna Rose so she could inquire about his whereabouts.

But the town appeared empty.

Sadie contemplated walking to Anna Rose's house. However, she felt strange just dropping by. While she was friendly with Anna Rose, they weren't close enough for Sadie to visit her at her parents' home.

So, instead, Sadie walked through the center of town and headed to Troyers' General Store. If Ella was working, she, too, might have heard something about Frederick, or even seen him at the store.

The bell over the door jingled and Linda Troyer greeted Sadie when she walked inside.

"Sadie Whitaker!" Linda smiled at her. "How are you doing today?"

"Right as rain," Sadie replied cheerfully. She glanced around the store. "I was wondering if Ella's working today."

Linda's smile faded, and she pursed her lips. "She's doing inventory in the back. I'll fetch her, but don't keep her long, Sadie. She has much work to finish." Without waiting for a response, Linda turned on her heel and disappeared into the back stockroom.

Sadie wandered down an aisle, perusing the many different items on the shelves. Kerosene lanterns, pots, pans, even glasses. Everything a person could need for their home, as well as a section of dry goods in the back.

She wandered over to the fabric section and looked through some of the remnants. Oh, how she would have loved to purchase some, especially the dark blue with white flowers. But she knew that would be wasteful, since she hadn't finished the quilt that she was currently making.

"There you are!" Ella smiled at her as she hurried around the corner. "I've only a few minutes." She glanced over her shoulder as if making certain that her stepmother wasn't standing there. "I haven't seen you all week."

Sadie made a face. "Rachel's been angry with me and I've had to pick up extra chores to appease her."

Ella sighed. "Sounds familiar."

It was one thing that Ella and Sadie had in common: stepmothers. However, Linda had never treated Ella well, while Rachel had at least pretended to do so.

"Things haven't been going so well with her," Sadie started. "I need to talk to someone, Ella. But you know I don't like to gossip—"

"I know that. Whatever you tell me won't go any further," Ella promised, a solemn expression on her face.

Sadie counted on that. Ella had always proven to be a true friend in the worst of times. "Rachel's been awfully hard on me these past few weeks. Ever since she found out that she's"—Sadie bit her lower lip, hesitating before she confided the rest—"not with child again."

"Oh help."

Sadie sighed. "When she first married Daed, she was so kind and friendly toward me. Everyone seemed so pleased with their marriage, although some commented about her being so much younger than he."

"And quite pretty," Ella added. "She could've married anyone."

That was true, too. In fact, Sadie often wondered about that. Even though she was no longer in her twenties, Rachel could have married any widower in Echo Creek, or even Liberty Falls. But she had married Jacob Whitaker. From what Sadie knew, their courtship had been brief, and several people had whispered that their introduction had been arranged by the bishop.

"*Ja*, she could have married anyone, but she chose my *daed*." Sadie scratched the back of her neck. "Now, she's behaving so strange. She was angry and hostile for a while. Then, since Belle's wedding, she's been overly kind. And yet, something is amiss. It's as if she wants me out of the *haus*."

Ella's blue eyes widened. "Whatever for?"

"I don't know exactly." Sadie raised her eyes and stared at Ella. "But she arranged for me to watch John Rabor's children that one week and tried, again, to get me out there this week."

"Oh!" Ella shook her head.

"But I refused this time. And she's been even harder on me ever since."

Ella sighed. "Mayhaps she's just upset because she hasn't had a *boppli* yet."

Somehow, Sadie knew that was at the heart of the matter. But she certainly didn't know why Rachel would be upset with *her* over her failure to conceive.

"Well, I certainly hope things get better for you," Ella said at last. She glanced again in Linda's direction and whispered, "I know what it's like to have a hard-to-please stepmother."

As if she had been listening, Linda called out, "Ella! It's time to get back to work now. You must finish inventory before noon and get home to clean the *haus* and cook supper!"

Ella gave Sadie a look of despair. "See what I mean?"

Realizing that she hadn't even inquired about Frederick, Sadie watched as Ella walked away, her shoulders slumped forward. Oh, how her heart wept for Ella. Long ago, Sadie had learned how Linda Troyer overworked her stepdaughter while letting her own two daughters do whatever they pleased. It wasn't fair, but neither was life.

God's plan was not always easily identifiable, but Sadie knew that there was a reason for everything, even if one couldn't quite understand what it was.

After finishing with her shopping, Sadie tucked the sack of items under her arm and headed out of the store.

She took her time walking back to the lane that led to her father's farm. As she made her way out of town, she heard the sound of schoolchildren playing during recess. Behind her, the gentle clip-clopping of a horse's hooves made her look over her shoulder.

She smiled when she recognized Frederick's horse. How fortunate! Moving toward the side of the road, she waited for him to get closer.

"My little songbird," he said by way of greeting.

"I'm so glad to see you," she said in a soft voice.

He gestured with his hand. "Climb in and let me take you home."

"I'll agree to the first part," she said as she started to get into the buggy. "But please, Frederick, don't make haste to the *haus*."

He tilted his head and studied her. Then, without asking any questions, he nodded.

Instead of continuing down the road, he turned at the first fork and they rode in the opposite direction from her father's farm. Sadie stared out the window in silence.

"Everything all right, then?" he asked at last.

She shook her head. "*Nee*, Frederick, it's not."

He waited, as if to see whether she would volunteer information. When she didn't, he prodded her. "Care to tell me more?"

How could she do that without disparaging her stepmother? Despite her temper and moodiness, Rachel was still her stepmother, and the Bible commanded her to honor both her father *and* mother.

"At the risk of sounding impertinent," she began, carefully selecting her words, "I've somehow offended my stepmother, and it hasn't made life very pleasant at home."

He pursed his lips. "Go on."

Sadie sighed. "It has to do with John Rabor."

Out of the corner of her eye, Sadie saw the muscles tense along the side of his jaw.

"He came visiting after worship on Sunday last. He needed more help with his *kinner*, and when I refused to watch them again, Rachel was not happy with me at all." Sadie glanced at him, but Frederick continued staring straight ahead. "After the rumors that started circulating last week, I knew I couldn't agree to help. And I know that God wants us to love our neighbors, but haven't I already fulfilled that by helping the week before?"

Frederick remained silent and Sadie twisted her hands on her lap. Why wasn't he saying something?

"Now," Sadie continued, "Rachel's behaving strangely. All week she gave me chore after chore, things that were nonsensical, Frederick, as if to punish me for something."

He lifted his chin and she thought she saw his eye twitch.

"I fear she wants me out of the *haus* and that it was she, not John, who originally thought to get me to help him." This time, when Sadie finished speaking, she remained silent. Oh, how she prayed Frederick didn't find her accusations disrespectful toward her stepmother.

The horse and buggy approached another crossroad. Frederick pulled the horse to a stop, and for a moment, Sadie thought he was wondering which way to turn. But she soon realized that he wasn't lost, merely thinking.

He guided the horse to continue straight down the road, rather than turn toward Sadie's house.

"There's a nice stream over here," he said. "Just down the road a spell. Let's go there and walk a bit, *ja*?"

"That sounds *wunderbarr*." She couldn't think of anything she would enjoy more than walking along a stream with Frederick.

The leaves were beginning to turn and the trees that lined the stream were reflected in the water. After tying the horse to a tree, Frederick helped Sadie get out of the buggy. He held her hand for just a minute longer than he should have, but Sadie found that she didn't mind.

"There's a path over here, I believe."

She walked beside Frederick as they headed toward the narrow dirt path.

"I'm sorry to hear about your stepmother," Frederick said at last. "Believe it or not, I was actually headed to your *haus* when I ran into you."

"You were?"

He nodded. "*Ja.* I hadn't seen you all week and I was

worried that something had happened." He took a deep breath and exhaled. "When I came to town earlier in the week, Anna Rose hadn't seen you, either. And I knew I couldn't go an entire week without seeing my little songbird."

She looked up at him. "But you'd already driven past my *haus* when you found me."

"I talked with your stepmother."

Immediately, Sadie felt uneasy. Surely Rachel had told Frederick that she'd gone to town. And Rachel would know that he had picked her up. She'd be angry that Sadie hadn't gone straight home.

"She didn't look very happy, now that I think of it."

Sadie made a small noise.

He glanced at her. "Whatever is bothering her, you just need to have faith that she'll find her peace, Sadie. And you can pray for her, too."

Immediately, she felt guilty. She hadn't been praying for Rachel enough.

"God will make it right, Sadie."

Out of the corner of her eye, Sadie saw movement on the other side of the stream. She turned just in time to see a rabbit dipping its head to take a drink of water.

When it lifted its head, it stared at her for a moment before hopping back up the embankment.

That was the moment when Sadie stumbled on a rock and fell. Frederick reached for her arm, but it was too late. Sadie fell into the stream, putting out her hands to stop herself from being immersed in the cold water.

"Sadie!"

Frederick jumped into the stream and quickly helped her get to her feet.

"Are you all right?"

"*Ja*, I'm fine." She glanced at her hands. Her palms were cut from the rocks in the stream bed. "Bruised a little, but fine."

He guided her back onto the path. "Let's get you home right quick, Sadie. It's too cold for you to be wet."

How careless of me, she thought. She had been enjoying herself just being in Frederick's company and now she had no choice but to return home. But he was right. The last thing she needed was to catch a cold.

Chapter Seventeen

By Saturday morning, Sadie had taken ill. She had known it was coming, for she'd begun sneezing the previous evening. By morning, her body began to ache.

"You can't catch a cold that fast, can you?" she asked her father as she shivered under her blue blanket while sitting at the table for breakfast.

"I reckon you can." He reached over and pressed his hand to her forehead. A look of concern crossed his face. "You're feverish. You best get up to bed and rest." He glanced at Rachel. "No work for Sadie today."

Rachel nodded her acknowledgment to Jacob, but when he returned his attention to his coffee, she scowled.

Sadie wasn't certain what to make of that. Perhaps Rachel thought that she'd have too much work to do without Sadie's help. In reality, there was not much to do. The previous day, Sadie had finished all of the laundry, and the house was always pristine and clean.

Excusing herself from the table, Sadie retreated to her bedroom, snuggling under two quilts and wrapping the blue blanket around herself as well. She felt safe and comfortable in her room, Frederick's blanket keeping her warm.

She couldn't remember the last time she had been sick. Usually she was so healthy. With her head feeling as if it were being squeezed by a vise, Sadie sought comfort through sleep, which, fortunately, came easily.

Later that afternoon, her father knocked on her door. When he peeked into the room, he wore an expression of grave concern. "Not feeling any better?" he asked as he walked into her room. Sadie saw that he carried a bowl of soup with a piece of bread.

Sadie sat up and adjusted the pillows behind her back. "*Nee*, I'm not, Daed."

Her father pulled up a ladder-back chair and sat down, handing the soup bowl to her. "Reckon that's what happens when you decide to go swimming in October."

Sadie managed to laugh. "Oh, Daed!" She took the bowl of soup. It was a thick puree of root vegetables with pieces of translucent onion and chunks of potato in it. She inhaled, the steam warming her cheeks. "Smells *gut*. Did Rachel make it, then?"

Jacob nodded. "She did, *ja*. Seems she must be feeling better."

Of *that* Sadie wasn't so sure. She didn't want to tell her father that Rachel hadn't checked in on her at all. In fact, Sadie had awoken in the middle of the morning and walked downstairs to fetch herself a glass of water. Rachel hadn't even inquired as to how she was feeling. But Sadie wasn't about to complain to her father about his wife. Instead, she reached for the spoon and dipped it into the bowl.

Leaning back in the chair, Jacob put his hands behind his neck. He looked tired, dark circles shadowing his eyes. "I mowed the back field today. Reckon that's the last cutting for the season. Should have enough hay for the winter, though."

"Mayhaps I can help you bale it?" Sadie dipped the spoon into the bowl.

She knew that he'd need to bale it after it sat drying for

a few days. Baling damp hay meant risking mold which, if left unattended, could make horses sick. Even worse, sometimes hay that was baled before it dried properly could smolder into a fire, burning the barn in which it was stored.

"You know how much I love working in the fields," she added as she lifted a spoonful of the soup to her mouth. Baling hay was one of her favorite farm chores. She loved the scent of freshly cut and dried hay.

Despite her request, Jacob didn't immediately accept her offer. That surprised Sadie. Usually he wanted her help, especially with some of the more strenuous chores. And he couldn't bale hay alone. One person had to drive the mules while another lifted and stacked the bales.

"Let's just see about that, Sadie. Seems Rachel thought she'd help me."

Rachel? Nothing could have shocked Sadie more. Rachel *never* helped Jacob with anything outside the house. She definitely favored working inside and usually wanted Sadie working beside her.

At least until last Monday.

"Fresh air might do her good," Jacob explained as he rubbed his temples with his thumbs. "She's always cooped up inside the *haus*. Never works outside, except to garden with you. I think her offer is her way of trying to come around a bit."

Sadie wasn't so sure about that, but she also wasn't certain what was driving her stepmother's recent odd behavior. The only thing she knew was that Rachel was definitely trying to drive a wedge between her and her father.

"Baling's hard work," Sadie commented before she took another taste of the soup. It was warm and spicy with a hint of sweetness. She loved soup, and this soup was particularly good. "She's not used to it."

Her father rolled his eyes. "Well, I sure won't hint that she's not strong enough—"

"—or young enough—" Sadie added.

"—or young enough to start baling hay." Jacob winked at his daughter. "She wants to try, so I say let her."

After taking another spoonful, Sadie set down the bowl on her nightstand. She wiped at her mouth with the back of her hand. "Daed, may I ask you something?"

"Of course, Sadie."

She wasn't certain how to ask the questions that were on her mind. But she knew that this was the perfect opportunity to do so. Rachel rarely left Jacob's side when he was in the house. "Why is Rachel acting so . . ."

She hesitated, searching for a word that would describe her stepmother's behavior without sounding too critical. Whatever she thought of Rachel, Sadie knew that the woman was still her father's wife.

". . . well, so peculiar?"

Her father sighed and lowered his hands from behind his neck. Leaning forward, he put his elbows on his knees and stared directly at Sadie. There was a sadness in his eyes. "Some things can't be explained, Sadie. But I've noticed it, too." He paused, suddenly deep in thought. "I've thought long and hard about this. And I reckon Rachel's just having a tough time with growing older."

"I thought it was about not having a *boppli*."

Jacob nodded. "*Ja*, that too. But the two go hand in hand, don't you think? You know, when she was your age, her *daed* was in that accident and lost the use of his legs. Her *maem* died soon after, and Rachel's older siblings were all married. She was left to care for him."

"I don't understand."

He reached up and scratched his cheek, just above his beard. "You've heard her stories, about not going to singings or volleyball games. She didn't get to court anyone. And when her *daed* finally passed, she was thirty years old. A *maedel*. And with few prospects, Rachel." He gave her a weak smile. "She's a fine woman, both inside and out. But unless she wanted to marry an older widower . . ." He left the sentence unfinished.

"You're a widower," Sadie pointed out. "I don't think marrying you was such a bad thing." *For Rachel, anyway,* she wanted to add, but refrained from doing so.

He laughed, but the sound wasn't filled with his usual joy. "I'd like to think so. And I'm certainly younger than most widowers. But I reckon she had dreams of having her own family and *kinner.* Most widowers remarry because they have too many *kinner* and need help to care for them."

Sadie cleared her throat. "Not you."

"That's right. I might be older than Rachel, but I only had one *dochder.* In her mind, you were more her own age and mayhaps she thought of you as a friend. Now, however, she's realizing that she's not a typical Amish wife. She wasn't nineteen when she married, and from the looks of it, she might never have her own family besides you and me. And she sees you going to all of these youth gatherings and living a life she never had."

Suddenly it began to make sense to Sadie. Rachel was jealous of Sadie's youth. She was also envious of Sadie's future. Unlike Rachel, Sadie was able to attend singings and picnics. Unlike Rachel, Sadie also had a suitor. And Sadie was young enough to have children when the time came.

But she couldn't articulate any of this. Something tickled the back of her throat. She tried to swallow but couldn't. If felt as if she had a puff of cotton blocking her breathing passage.

"You okay?"

Sadie frowned. She tried, again, to clear her throat. "I could use some water, I think."

Quickly, Jacob left the room and hurried to the upstairs bathroom. As Sadie heard the faucet turn on, she wondered what she could do, if anything, to improve her relationship with Rachel.

Her father returned and handed her the glass.

"*Danke.*"

Sadie took it and drank some, feeling the cool wetness soothe her scratchy throat. She lowered the glass and looked up at her father.

"I think I understand," she said.

"That's a *gut* girl." He leaned over and patted her arm. "I knew you'd have compassion for Rachel."

Sadie raised her hand and pressed it against her throat. She frowned and tried to swallow. "Daed?"

"*Ja?*"

"I . . . I can hardly breathe," she managed to say. She tried to swallow once again. "My throat. It's swelling shut."

Jacob straightened his back and stared at her. "Your lips. They're swelling, too." He hurried to the open doorway and called out for Rachel.

Sadie didn't hear her respond. After what felt like minutes, but was probably only seconds, Rachel appeared in the doorway. Her black apron was streaked with flour and she dried her hands on a dishcloth.

"Everything okay?" she asked, peering into Sadie's room at Jacob.

"What was in that soup?" Jacob demanded.

Rachel looked from him to Sadie, who, by now, was gasping for breath. Rachel's eyes widened. "Wh-what's happening to her face?"

Sadie didn't need a mirror. She knew from past experience that her skin was patchy red. She began to panic, fighting to gulp some air into her lungs. But it was nearly impossible.

"Answer me!" Jacob shouted. He placed his arms on Rachel's shoulders and gave her a slight shake. "Were there apples in that soup?"

Rachel's eyes returned to him. She hesitated and licked her lips. "I . . . well, there's onions and celery and potatoes—"

"Apples!" he demanded. "Were there apples in it?"

Her eyelids fluttered rapidly. "*Ja*, th-there were. Just some juice to add a little sweetness."

Abruptly, Jacob released her. The force of his action caused Rachel to stumble into the wall. He glared at his wife. "You know she's allergic to apples! Deathly allergic! Why would you have done such a thing?" When he turned to look at Sadie, his cheeks drained of all color and his eyes went wild with fear. "I'll get you some allergy medicine and then fetch the doctor."

Sadie nodded, her hands still pressed against her throat. Try as she might to gulp air, she couldn't. Her throat was dry and itchy, swelling shut. *Please hurry,* she prayed. She couldn't remember the last time she had had such an allergic reaction, and never had it been this strong.

When her father returned with a small cup of pink liquid, Sadie eagerly did her best to swallow it.

"Stay with her!" Jacob gave Rachel a not-too-gentle shove into the room. He was angry, that was clear. And Rachel looked fearful of his fury. "Don't leave her side. You hear me?"

Meekly, Rachel nodded and stepped into the room. Sadie noticed that she barely made any eye contact with her and, for the briefest of moments, she wondered if Rachel had truly forgotten about her stepdaughter's allergy to apples. Perhaps she had included the apples on purpose.

But when Rachel finally sat down, she folded her hands and shut her eyes, her mouth moving in a silent prayer.

No, Sadie realized, no matter what was going on with her stepmother, not even Rachel was so cruel as to deliberately try to harm her.

Chapter Eighteen

"Sadie, I need you to do me a favor."

Sadie glanced up from the table where she had been sitting, reading the most recent issue of *Family Life*. Her father sat nearby, in his reclining chair, reading the *Budget* newspaper. He barely looked up at the sound of Rachel's voice as she walked up the basement stairs, a glass pan in her hands.

"What is it, Rachel?" Sadie set down the little magazine, wondering what her stepmother could possibly need from her at this late hour in the day.

Shutting the basement door behind her, Rachel walked to the table. "Would you run this pie over to John Rabor's *haus*?"

Immediately, Sadie knew that something was amiss. She eyed the pie with suspicion. "John Rabor's *haus*?" She clenched her teeth. The last thing she wanted to do was go anywhere near that man. "Is something wrong with him?"

"He's feeling poorly."

"He seemed fine when he came to our church meeting last week."

Sadie couldn't help but wonder how Rachel would have known *anything* about John Rabor. It wasn't as if Amish people in Echo Creek socialized on the telephone. In fact, Sadie had never seen her stepmother use the telephone in the small shanty that they shared with their neighbors. She had no one to call, after all. In Echo Creek, the phones were usually just for emergencies and, even then, rarely used unless someone needed to call for help from Liberty Falls. With everyone's phones located outside of their houses, who would hear a phone ring anyway?

Her father, however, used the phone to contact *Englischers* when it was time to pick up milk or when he needed a special part for his cooling system. And, of course, whenever he needed more diesel fuel, he'd call the supplier for a delivery.

Other than that, the phone remained unused.

So how would Rachel have heard that John had taken ill?

Apparently Rachel didn't find Sadie's comment charitable. She set the pan upon the table and put her hand on her hip. "Honestly, Sadie. It's the neighborly thing to do when someone is ill."

Sadie wanted to quip back that Rachel had never sent anything to anyone else's house when they were ill, but she knew better than to disrespect her stepmother.

"It's getting late." Sadie glanced at the clock. It was almost six and the sun was already setting. "And it's a long walk."

Rachel gave her a dark look.

She heard the rustle of the newspaper. "Sadie," her father said in a firm voice, "take the horse and carriage if you want."

Getting up from the table, she reached down for the pie and headed toward the mudroom. She paused to grab her shawl, knowing that the night air would be cool. She didn't want to get sick again.

Ever since the weekend, when Rachel had accidentally cooked with apples, Sadie had noticed that something was amiss in the house. She knew that her father had exchanged words with Rachel about the apples, for she had heard him arguing with her. For the past four days, there had been an uneasy feeling lingering in the atmosphere.

Almost thirty minutes passed before she arrived at John Rabor's farm. The sun was setting behind the barn and a light burned inside the kitchen window. Sadie stopped the buggy and took a deep breath before she climbed out.

"I'll only be a minute," she mumbled to the horse as she tied it to a hitching post. "Trust me on that."

The horse whinnied in response.

With the pie in hand, Sadie crossed the driveway and climbed the stairs to the front door. Dread built in her chest as she lifted her hand to knock on the door. As if she had been expected, the door immediately opened.

John Rabor stood there, his gray beard covering the front of his white shirt and black vest. Sadie didn't know what to make of the fact that he was wearing his Sunday best. Clearly he wasn't sick at all.

"Come in, Sadie," he said, gesturing with his hand for her to enter the kitchen.

Behind him, she saw the faces of the children, all of them wearing fresh clothes and scrubbed faces. Owen scowled a little, but the younger children beamed at her.

"My *maem* told me you were feeling poorly," Sadie said as she handed him the pie. Her eyes returned to the children. Not one of them moved. They were on their best behavior. Yes, they had known she was coming. "I'm pleased that she's mistaken."

John took the dish from her. He lifted it to his nose and inhaled. Then, as if he remembered that she was there, he looked up and stared at her. "You will stay and have some, *ja*?"

Sadie swallowed. She knew that he expected her to say

yes, but she couldn't. "I . . . I really must return home. It's a long drive and it's getting dark."

But he acted as if he hadn't heard her.

"Come sit. Let me fetch the plates." But he didn't fetch the plates. Instead, he motioned with his head, and Owen sighed, grumbling under his breath as he moved to the cabinet to fetch some plates.

John escorted Sadie to the table and seated her to the left of his spot at its head.

Feeling uncomfortable, Sadie folded her hands in her lap and stared at the clock on the back wall. She felt the warmth of a hand in hers. Wilmer. The gesture was too familiar for Sadie, but she couldn't extract her hand without hurting the child's feelings.

"You've had a *gut* week, *ja*?"

Her eyebrows twitched and she fought the urge to furrow them. John's question smacked of familiarity. It was as if they were having a family discussion. "I have." She felt beads of sweat on the back of her neck.

"But you were sick, I hear."

This time, she couldn't help but frown. How had he known that? As far as she knew, he had no telephone in the barn. Had he visited with Rachel? And, if so, how could Sadie not have known?

"I . . . I was, *ja*."

"We prayed for your recovery." He glanced at the children. "Isn't that so?"

Nine heads nodded in unison.

"*Danke*." Feeling awkward, Sadie watched as John began to cut the pie. He gave her the first piece, a tiny sliver that crumbled apart when he put it on a plate, and then cut a larger piece for himself.

John quickly cut pieces of pie for the children and then bowed his head to pray before lifting his fork. At first, he took a few bites, silently chewing as if savoring the taste of a homemade pie. The children, however, quickly gobbled their pie and then used their forks to scrape their plates clean.

"This is right *gut*," John said at last. He smacked his lips, and the noise repulsed her. "Rachel surely knows how to bake."

Solemnly, Sadie nodded her head twice. She took a piece of pie and ate it.

"Has she taught you as well?"

For a second, she stopped chewing the pie and merely stared at him. Had he truly just asked her that? Sadie wanted to remind him that she had baked bread, cookies, and a pumpkin pie when she had watched the children for the week. Was it possible that he had forgotten? Or was he merely trying to make conversation? Either way, it was an awkward question that Sadie found offensive.

"We often bake together, *ja*."

"*Gut*." He jabbed his fork into the pie. "That is *gut*!"

She lost her appetite.

After a few minutes of silence, Sadie pushed her mostly uneaten pie away from her and cleared her throat. "I . . . I really must be going." Before he could respond, she stood up and started toward the door.

But John was quick to join her.

"Let me help you with the horse."

That was the last thing she wanted. "The horse is fine. Really." She tried to smile. "It's already hitched."

But he ignored her comment. Pausing at the door, he grabbed his black hat and plopped it on his head.

Outside, he held her arm as she walked down the stairs. She tried to free herself from his grasp, but he didn't let go until she was on solid ground.

"I wish to speak to you, Sadie."

The tone of his voice, so serious and restrained, made her heart begin to race. An eerie sensation swept her and she suddenly realized what he was about to do.

"I have given much thought to this, and have decided that you would make a right *gut* mother to my children."

No, no, no. She wanted to scream it out loud, but held it inside.

"And a *gut fraa* to me." He took a deep breath, his chest puffing up a little. "I'm sure you see the benefit of such a marriage."

She felt sick to her core.

"So, with your permission, I'll speak to the bishops about announcing the banns at our respective churches this Sunday."

For a moment, she couldn't speak. How could John Rabor possibly think she would make him a good wife? They had nothing in common. Besides, she was young and not in need of a widower with a ready-made family. And even if she were a forty-year-old spinster, she would have found his "proposal" boorish and rude. He had focused on what *he* was to gain from such a marriage and not on what he might give to her.

In the darkness, she realized that he was staring at her, an expectant expression on his face. He was waiting for her answer.

Still stunned, Sadie fought to clear her mind of the self-centered proposal that John had just made. Somehow she managed to find her voice. "You do not have it."

He blinked. "Excuse me?"

She tilted her chin, meeting his gaze so that there could be no misunderstanding. "You do not have my permission to speak to either of our bishops, for I will *not* marry you."

He appeared stunned. His mouth opened and then shut again. He raised his hand to rub his eyes. "This is unbelievable," he muttered under his breath. "Rachel assured me that you would say yes."

Sadie grimaced. His words felt like a physical blow. So her stepmother was, indeed, behind this ridiculous proposal. Suddenly she remembered what her father had said to her when she had taken ill the previous weekend. John Rabor was the type of man everyone had probably thought would marry Rachel. But she had found Jacob, instead. Now Rachel was trying to get rid of Sadie by marrying her off to an older widower?

"I can assure you that I will never agree to such a marriage. I'm sorry." And she meant it. She didn't want to hurt his feelings, if that were even possible. It was more likely that she had hurt his male ego. But she couldn't give him any room to hope that she might change her mind.

Without another word, she hurried to the horse, untied it, and quickly got into the buggy. She couldn't get away from the Rabors' farm fast enough.

She took her time driving back to her father's farm. She didn't want to face Rachel and hoped that her parents would have retired by the time she arrived.

But as she drove the horse down the driveway, she saw the familiar glow of a light from the kitchen window.

Sighing, Sadie resigned herself to the fact that she had no choice but to deal with the situation that evening.

As soon as she walked into the house, she saw Rachel and her father seated at the table. They had been waiting for her.

"Well?"

Sadie could hardly look at her stepmother. Clearly she had orchestrated the proposal. "I refused his offer."

Rachel's face paled. "What do you mean you said no?"

Sadie tried to remain calm, keeping her head held high. "I will not marry John Rabor. And that's exactly what I told him."

"Jacob!" Her stepmother turned toward Sadie's father. "Do something!"

Sadie watched as her father took a deep breath, a frown covering his face. "I think you should reconsider," he said in a tight, even voice. "John could provide a right *gut* living for you, Sadie."

She felt as if the bottom of her world had just fallen out from beneath her feet. Her father was siding with Rachel? "How could you possibly want me to marry a man that I don't love?"

He shook his head. "Love often comes later, Sadie."

"Or maybe not at all!" she snapped back and stared at Rachel.

Gasping, Rachel placed her hand over her heart. "What's that supposed to mean?"

Jacob held up his hands. "Enough!" His voice boomed through the kitchen, and Sadie, stunned at the ferocity of his command, faced him. His frown deepened. "There is nothing wrong with John Rabor," he said. "And, at eighteen years of age, you need to start thinking about settling down."

"Daed!"

He raised an eyebrow, but there was a distant look in his eyes. "You haven't courted anyone, Sadie, and it is time that you decide on a husband."

"Not John Rabor!"

"That sounds very much like pride," he chided her.

Oh, how she wanted to tell them about Frederick. But she knew better than to presume anything about her relationship with him. After all, he hadn't asked her to marry him, and he hadn't come calling on her at the house. Not formally, anyway. However, he had stopped by that one time and Rachel had spoken with him. Surely *she* knew that a young man was interested. Hadn't she shared that information with Sadie's father?

Apparently not.

Defiantly, Sadie lifted her chin. "I'm eighteen, *ja*," she said, agreeing with her father, "but that doesn't mean I should settle on marrying someone just for the sake of getting married. I do not love him. I could *never* love him." She looked pointedly at Rachel. "When and if I get married, it will be a man of my own choosing, not one selected for me by any other person. And I would think that my own *daed* would support that decision."

He shut his eyes and exhaled. He appeared defeated and Sadie couldn't help but wonder what, exactly, Rachel had said to convince him that a marriage between his daughter and John Rabor was a good idea.

She didn't bother to say anything else. Enough had been said already.

Turning away from them, she walked to the staircase and quietly ascended. Her nerves were rattled from the events of the evening. She didn't know which bothered her more, that John had proposed, that Rachel had encouraged it, or that her father had supported it. For the first time in her life, Sadie felt utterly alone. She couldn't wait for the morning. She would slip away and find Ella. She needed to talk to someone about the emotional turmoil she felt.

Chapter Nineteen

In the morning, Sadie stayed upstairs as long as she could. She didn't want to face her stepmother, and she most certainly did not want to see her father. After a sleepless night, Sadie knew that his decision to side with Rachel disappointed her more than words could say.

She had hoped her father would have been outside already. Her plan was to walk past Rachel and leave the house without a word. She would spend the day with Ella, or, if her friend was working at the store, she'd escape to the stream. She'd rather be anywhere than the farm.

But, to her surprise, when she walked down the stairs, she discovered that both her father and stepmother were in the kitchen as if they had been waiting for her.

And with them was John Rabor.

Sadie stood on the bottom step, staring at the three of them. It was an ambush, of that she was sure and certain.

"Sadie," her father began. "Please come sit with us."

She shook her head. "I don't know what this means, but I can assure you that I will not change my mind."

John averted his eyes.

Rachel's gaze, however, never wavered. "You will sit down and discuss this."

Sadie refused to move from where she stood.

"Sit." Her father's voice was stern.

Frustrated, Sadie crossed the room and sat down, choosing the chair that was as far away from John as possible.

"Now," Jacob said slowly, "John has presented you with an offer."

"An offer I have refused."

Jacob pressed his lips together. His eyes flickered in Rachel's direction. "Your stepmother and I feel strongly that you should reconsider."

Sadie remained silent.

Rachel tossed her hand into the air. "I told you, Jacob. She's far too proud. That's what happens when a young girl becomes too confident in herself."

Sadie's mouth opened, shocked that Rachel would think such a thing, let alone say it. After all, it was Rachel whom Sadie had caught numerous times preening in the mirror.

Jacob looked miserable. For a moment, Sadie wondered if he was agreeing to go along with Rachel just to keep peace in his house. If that was the case, Sadie felt a momentary wave of empathy for him.

"John Rabor is a prosperous farmer," her father said in a slow, even voice. "He would provide for you and any *hopplin* you might have."

At the mention of babies, Sadie's empathy disappeared.

"Rachel has asked John to take you for a drive. To spend a little time together so that you can see the wisdom of accepting this generous proposal."

Stunned, Sadie stared at her father. Did he truly think that she would *ever* see any wisdom in such a match? Hadn't he heard what she had said the previous evening? "*Nee*, I won't go."

John furrowed his brow. "Such insolence!" He turned toward Rachel. "You told me she was obedient and hardworking. I've seen no signs of either trait."

Sadie gasped. "Because I won't agree to marry you?"

"Because of how you are behaving," John replied in a harsh tone.

Sadie pressed her lips together. The last thing she needed was for John Rabor to go to the bishop and inform him that she was disrespectful to her parents. She wondered if the bishop would side with them, too.

Jacob gave her an imploring look. "Please, Sadie. Do this for me. Just go for the buggy ride. Perhaps you will see things differently when you return? Perhaps you may even thank me, *ja*?"

She hesitated. She needed to get out of the house and away from Rachel. If she agreed to go on the buggy ride, she would at least solve the immediate problem at hand. Perhaps she could convince John to take her to town and she could slip away when he halted the buggy at a stop sign.

"Fine." She stood up, her body rigid and her muscles tense.

Minutes later, she found herself seated next to John Rabor, heading down her father's driveway. Unlike Frederick's buggy, this one was old and poorly taken care of. There was hay on the floor and a tear in the seat cushion.

When John got to the end of the driveway, he turned right, heading in the opposite direction from town. Her heart sank. There was nothing but forest in this direction, at least until the road reached John Rabor's farm.

"Do you have any idea how impudent you are?" he said. "Mayhaps you are too young to realize it. But you'll learn soon enough that any fancy ideas of romance filling your head are nothing but fantasy."

Sadie stared out the window.

"Romance fades, Sadie, and then what do you have?" He scoffed. "You have your place in your marriage, and that place is in the home, tending to the *kinner* and your husband."

She felt as if she were suffocating. She leaned forward and slid the door open so she could get some fresh air.

"God commands it to be so."

Sadie stiffened at his words. Slowly, she turned to face him. "'For husbands, this means to love your wives, just as Christ loved the church.' He gave up his life for her."

John Rabor clenched his teeth, the muscles in his jaw tightening.

"I agreed to ride with you," Sadie said, "but I will not agree to marry you."

"Your parents wish it to be so."

"But *I* do not."

"Rachel said you would agree, in time."

Sadie shook her head. Why would Rachel have said such a thing? "I find that hard to believe." And yet, Sadie knew that John spoke the truth. "If she said it, she was lying."

"You accuse your stepmother of lying?" He sounded shocked.

Sadie did not reply.

"Rachel supports this marriage and so does your father. Your refusal is disrespectful, and I can assure you that the bishop will hear more about this."

Sadie fanned her hand at her face. She felt too hot despite the cold temperature. "I have never heard of a bishop getting involved when a woman refuses to marry someone. It is my right to decide who I choose for my lifelong partner. Not anyone else's."

"You silly girl."

Sadie couldn't sit there for one more moment. Listening to him with his pompous speech and idle threats made her feel physically ill and emotionally drained. Her head began to feel fuzzy and her vision began to change, a darkness filling the edges of her sight as if she were falling down a dark hole.

In a moment of impulsiveness, Sadie started to climb out of the moving buggy.

"What are you doing?"

Fortunately, he pulled back on the reins and the horse slowed down, giving Sadie the opportunity to jump onto the road. She didn't look back as she darted into the woods, putting as much distance between her and John Rabor as she could.

"Sadie! Come back!"

But she wouldn't turn around. Instead, she ran as fast as her legs would carry her. She didn't care where she was headed, as long as she could put distance between herself and John Rabor's buggy.

Sadie had no idea how much time had passed. She emptied her mind as she ran until her legs ached and she had no choice but to slow down and take a break for a few minutes.

Returning to her father's farm was not an option. Rachel had clearly lost any sense of tenderness toward her. Instead she was intent on removing Sadie from the house. And she apparently wanted her stepdaughter to enter a loveless marriage, rather than wait to find her one true love. In fact, Rachel seemed to enjoy seeing Sadie suffer.

Confused by the radical change in her stepmother's affection, Sadie gave up trying to understand it. But it was hard to understand how Rachel had infected Jacob, and Sadie found that thought even more alarming.

Sadie could never return home. Of that she was sure and certain. Rachel's resentment of Sadie's youth and her willingness to marry her off to a man like John Rabor proved that, beneath the sweet veneer her stepmother had shown for the past three years, Rachel was nothing more than a self-absorbed tyrant who wanted Jacob to herself. Perhaps that had been her plan from the very beginning.

The thought saddened Sadie.

For three years, she had given Rachel no reason to resent her. But it was clear to Sadie now that Rachel viewed her as competition for Jacob's love.

Sadie had no allies in her father's home.

The tears started to fall from her eyes and she swiped at them with her fingers as she continued on, walking south, deeper into the forest, always putting distance between herself and Echo Creek.

When finally the sun began lowering in the sky Sadie knew that soon it would be evening. Wrapping her arms around herself, she stopped walking once again and sat down on a fallen tree. For a long time, she sat there, her eyes shut and her mind devoid of any thoughts. She listened to the sounds of nature: wind through the tree branches, songs from the birds, chatter from the squirrels.

Suddenly, she felt a strange sense of peace overcome her.

She opened her eyes and, to her surprise, saw the six-point buck standing before her, no more than fifteen feet from where she sat. A sparrow flew over the deer's rack and landed on a tree branch, its head nervously twitching as it stared at her.

The deer's dark eyes studied her, its nose twitching as it took in her scent. It blinked and then lowered its head to graze on a nearby bush.

Suddenly, as if a voice were whispering in her ear, Sadie felt encouragement from God: "Be strong and courageous. Do not be afraid or terrified because of them, for the LORD your God goes with you; he will never leave you nor forsake you."

Sadie took a deep breath, reflecting on God's word. Surely, he was with her in the forest. He had guided her to this place and wrapped his protective arms around her.

Her fear waned as she sat on the log in the company

of the deer and the little bird. She stayed there until the
sparrow flew away and the deer slowly meandered in
another direction.

Rising to her feet, Sadie followed the deer, careful to
maintain a safe distance, for she didn't want to frighten it.
The deer wandered deeper into the woods, but Sadie remained courageous. She had nowhere else to go anyway.
Moving forward was the only path to take.

Sometime later, the deer stopped walking by a small
stream. Sadie wondered if it was the same stream that
flowed from her father's farm, but she doubted it. While
she had lost all sense of direction and time, she knew
that she had walked many miles into the forest and was
most likely too far away for this to be the same one.

She knelt on the bank and dropped her cupped hand
into the cool water. Taking a drink, she shut her eyes as it
soothed her parched throat.

She hadn't eaten all day and her stomach began to ache,
along with her legs, from having walked so far through the
woods.

And she was so very tired.

Shivering, Sadie rubbed her arms. She looked around,
amazed at how beautiful the sunset was. Overhead, the sky
was darkening and a fine mist was settling on the earth.
Birds were beginning their evening songs and several
rabbits nibbled on the leaves from a bush nearby as the
sky turned darker and darker.

The deer turned to look at her and then began its
journey again. Sadie rose to her feet and followed it
once more.

As the sun continued to set and the evening air turned
even colder, Sadie walked on, forging new paths. She
had no idea where she was going or what she would do.
But she knew that she would never marry John Rabor, no

matter what her stepmother, her father, or even the bishop thought of her impertinence.

Obedience only went so far, she told herself. Nowhere in the Bible did it say that a grown woman *had* to marry a man she did not love. Unlike Belle, her family was not in dire straits. Rachel could quote the Book of Ruth all she wanted, but there was no parallel between Sadie's situation and Ruth's.

God would forgive her defiance. She could only pray that he would help her learn how to forgive *them* for pressuring her against her will.

She walked until she rounded a big pricker bush and found herself facing a wall of large rocks. Too large to climb. Frustrated, Sadie began walking around them but grew disheartened when she realized that they were a formation that went on for as far as the eye could see.

Please, God, she prayed, *show me the way.*

Her stomach grumbled and she felt light-headed. She needed to find shelter to warm herself and food to feed her body.

She stumbled and fell to her knees.

With her eyes closer to the ground, she noticed that some of the leaves ahead of her had been disturbed. Intrigued, she scrambled to her feet and carefully tried to follow the almost-invisible path.

She walked around a large tree and noticed that there was a break in the rocks. And, sure enough, there was a dirt path that led through it.

Curiosity, as well as hope that it might lead to a house with provisions, got the best of her. Throwing caution to the wind, Sadie walked through the break in the rocks and followed the trail.

The trees that lined it seemed to shelter her from the night. It was beautiful, and she found herself staring up into the overhead canopy. She had never been this far into the forest and wondered how many people had traveled through this section. The path indicated that someone knew of this little piece of paradise, but who?

Night had fallen and Sadie needed to find a place to sleep. A sense of panic overtook her. She hadn't considered that she would be alone in the woods all night.

Exhausted, Sadie stumbled over a vine as she came to a little hollow where pine needles were soft underfoot. She practically fell down, her back to a fallen tree trunk as she burrowed into the leaves. It would have to do.

Shutting her eyes, she felt the magnitude of what had happened. Never in her wildest imagination would she have thought she would run away from home. But she knew she had no other options.

Tears welled in her eyes, but she willed them not to fall. She was too tired to cry anyway.

Taking a deep breath, Sadie felt herself float away, sleep overcoming her as darkness cloaked the forest for the night.

Chapter Twenty

When she awoke on Saturday morning, she felt warm for the first time since she had run away. She nestled under the blankets and imagined that she was at home in her own bed. But as soon as she heard the crackle of a fire, she startled. Her father's house did not have a fireplace in any of the bedrooms. Suddenly, the events of the day before came rushing back and she remembered what had happened: that she had run away and gotten lost in the woods. And she knew there was no way she was in her own bed.

Sitting up, Sadie yanked the covers to her chin. With wide eyes, she stared around the room.

A fire burned in a stone fireplace and there was a long wooden table that was set for breakfast. And yet, she was alone in the house.

She tried to remember how she had gotten there. The last thing she recalled was hunkering down on a pile of soft pine needles and covering herself with some leaves to stay warm in the biting chill of the night air.

Swallowing her fear, she slid her legs over the side of the cot she lay in and stood up. The house was smaller

than any other she had ever been in. Had she been any
taller, she would have hit her head on the rough-hewn ceiling beams.

And it was dirty.

Very dirty.

Wrinkling her nose, Sadie wandered over to the fireplace. There were several logs on the hearth, but the fire
was dying out. There were just embers that glowed orange
from beneath the sooty stone. Sadie bent down to throw
another log onto the fire.

Where am I? she wondered as she looked around one
more time. She remembered falling asleep in the pile of
leaves, but that was the last thing she could dredge up
from her memory. Someone must have found her, but
who? Had someone carried her into this house?

Curious, she walked to the front door. It was lower
than the average door and she had to stoop down to walk
through it.

Once outside, she recognized nothing. She wasn't in
a town or even on a farm. When she looked up, she was
surprised to see that she stood in a clearing beneath a
canopy of trees, their leaves shielding her from the early-
morning sun.

Turning around, Sadie caught her breath as she saw
the house she had just emerged from. It was the most
charming of homes. A cottage, really, made from logs that
had most likely been cut from the forest. The bark had
been removed and the logs lay upon each other, their ends
crisscrossing. In between each of the logs, the gaps were
packed with cement and then the walls whitewashed.
While it appeared to be only one story high, there were
two dormered windows on the shingled roof. Truly, it was
one of the smallest houses she had ever seen.

She looked up at the roof again and suspected the shin-
gles had not been purchased in a store but made by hand,
as the cedar was heavy and thick. Patches of moss grew

along the edges, and there was even a bird's nest tucked under one of the eaves.

"Hello?" Sadie called out, wondering if someone might be lingering on the other side of the cottage.

There was no response.

The yard had been trampled down so that it was mostly dirt, although there were sections of grass growing here and there. An ax rested in an old tree trunk that sat in the middle of the yard and there was a stack of wood piled in a heap nearby.

But there was no sign of life on the property.

She wandered to the rear of the house, where she spotted a clothesline tied between two large trees, but it was lower to the ground than usual. Several wooden clothespins lay scattered in the dirt, and an old tattered wicker basket lay on its side nearby.

Whoever lives here is not very tidy, she told herself.

Her eyes traveled to the side yard. There was a well with a wooden frame around it. And a platform for someone to step up in order to get the bucket of water. With a wooden pulley and long rope being used to retrieve the water from the depths of the earth, it was a very antiquated system for retrieving water.

The rumbling in her stomach made her return to the house. She was anxious to find something to eat, but she knew that she couldn't take someone else's food without an invitation to do so. That would be stealing.

Hopefully the owners would return shortly.

Once inside again, she noticed a narrow ladder in the rear of the room that led to a hole in the ceiling. Curiosity got the best of her and she walked over to it. Because of the low ceilings, she only had to climb one rung before she could peer through the opening.

When she popped her head through it, she saw that it was a large room with a floor of wide planks that were random in size and width. The ceiling was pitched and there were only two small windows in the eaves. But on the rough-hewn floor lay several mattresses with tattered quilts. She counted them. Seven mattresses in total.

Carefully, she stepped off the ladder and assessed the main floor. Just one large room with a sink, table, seven chairs, and the cot where she had slept. Only, upon closer inspection, she realized that it was not a cot at all. Instead, it was made up of several planks that were resting on two large logs. On top of the planks were piles of blankets and quilts.

She couldn't help but wonder how had she gotten to this strange little house? And where were the occupants?

Whoever lived here certainly had been kind to bring her in out of the cold. They had set up a makeshift bed for her and left a fire burning to keep her warm.

Sadie knew that she had to repay their kindness and thought the best way to do that would be to clean the house. After all, cleanliness was next to godliness, or so her father always told her. And, if truth be told, this was one of the dirtiest homes she had ever seen.

Once she decided, it took her a while to find the cleaning supplies, which consisted of one bucket, several dirty rags, and bar of homemade soap—lavender-scented, at least! The sink was an old hand pump and it took her a while to fill up the bucket. But once she did, Sadie set to work washing the table and chairs, careful to reset the table just the way she had found it, and then washed the walls and floors.

With the sudden burst of lavender overshadowing the previous smell of grime and dust, Sadie felt a little more at ease. Only then did she venture to the little loft and tackle the chore of making the seven beds. She had to kneel down in order to do so, as to keep her head from bumping the ceiling.

"What ho!" a voice called out from downstairs. "What manner of whirlwind hit here?"

Sadie stiffened and crawled over to the ladder.

"Whatever it was, I don't like it one bit."

Another voice grumbled, "It doesn't smell like our house at all!"

"Stop being so grumpy all the time," a third voice laughed. "That smell you smell is the scent of clean. Remember it?"

"Barely."

Sadie's heart began to beat rapidly. She didn't know what to do. She didn't dare stay on the second floor, but she feared venturing down below.

"Fire's still burning," the first voice called out. "But we need more wood. Hey, Sleepy! Stop lollygagging and get more wood from outside."

The sound of feet shuffling across the floor was followed by the slamming of a door.

Sadie took a deep breath. She had to make her presence known. Despite her fears, she began to back down the ladder.

"What's that now?"

Sadie waited until she was on the ground before she shut her eyes, said a quick prayer to God to protect her, and slowly turned around.

What faced her was six pairs of large, brown eyes from six rather short, stout men. All of them, except one, wore gray mustache-less beards, typical of the Amish, and their clothing appeared plain, too. But they were unlike any Amish men she had ever met.

For a long moment, she stared at them, bewildered at the sight of the row of men facing her. Not one of them was taller than she was. In fact, she realized that all but one of them were no more than four feet tall.

They, too, stared at her in amazement, as if they had never seen a woman before. Finally, the door opened, and a seventh man entered the room, his arms laden with logs.

When he saw Sadie, he stopped walking and dropped the logs onto the floor. Dirt and leaves spilled all around him.

"Oh!" She hurried forward to start gathering them. "I just washed this floor!"

One of the men scowled at her. "So you're responsible for this dreadful smell?"

Another one nudged him. "Don't be such a grump!"

With the logs in her arms, Sadie stood up and stared at the men. "I . . . I suppose I must thank you for letting me sleep here last night."

The tallest of the men pointed his thumb at his own chest. "I found you in the woods." He gestured toward the others. "But my *bruders* helped to bring you into the *haus*."

Another of the men added, "I covered you with that blanket." He grinned at her, with a sense of pride on his face that made her smile.

"Then *danke* for your kindness." She took a step closer to the heap of logs on the floor, bent down, and neatly stacked them on the hearth by the fireplace.

"What were you doing sleeping in those leaves anyway?" the tallest one asked, removing his glasses and cleaning them with the edge of his untucked shirt. "That's an odd place to spend the night, don't you think?"

"I suppose it is," she admitted as she stood up straight. She wasn't certain how much she should confide in them. Even though she knew they were Amish, she had no idea *who* they were.

"Why were you sleeping there, then?" he asked, sliding the glasses back onto his nose.

Sadie frowned. These men were strangers, after all. So, rather than answer, she tried to change the subject. "Perhaps you might tell me where I am?"

He glanced around and gestured with his hands. "At our *haus*, of course."

"And who *are* you?"

The man removed his hat and, immediately, the other

six men did the same. "My name is David Grimm. And these are my *bruders*. Stevie, Samuel, Gideon—but we call him Grumpy because, well, that's just what he is—"

"Bah!" Gideon waved his hand at David and, after plopping his hat back on his head, crossed his arms over his chest.

"—Ben, Dan, and Hank—we call him Happy, and I bet you can guess why."

The one named Hank began to laugh, the sound filling the small house with joy. Even Sadie couldn't help but smile.

"We're the *bruders* Grimm."

As soon as David said that, Sadie immediately sobered. "Of course," she said under her breath. She had heard of these men, seven unmarried self-proclaimed bachelors who lived deep in the forest to the south of Echo Creek. They never ventured to town, and for good reason, apparently. Born into a family of twelve, the seven brothers had been born with short limbs and, reportedly, two of them had polydactyl hands.

They were distant cousins of Anna Rose's and Elizabeth's, which was how Sadie knew about them. But, then again, the Grimm family was so large that Sadie hadn't met most of their relatives and probably never would. They were spread out across the county and Sadie had heard that a few of them had even moved to other states.

"So *you're* the infamous Grimm *bruders*?"

Hank grinned at her.

David, however, appeared somber. "You've heard of us, then." It wasn't a question but a statement. "I'm not surprised. Seven old *buwes* living alone in the woods."

"Seven old, small *buwes*," Stevie added, emphasizing the word "small" before he sneezed and wiped his nose on the back of his sleeve.

"*Ja*, small *buwes*." David nodded his head. "I reckon we're the cause of some tongue wagging."

Quickly, Sadie shook her head. "*Nee*, not like that. I know of you because I'm friends with Anna Rose and Elizabeth. They're your cousins, *ja*?"

Samuel yawned and Gideon elbowed him.

"What? I'm tired," he complained.

"Then go nap instead of being so rude!"

David ignored his two brothers. "We don't see much of Anna Rose or Elizabeth, but *ja*, they're distant family. Our parents live farther south of here. Or, rather, they did live there. But they passed long ago."

Sadie lowered her eyes. "I'm sorry."

Gideon grumbled, "Daed's youngest *bruder* inherited the farm. And we're stuck living here in this old rickety *haus*!"

David gave him a stern look. "*Nee*, Gid, we're stuck nowhere. It was our choice to move out here long before Daed passed on," he reminded his grumpy brother, and then he turned to Sadie. He wiggled his fingers at her. "Can't farm much with such short arms and legs, you know."

She *didn't* know, and she also didn't know how to respond.

"But we sure can live off the land," Hank said with another big smile. "Me? I love to hunt for wild mushrooms with Dan."

His brother Dan, the only one without a beard, nodded his head, a lopsided grin on his face, but said nothing.

"And Stevie and Ben collect firewood for the cottage and to sell to folk in town," David added. "As for the rest of us, we fish when we can and sell that to town folk, too."

Sadie wondered how they got their products *to* town. But she didn't want to appear too inquisitive. If what they said was true, they could, indeed, live off the land. There wasn't much they needed beside food and firewood.

"Now, tell us your story," David said. "Why *were* you sleeping alone in the woods?"

Sadie sighed and moved over to the fireplace. She reached for the iron poker, pausing long enough to nudge some of the logs. Only when she had replaced the poker on the hearth did she respond.

"My stepmother wants me to marry a man that I . . ." She paused. How could she explain without sounding impertinent? "Well, I just don't find favor in him."

For a moment, seven pairs of eyes stared at her from seven faces that wore blank expressions. Sadie could only imagine how silly she sounded. Petty, juvenile, disobedient. She knew that she needed to explain the situation further so her rescuers could understand. Taking a deep breath, she continued with her story.

"She . . . she just wants me out of the *haus*. She wants my *daed* to herself. She thinks that I'm the reason that she can't . . ." Sadie stopped herself mid-sentence. Even though she had heard *about* the Grimm brothers, she didn't *know* these men. "Well, suffice it to say she is blaming me for something that isn't right in her life. And she's intent on my marrying John Rabor—"

At the mention of John Rabor's name, the seven men cringed.

David held up his hand to stop her from continuing further. "Say no more. You are welcome to stay here as long as you need. You won't be bothered here."

"You know John Rabor, then?"

The smile faded from Hank's face, and the other brothers looked just as serious.

However, it was David, the apparent spokesman for the others, who responded. "*Ja*, we know him. He hunts these woods and kills the animals." He frowned. "Sometimes he leaves the carcasses behind, taking just what he needs, leaving the rest to rot on the ground."

"The deer," Ben said in a sad voice. "How can he kill the deer?"

Sadie understood just how he felt.

David shook his head. "But even worse, he was married to our half *schwester*'s *dochder*. He didn't treat her kindly."

"And he made fun of us at their wedding!" Gideon added.

Sadie gasped. John Rabor's deceased wife had been their cousin, too!

"So you will find yourself safe here," David said. "But only on one condition."

Startled, Sadie blinked. A condition? "And what would that be?"

David leaned forward and, with a twinkle in his eye, he whispered, "If you tell us your name."

Chapter Twenty-One

For the next few days, Sadie found herself in a state of unexpected bliss. Living in the Grimm brothers' cottage, so deep in the woods, and surrounded by nature, was like a dream come true for her. Sadie felt she could finally be herself amidst nature and she relished in the songs of the wild birds, the scents of the many plants, and the peace and quiet of the forest.

Every morning when she awoke, the Grimm brothers were already gone from the house. She didn't know where they went each day, but in the evenings, they returned with baskets full of things they had collected from the woods. Some nights there were wild mushrooms and herbs, and she would sauté them in lard for their supper. Other nights they would return with trout or catfish from the stream, which she would pan-fry in a cast-iron skillet and sprinkle with herbs. And yet other times they would return with their arms laden with kindling and firewood, which they would stack at the side of the cottage in anticipation of the long winter ahead.

She learned that, like her, they loved nature and refused to hunt any of the wild animals. It wasn't that they were vegetarians, but, rather, that they had come to think of the deer and rabbits and even the pheasants as members of their household.

On her second morning there, it surprised Sadie to see that the deer would wander up to the house, grazing on whatever they could forage from the clearing by the side of the cottage. They showed no fear of her presence and would often approach her, coming within several feet of her before dipping their heads to eat the tender dandelion shoots.

Even the rabbits showed no fear. Sadie set out some old carrot tops and celery leaves that she saved after she made a vegetable stew and watched as the rabbits hopped right up to her to nibble at them from her outstretched hand.

For Sadie, being around so many wild animals that considered her a friend and not a foe was magical. She found herself often lost in time, watching them throughout the day.

The Grimm brothers usually left before she even woke and, more times than not, would arrive home just as the afternoon sun was setting. During their absence, when she wasn't cleaning the house and doing their laundry, she would sit among the animals and spend time with them as they foraged for food. In the solitude of the cottage, Sadie found a new sense of inner peace. She sang her songs, often peering out the open door to see the birds eating the bread crumbs she would scatter on the ground. And in the evening, she looked forward to sharing a meal with the Grimm brothers.

The biggest problem she encountered was when she washed their bedding. The seven small beds in the loft had not been tended to in a long time, so with the first washing of their dirty, tattered quilts, she found that they practically disintegrated from being handled.

When she hung them to dry in the early October sun,

she stood back and knew that most would not survive another washing.

"Oh help," she muttered.

Fingering one of the quilts, an idea struck her. The Grimm brothers had been very caring and understanding of her situation. Suddenly she knew exactly what she could do to return the brothers' kindness: she would make them each a new quilt.

The morning after she had made that decision, she searched the small house for fabric and found a closet full of old clothing. There would be more than enough material to make seven small quilts. Smiling to herself, she took the torn and worn-out shirts and pants outside to wash. By the afternoon, she was able to start cutting them into four-inch-by-four-inch squares. When the brothers came home from their day of foraging and hunting, Sadie had hidden her secret beneath her makeshift bed on the first floor.

The following Friday, in the early afternoon, she sat under the shade of a large tree and went about piecing together the first of the seven quilts. She had decided that she would make tie quilts, using large quilt blocks and sewing them together. Then she would use the old quilts as batting. With new backing, she'd be able to place simple tie-knots in the center of each block. While it wasn't exactly what she would have liked to do, it was certainly an improvement over what they had previously had. And the quilts would keep them warm in the loft during the cold winter months.

While she sewed, she listened to the songs of the birds, often setting down her work to stare into the sky as the lilting tunes graced her ears. It was beautiful, truly, to listen to the many sweet sounds of nature.

Returning her attention to the quilts, Sadie began to

hum a hymn in a soft voice. Within a few minutes, she noticed that several birds were perched on a nearby tree limb, their heads cocked to the side as if listening to her.

Sadie gave a soft laugh. "You probably haven't heard anyone make music like you do," she said out loud. And then, feeling silly for having talked to the birds, she bent her head down and focused on her work.

Her mind wandered to Frederick. She wondered what he was doing. Had he heard that she had run away? Was he worried? She wished there was a way to contact him, to let him know that she was okay.

Another thought struck her. What if he *didn't* know?

A moment of panic washed over her. What had her father and Rachel told people? Had they told the truth? Perhaps no one knew that she had run away? Family problems were not often shared with others in the community. They were considered private matters, and most Amish people liked to keep them that way. And because she was older and lived outside of the town proper, it wasn't as if people would *immediately* miss her presence. She didn't visit the stores in Echo Creek but once a week, if that. And her attendance at social gatherings was infrequent, or, rather, it had been irregular until she had met Frederick. No one would think anything of not having seen her, at least not right away.

That thought resonated with her, for if people didn't know where she was, she wondered what Frederick would think had happened to her. Perhaps he would assume that she was avoiding him or, worse, was not interested in courting him. Would he take her absence to mean just that? Or would he go to her house to seek her out? And if he did, what would Rachel tell him?

Knowing what she now knew about her stepmother, Sadie suspected that Rachel would not confess the truth. She couldn't imagine Rachel admitting that she had tried to force her stepdaughter to marry John Rabor against her will. Instead, Rachel would most likely make up a story to send Frederick away with a heavy heart.

"What ho!" David called out as he approached the cottage.

Sadie stuffed the quilt top into the basket by her feet, hiding it from view, and jumped up, then raced ahead into the cottage to check on the fire she had started earlier. She wanted to make sure the house was pleasantly warm when the rest of the brothers arrived home. After she stoked the fire and threw on another log, she looked out the window and saw the line of brothers walking down the trail toward the house. The image made her smile. She almost felt as if they were her own brothers returning home after a long day of work.

"Do I smell fresh bread?" Ben asked shyly.

Stevie sniffed at the air as he stepped through the front door. "I can't smell anything," he said in a muffled voice before he sniffled and wiped his nose with the back of his hand.

"Take your allergy medicine!" Gideon snapped.

Sadie reached onto the kitchen shelf for the bottle of allergy medicine. "It's almost empty," she said as she handed it to Stevie. "You'll need to get more."

He took it, shook it, and sneezed.

"Bah!" Gideon gave his brother a look of disdain. "Might as well buy a carton of it! The worst of the autumn allergy season hasn't even hit yet and already he's sneezing up a storm! We should call you Sneezy instead of Stevie," Gideon joked as he sat down and pulled off his work boots.

Sadie watched as Stevie drank the rest of the medicine. "There must be some other treatment, *ja*?" She tried to think of some natural remedy that she could make for him. "Perhaps some wild honey would help. I've often heard that from some of the older women down in Echo Creek."

Hank snapped his fingers, a broad smile breaking out

on his face. "That's a right *gut* idea, Sadie. I know just the place to get some honey."

But David, ever the wise one of the brothers, shook his head. "Too late in the season, I'm afraid. Those bees are all hunkering down for winter."

Sadie felt sorry for Stevie. His constant sneezing and sniffling was a source of many arguments among the brothers. Without his medicine, she imagined it would only get worse.

"Let me make you some hot tea, then. At least the steam and warmth might help," she offered and hurried to put on a kettle of water.

That evening, the brothers sat around the table, eager to sample Sadie's vegetable soup and fresh bread. She had made two loaves, and by the time the evening meal was over, the only thing left of it was the lingering scent of yeast in the large downstairs room.

"You'll make more bread tomorrow, *ja*?" Ben asked in a soft, shy voice.

His request startled her. Ben always avoided making eye contact with her and, whenever she did speak to him, he blushed and smiled shyly to himself. She had never met anyone as bashful as Ben and made a mental note to be extra kind to him. Perhaps if she treated him a little more specially than the others, she could bring him out of his shell. His soft eyes mirrored his kind heart, but the shroud of silence that engulfed him hid both, it seemed.

"I'd be happy to make more bread tomorrow," she told him with a smile, happy to be so appreciated. "And cookies."

"Cookies?" Hank lit up at the suggestion. "Why, I can't remember the last time we had homemade cookies." He rubbed his hands together and grinned. "What kind will you make?"

Sadie pursed her lips. From her exploration of the

kitchen in preparing the meal, she knew that the pantry held limited ingredients. Clearly the Grimm brothers lived mostly off of the gifts from the forest. But she had seen basic supplies such as oats and cinnamon. And, of course, she knew they had flour, sugar, and baking powder from having made bread earlier.

"If you have molasses, I could make oatmeal cookies," she suggested.

"Oh joyous day! I can hardly wait for tomorrow!"

David pushed his plate away and leaned back in his chair. He rubbed his stomach as his eyes scanned the room. "I must say," he began, "I can't remember ever seeing the cottage so clean."

"It stinks," Gideon mumbled.

David ignored him.

"I like having a clean *haus*," Ben said, his voice soft and high.

"Me, too," Hank added, laughing. "Why, the floor's almost a completely different color!"

Clearing his throat, David stood up. His eyes swept across the eager faces of his brothers—all but Gideon, who still scowled, his nose wrinkled as if bothered by the scent of the soap. Then, with a stoic expression on his face, David faced Sadie as if he had an important announcement to make. "We've been talking, Sadie, my *bruders* and I." The other brothers, except for Gideon, all nodded in unison. "We've decided that you're welcome to stay for as long as you'd like."

While his announcement warmed her heart, it also tore apart her soul. How on earth was such a solution possible? As much as she loved the thought of accepting their offer, Sadie knew it wasn't workable for the long run. How could she possibly stay in the middle of the forest, living with seven bachelors? When people found out, tongues would be wagging. Why, if the townspeople had stooped so low as to gossip about her and John Rabor, Sadie couldn't begin to imagine what they would have to say about *this* living arrangement!

"David, that's a very kind offer," she began slowly, not wanting to hurt their feelings, for the invitation was not just generous, but also truly Christian in spirit. However, she had to tell them the truth. "But I fear my reputation would be in tatters if I were to stay much longer."

Gideon surprised her by making a noise of disapproval and scowling. "Oh, stuff and bother!" He waved his hand as if swatting away her words. "Those gossipmongers. Who gives a care about what *they* think?"

David seemed to agree with him. "Sadie, we're old *buwes*. No one would ever think that something inappropriate was going on here."

Even Dan nodded his head emphatically.

But Sadie wasn't so sure. She knew far too well how gossip started.

"Besides," David continued, breaking her train of thought, "where else would you go?"

It was true. She knew that she couldn't return to her father's house, not with Rachel in her current state. Surely nothing good would come from Sadie's returning home. Not now anyway. Rachel's increasingly irrational and unpredictable behavior supported Sadie's fears.

"Perhaps just for a few more days," Sadie relented, knowing that her options were, indeed, limited.

While her acceptance of their offer appeased the Grimm brothers for the moment, it left Sadie in a quandary. How long could she stay hidden in the woods with them? Surely someone would come looking for her eventually. And then what? She'd have no choice but to return to her father's farm. Surely Rachel would not greet her with open arms. Instead, her anger would have increased because of Sadie's disobedience. What would Rachel do to her?

The reality of the situation sank in. Her options were limited. Unless she chose to return to her father's house, what else *could* she do but agree to stay with the Grimms? Despite the joyous way in which the Grimm brothers greeted her acceptance of their offer, her heart felt heavy. Not for the first time since she had fled from John Rabor, Sadie felt the weight of an invisible chain hanging from her neck. No amount of good cheer and Christian generosity from the seven brothers could remove that burden from her.

Chapter Twenty-Two

"What ho!" David called out late one afternoon during the second week of Sadie's stay. He had been feeling poorly that morning so had decided not to join his brothers in the forest that day. At a sound coming from outside, he shuffled to the front door and peered down the lane. "Someone's here to visit."

From the table where she sat folding clean laundry, Sadie looked up and tilted her head, listening. She heard nothing unusual. Just the rustle of leaves and the song of the birds. Earlier that morning, she had sprinkled some bread crumbs near the big log where the brothers cut wood. All day, the birds had lingered in that area, pecking at the ground and gracing Sadie with their songs of gratitude.

"I think you are imagining things, David," Sadie said.

He gave her a knowing smile. "Oh *ja*?"

Concerned, Sadie stood up and walked to the door. She knew that the Grimm brothers had lived among the woods for so long that she probably should not doubt them. As she stood beside him, she listened for anything unusual. As far as she could tell, there was no noise to indicate that anyone had approached the small house. But that didn't lessen Sadie's sudden wave of concern.

The Grimm brothers' house was so deep in the forest that she had felt protected there. Now, however, she realized that she might have reason to be worried. Over the past week, there had been no news from Echo Creek, which had lulled her into a sense of security. She had taken the silence to mean that her sanctuary was safe. However, just because they hadn't heard anything didn't mean that her father wasn't searching for her. She hadn't given much thought to that possibility.

And, by now, surely people knew that Sadie was not at her father's farm. Enough time had gone by that *someone* would have noticed.

Sadie had no idea how the rest of the town might have reacted to the news of her disappearance. The previous week, she had suspected that Rachel might not admit the real reason for her stepdaughter's flight. To do so would be to admit to trying to force her to marry John Rabor, and *that* would put Rachel in a bad light, for sure and certain. People might believe that the normally levelheaded Sadie had just run away. However, *that* didn't mean people weren't looking for her. Surely her friends were concerned about her welfare.

Suddenly the silence of the forest broke and the sound of footsteps could be heard. Leaves crackled and twigs snapped under the weight of someone's footsteps.

David turned his head away from the door, a pleased grin on his face. "See? I told you I heard someone. You can't live out here in the forest without knowing when someone's approaching."

Despite David's self-satisfaction, Sadie felt a wave of panic. In the short time she had been at the Grimm brothers' house, no one had come to visit them. Who could it possibly be?

Immediately, Sadie turned away from the door. She stepped into the shadows and stared around the room. "I must hide!" In the one large open room, there were few places where she could conceal herself.

"Hide? Whatever for?"

Sadie felt as if every nerve in her body were on fire. How could David, the most intelligent of the brothers, ask such a question? "What if it's my stepmother? What if it's John Rabor?"

But David didn't appear concerned. He merely shook his head at her. "*Nee*, no need to fret. It's probably our cousin, bringing us supplies."

Cousin? Though she had never thought about how the brothers got their basic supplies, she also knew that they had never mentioned a cousin who regularly visited.

Sadie wasn't about to take any chances. She retreated to the far corner of the room and tucked herself in the shadows behind the ladder that led to the loft.

"Good day, Cousin!" David called out to the approaching visitor.

"And to you, David," a male voice responded—a voice that sounded familiar to Sadie.

David hesitated and then asked, "What's wrong? Why so long in the face?"

"Too much to explain, I reckon."

Frederick? For a moment, she couldn't make sense of why Frederick would be standing outside of the Grimm brothers' cottage. And David had called him "Cousin."

Suddenly a memory came to mind. Sadie recalled the day she had met Frederick, just moments after she had spotted that beautiful deer near the stream. Hadn't he told her that he was coming from his cousins' house, having stopped to visit on his way to Echo Creek? And, of course, both Anna Rose and Elizabeth Grimm, also cousins to the Grimm brothers, were related to Frederick. Their fathers had been Frederick's uncles.

In her mind, Sadie envisioned the family tree. Like every Amish family, it was convoluted with twists and

turns, interwoven branches that made a complicated mess
when it came to genealogy. Because of frequent intermar-
riage, there was a tendency for certain genetic diseases,
including dwarfism, to be prevalent in some communities.

Regardless, it made sense that, if Frederick's mother
had been a Grimm and Frederick was related to Anna Rose
and Elizabeth, then he, too, was a cousin to the Grimm
brothers.

She felt foolish that she hadn't made the connection.

"I'm on my way to Echo Creek and have come to fetch
your list of supplies," Frederick said as he neared the front
door of the house.

"*Wunderbarr.* We're out of many things." He gave a
jolly laugh. "Allergy medicine being one of the most
important, of course." The jovial tone of David's voice
indicated his pleasure at seeing Frederick.

Frederick didn't respond to David's mirth. Instead, he
paused, the silence feeling heavy to Sadie as she hid from
view.

"I have a question to ask," he said, his tone solemn.

"Ask away, Cousin. Hopefully I might have an answer."

Sadie heard Frederick clear his throat, hesitating for
just a moment before he spoke. "There's a girl. A young
woman, rather. She's missing from Echo Creek. Have you
seen her?"

Now it was David's turn to pause. She was glad that the
rest of the brothers were still off in the woods gathering
their daily treasures. Surely one of them would have given
away her presence in their home—probably Hank, since
he always joked and laughed about everything. He'd never
have been able to keep the secret. However, Sadie held her
breath, wondering how David would respond to Frederick's question.

"Missing?"

Frederick cleared his throat and exhaled. His voice
sounded forlorn when he responded. "*Ja*, run off, I reckon,

although no one seems to have a straight answer as to why that might be."

"I wonder about that," David said slowly.

"*Ja*, me, too."

Sadie realized that David had answered by not answering at all. It warmed her heart that her protector had not lied, but he had also not given away her secret. Not even to Frederick.

There was a slight pause and the sound of heavy footsteps on the wooden floor. Sadie knew that Frederick had entered the house.

"What's this?" Another pause. "Has one of you suddenly taken an interest in cleaning?" Curiosity underlaid the question. He took another few steps into the room, apparently approaching the table. "And washing your clothes?"

David stuttered. "*Ja*, well . . ." He hesitated as if searching for an answer. "You always tell us what a pigsty it is in here." He gave a nervous laugh. "You could say we've decided to do a bit of housekeeping," he added.

But it was clear that Frederick was not fooled.

"*Nee*, I don't think you have." His voice suddenly sounded more hopeful. "Someone else is here!"

"Wh-why would someone be here?" David stammered.

"Oh! I should've thought to check here sooner." Frederick sounded desperate as he called out, "Sadie! I know that you're here!"

For a moment, she hesitated. Would he be angry with her? Would he tell her family? Still, she knew that she couldn't remain hidden much longer, not from Frederick or anyone else. Even if she did not reveal herself, Frederick would be suspicious and might tell others, and then there was no telling who would come. Perhaps Rachel or John Rabor would show up next!

Certainly, it would be better to face Frederick and explain it to him herself, rather than allowing him to hear it from anyone else. Perhaps he might understand and help her find a more permanent solution to her problem.

Hesitantly, Sadie emerged from the shadows and, with her head hung low, stepped into the center of the room.

"Oh, Sadie!" Frederick rushed toward her and, to her shock, pulled her into his arms. "How worried I've been!" His voice filled her with both relief and joy. If she had felt protected during her stay at the Grimm brothers' house, she suddenly felt completely safe in Frederick's embrace.

"You know each other?" David seemed taken aback by the unusually friendly greeting. And then he softened his tone. "Ah, of course you do."

After what felt like a lifetime but wasn't nearly long enough, Frederick pulled away. Gently, his hands pressed against her cheeks and he tilted her face so that he could stare into her eyes. "Have you been here the whole time?" His expression shifted from relief to guilt. "Oh, I should have known my cousins would've found you and taken you into their care!"

"I'm so sorry, Frederick." The words were just a whisper on her lips, but they were shouted from her heart. "I . . . I didn't mean to cause you any worry."

He bent his knees, just enough so that he was eye level with her. With his hands still holding her cheeks, he studied her face. "What happened, Sadie? Whatever could have caused you to just run off?"

David coughed into his hand. Sadie's eyes flitted over Frederick's shoulder, and she saw that David was backing toward the door. Clearly he was uncomfortable. "I . . . I reckon you young people have things to talk about. I'll just slip outside, then."

Sadie glanced in his direction and saw him shuffle out the front door. Alone with Frederick, she lowered her eyes, staring at the floor as shame overcame her.

"I . . . I didn't know what else to do. Rachel . . ." Sadie felt tears well up in her eyes. "She's been so terrible to me lately. So angry and hostile. And then she began inviting that man to our house and had me watch his *kinner* without asking me."

"That's no reason to run away," he said, in a soft tone but with a touch of reproach.

"*Nee*, it's not," she agreed. "But then she insisted that I marry John Rabor. She even convinced my *daed* that it was a *gut* idea." She felt tears well in her eyes.

A noise of displeasure slipped through Frederick's lips. "Marry him?"

"*Ja*, she was determined that I do so. And I would no sooner marry John Rabor than I'd . . ." She couldn't finish the sentence. How could she explain how she felt about one man without revealing how she felt about the other?

"Than you'd what, Sadie?"

Only then did she look up at him, her blue eyes now overflowing with tears. "Than I'd deny how I felt about you."

The expression on his face was transformed. The concern disappeared and he gave her a small smile filled with tenderness. "My little songbird," he said. He brushed away the tears that fell down her cheeks. "What you have been through."

The relief she felt at his reaction caused a sob to catch in her throat. "I was so frightened, Frederick," she wept.

He embraced her once again, soothing her as he rubbed her back and kissed the side of her head. "Oh, Sadie, how I wish you had come to me."

Another tear fell, this time staining his shirt. She pulled away and peered up at him. "I . . . I didn't want to be seen as brazen. Besides, how could I have gotten a message to you anyway?"

He must have realized the truth of her statement. She didn't know where he lived, and even if she did, it was too far away for her to walk there without being caught along the way. Frederick took a deep breath. "Well, I am here now and no further harm will come to you." He looked around the large room. "And I know you are safe here with my cousins."

Sadie lowered her gaze. "I . . . I worry, though. If people find out, what will they think?"

Her fear did not seem to give Frederick reason to feel anxious. "*Nee*, Sadie. No one knows that you are here. And if they did, no one would presume anything, I'm sure." He guided her to one of the chairs and gestured for her to sit. Only when she had seated herself did he take a seat next to her. "No one in town knows where you are. But I'll go to Echo Creek today and find out what I can. In the meantime, promise me that you will stay here. The cottage is deep enough in the forest that no one ever travels this way, only me when I stop on my way to Echo Creek to bring my cousins supplies."

She nodded. "I promise."

He reached for her hands and held them in his. "The relief that I feel knowing you're out of harm's way . . ." He sighed. "A great burden has been lifted from my shoulders."

"But not from mine," she confessed. "I know I cannot stay here forever, but I have nowhere to go."

For a short moment, he appeared to ponder her plight. His eyes narrowed as if deep in thought. While he reflected, Sadie waited, hoping against hope that he might have a solution for her.

Finally, he took a deep breath. "You leave this to me, Sadie Whitaker. Let me visit town, for I was on my way there to fetch supplies for my cousins. Let me learn all I can about what people are saying concerning your disappearance and what they say of your stepmother."

Sadie's eyes widened. How could he find out any news without giving away her location? "Promise me you won't tell anyone where I am!"

He gave a little laugh and pulled her hands toward him,

pressing them against his chest. "On my dying breath, I would never do such a thing. You're safe here, and I wish nothing more than to keep you that way."

There was something about the way he looked at her that made her feel as if butterflies fluttered inside her stomach. Surely God had led her to the Grimm brothers' house for a reason. He must've known that the one—and only—person who would help keep her safe was Frederick Keim. And, in that moment, Sadie knew, without doubt, that everything would be all right. With God's help, Frederick would straighten everything out.

Chapter Twenty-Three

The next day, Frederick returned, this time with a sack of dry goods. It was slung over his shoulder in such a way as to make it easier to carry, since he could not bring his horse and buggy into the woods to the brothers' house.

Stevie met him at the door. "Please tell me you have my allergy medicine," he sniffled.

Frederick laughed and swung the bag onto the floor. "Indeed I do."

Sadie watched as the seven Grimm brothers surrounded the burlap bag. For a moment, there was nothing but joy in the small house as they unpacked all the items that Frederick had purchased for them: flour, coffee, sugar, salt, yeast, and other things that could not be replaced by items found in the woods.

"We thought we might see you again yesterday evening," Sadie said as the brothers set the items onto the table.

Frederick nodded. "*Ja*, I usually return the same day when I fetch their supplies," he explained. "But I stayed over at Anna Rose's *haus*." He leveled his gaze at her. "I had much visiting to do in town."

She didn't need to inquire further as to what he meant. Surely he had been talking with people and trying to find out what he could regarding what folks knew of Sadie's disappearance. She was eager to hear what he had learned, but knew that patience was a virtue.

Oblivious to their exchange, the Grimm brothers began to clamor around her like small children on Christmas morning.

"Oh, Sadie," Ben asked, his eyes averted to the floor as he shuffled his feet nervously. "Might you make us some more fresh bread?"

"Of course I will," she promised.

Stevie sniffled as he tried to open the allergy medicine. "And those cookies? The chewy oatmeal ones?"

"How about a pie?" Hank asked hopefully. "I love pumpkin pie!"

Gideon rolled his eyes. "You and your pumpkins!"

Samuel yawned. "I don't see you complaining when you're eating her food."

Gideon nudged him with his arm.

"Now, now," Sadie scolded in a teasing tone. "I'm happy to make bread *and* cookies *and* pumpkin pie." She gave Samuel a kind smile. "Even if Gideon pretends not to want me to."

Several of the Grimm brothers snickered, and Gideon crossed his arms across his chest, scowling.

"Now, mayhaps you might put those things onto the counter," she said, "instead of the table?"

Eager to please her, Hank and Ben quickly complied with her request.

"Might we go for a walk, Sadie?" Frederick whispered into her ear. "I have some things to discuss with you."

Sadie wiped her hands on her apron and followed Frederick outside. He led her down the path, away from the noise of the seven brothers, who were arguing about what meal they'd like Sadie to make them for supper.

"Seems you've made quite an impact on my cousins," he said.

She laughed. "I'm not certain whether or not they are serious or pretending to argue. Seems they enjoy teasing each other."

"*Ja*, that's true. But I can assure you that no closer *bruders* ever lived. And I've never seen them so happy." He paused before adding, "Or their *haus* so clean!"

She laughed. "I imagine living alone, without much company—"

"Any company," he interrupted.

"*Ja*, any company, is sure to make them not care that the *haus* is so dirty." She stepped over a fallen branch. "I wonder that it's not lonely for them out here, alone in the woods in their little cottage."

"Mayhaps it would be, for you or me. But they live the way they want, free from the scrutiny of those who might mock their small stature."

Sadie knew only too well how some people tended to view those who were different. She had only to look at Belle and her husband, Adam. It was a shame that people judged others on their appearances and not on their substance.

"Such a shame," she mused. "And to think that those very people claim to be Christians."

Frederick raised his eyebrows and tilted his head. "Aren't we all sinners?"

"Some more so than others, it appears."

He laughed at her observation, but Sadie didn't join him. While she had enjoyed the peace and tranquility of living in the woods during her short stay, she was still bothered by the idea that such kindhearted, righteous men were not part of a proper community.

"But no family comes to visit them, then?"

Frederick pressed his hand on his chest. "I do."

"*Ja*, well, of course. But what of other siblings or extended family?"

Frederick shook his head. "*Nee*, just me and sometimes my family. They've no one else living nearby. They had two older sisters who are normal-sized. They married a few years ago and moved to Shipshewana."

Sadie hadn't known that. "That's far from here, no?"

"*Ja*, and their parents passed away many years ago. They were both older in years, you see."

"And you are related, how?"

"Ah, that." He smiled. "My *maem* and their *daed* were siblings. Half siblings, anyway. There's almost a thirty-year age difference between my *maem* and the *bruders' daed*. My *grossdawdi* took a second wife after his first had passed. He was over fifty when my *maem* was born. Several of my cousins are older than my *maem*."

She frowned, trying to visualize the extended family tree.

"Anyway, I wanted to talk to you about my recent trip to Echo Creek."

"Oh," she breathed at the sudden change of subject. "What news have you learned?"

He took a deep breath and shoved his hands into his pockets. His brow furrowed, and he gave her a regretful look. "In town, I heard an earful, Sadie. It seems Echo Creek is ripe with gossipers. Why, that Linda Troyer could speak of little else."

That didn't surprise Sadie at all. Linda knew *everything* that went on and enjoyed sharing it with anyone who might listen. Oftentimes, much of the town's gossip could be traced back to Linda.

"But one thing that I learned warmed my heart and, I trust, will warm yours, too."

"Oh? And what's that?"

Frederick sighed. "Apparently your *daed* is frightfully worried, Sadie."

It took her a minute to digest what he had just told her. While it made her happy to learn that her father cared enough to worry, she couldn't help but wonder at the underlying reasons. Was it possible that her father had realized the mistake he had made? Or was he merely concerned for her welfare? "How so, Frederick?"

"I don't want to give you reason to fret, but he's been unwell since your disappearance."

She took a short intake of air. Her father? Ill? "He's . . . he's going to be okay, *ja*?"

Frederick nodded. "It's nothing serious. According to Linda," he said, a scowl crossing his brow, "he's merely depressed. And apparently Rachel has been into the store, too."

"And how is she?"

He gave a little shrug. "Linda didn't say much more than that Rachel's told people how worried she is for your safety."

Sadie wasn't quite certain whether she believed *that* to be true.

And then Frederick's frown deepened. "But that John Rabor. He's been spreading stories, Sadie."

When she heard that last bit, she felt her stomach tighten. She was almost too afraid to ask. "Stories? What kind of stories?"

Solemnly, Frederick nodded. "*Ja*, stories, Sadie. Stories that he's to marry you. I learned that from my cousin, Anna Rose, who heard it from Elizabeth."

Sadie gasped. "How would Elizabeth come to know such a thing?"

"She's a teacher, *ja*? On Saturdays, she meets with the older students who are no longer studying at school but at home or in jobs during their final two years. Sometimes, apparently, the teacher from our school comes to Echo

Creek with her older students so that they can combine the effort for the school board."

Sadie hadn't known that. When she had been fourteen and stopped attending school proper, her teacher had met with the older students on Saturdays to review their journals in order to meet the state's guidelines, but they had never also met with students from the remote community where Frederick lived.

"What does that have to do with John Rabor?"

"Apparently the eldest Rabor boy—"

"Owen?"

"*Ja*, him."

Why wasn't Sadie surprised that Owen had something to do with this?

Frederick continued. "He told the other students that his *daed* was angry that his new *fraa* ran off. And the teacher spoke to John about Owen's story. She told Elizabeth that he was outright furious because you refused to marry him after Jacob and Rachel promised him you would. Several other people have spread the same story in Echo Creek."

Sadie gasped. "I don't believe it!" That was an outrageous thing for him to say. And it was almost more outrageous that anyone would choose to repeat it. "My *daed* would never promise such a thing."

"I don't doubt you, but apparently John believes otherwise."

And *that* made Sadie feel sad. Regardless of what she thought of John Rabor, he was still a person, and people needed each other. It was more than apparent that John needed a wife to help raise his *kinner* and, because he was older, had thought that an arranged marriage would be the answer to his problems. Surely Rachel had intentionally misled him into believing that Sadie had agreed.

Still, whatever Rachel had told John, Sadie knew what *she* had told him.

She pressed her lips together defiantly. "I would never agree to marry him, or anyone else for that matter, for the sake of convenience!"

Frederick stopped walking and faced her. There was a worried air about him. "So you say."

Sadie's mouth opened. What was *that* supposed to mean? "I haven't, Frederick. You must believe me."

"*Nee*, that's not what I meant, Sadie." He shuffled his feet as if he were nervous. "What I meant is that you say you wouldn't marry for convenience. But what *would* it take for you to agree to marry someone?"

Dumbfounded, Sadie gave him a blank look. Why would he ask such a question? "Well, I wouldn't marry someone *just* to get married, that's for sure and certain."

He swallowed, waiting expectantly for her to continue. "It would be for one and only one reason."

"And," he said slowly, "what might that be?"

"Because God led me to that man."

"I see."

Sadie wondered why he was behaving so evasively. "Why are you asking me this, Frederick?"

He took a few steps away from her, stopped, and then turned around. His cheeks were pale and his eyes wide. "I ask you this, Sadie, because I have every intention of making you my *fraa*."

She caught her breath.

"But I am fearful you will think that I ask because of the situation you are in and not for other reasons."

"What other reasons, Frederick?" she prodded him in a gentle tone.

"Oh, Sadie, surely you must know that I love you." Quickly, he closed the gap between them and reached for her hands. "And you must know that I have felt God's presence in bringing us together. Why, if I hadn't seen you at the stream and heard you singing to the little birds that morning, I might never have known you at all!"

Under his steady gaze, she began to feel dizzy.

"Surely you feel the same way? That God brought us together?"

Slowly, she nodded. "I . . . I do, Frederick. I have felt so from the very beginning. I just didn't want to presume that you felt the same."

He clutched her hands tight and pulled her toward his chest. "Oh, Sadie, your words are like music to my ears."

"Were you so uncertain?" It was an improbable thought that he hadn't known how she felt. Yet she, too, had doubted how deep were his affections for her.

"What matters, Sadie, is that now we each know how the other feels. And that you know I want you to marry me." He bent down just enough so that they were at eye level with each other. "You will marry me, *ja*?"

She felt giddy and her head spun. She savored the realization that everything she had been through had led to this moment with Frederick proposing to her in the middle of the forest. "Of course I will marry you," she whispered, feeling as if she might cry with joy.

Embracing her, Frederick kissed the side of her head. For a long moment, he held her, his arms wrapped protectively around her as they stood together in the quiet of the forest.

Finally, he loosened his hold on her. "Sadie, I want you to know that we will get through this together. I'll speak to your *daed* just as soon as I can. I have no doubt that our marriage will heal your relationship with your parents."

While her heart sang with joy that Frederick had made his intentions known, she still feared her parents' reaction. After everything that had happened, was healing really possible between them? Frederick had heard that her father was distraught, true, but was Rachel? Or was she merely pretending to worry about Sadie in order to protect her own reputation?

"Please be careful, Frederick."

He smiled. "Now Sadie, you must trust that people can change. Surely both your father and Rachel have seen the error of their ways. And God tells us to forgive, *ja*?"

Despite her apprehension, she nodded. "He does, *ja*."

"And that is what we both shall do!" He let his hand slip down to take hers. Holding it, he started to walk again, this time back toward the cottage. "Now, let's enjoy the rest of the day together. I must return home this evening and pre-pare to speak to your *daed* on my next trip to Echo Creek."

"When will that be, Frederick?"

From inside the cottage, Stevie sneezed, and one of the brothers, most likely Gideon, snapped at him to take his medicine.

"I did already!" Stevie replied, his voice nasally and hoarse.

"Then take more!"

Laughing, Frederick gestured toward the open door. "From the sounds of it, the sooner the better, for surely Stevie will need more allergy medicine within the next few days."

Together, they walked inside the house, Frederick joining his cousins near the fire while Sadie went about fulfilling her promise to make bread and cookies and pumpkin pie. While she worked, she realized that, for the first time, she would be cooking for Frederick. Her future husband. Reality struck her. He had truly asked her to marry him, for he loved her, just as she loved him. No matter what her current situation, her future looked bright, with the promise of a marriage based on tenderness and warmth, friendship and affection. Joy overcame her and she began to sing while she worked, unaware that the brothers and Frederick grew silent, listening to her song as they stared at her, complete adoration in their eyes.

Chapter Twenty-Four

"Such *wunderbarr gut* news," Frederick called out as he approached the Grimm brothers' house, a small bag in his hands.

Two days had passed since his last visit and the day on which he'd proposed to her. Sadie hadn't known that he had gone to Echo Creek that morning, for he hadn't stopped at the cottage beforehand.

Now, he practically jogged down the lane toward her. "I've spoken to your *daed*, Sadie!" He grinned as he set down his package and swept her into his arms, twirling her around. "And you'll never imagine what has happened!"

She laughed, her hands on his shoulders. His jubilant mood felt contagious and she smiled from ear to ear. Surely he had something fantastic to share with her.

"Perhaps if you set me down, you could tell me when my head stops spinning."

Immediately, he stopped and gently released her, careful to keep hold of her in case she was dizzy. But the grin remained on his face.

Once she steadied herself, Sadie took a step backward, too aware that the Grimm brothers had witnessed their display of affection. She ran her hands down the front of her dress, trying to adopt an air of propriety that Frederick had forgotten.

"Now, come inside and tell us your news, then," she said primly as she turned toward the cottage, ignoring the curious looks upon the Grimm brothers' faces.

Frederick couldn't contain his excitement as he bent down to retrieve the package and then followed her inside the house, where the fire warmed the first-floor room, which smelled like yeasty fresh bread and nutty pecan pie. She had cooked both earlier and, despite the eagerness of the Grimm brothers, had refused to let them taste anything until suppertime.

Frederick placed the package onto the counter.

"I rode into town today," he started.

"Where's your horse?" Ben asked.

"I tied it to a tree near the road," Frederick responded. "But that's not important."

"Did you get more allergy medicine?" Gideon asked, a grumpy tone to his voice. "Stevie kept me up all night with his sniffling and sniveling."

Impatiently, Frederick gestured to the bag. "*Ja, ja*. It should be in there." And then he returned his attention to Sadie. "After I went to the store, I stopped at your *daed*'s farm."

Sadie felt her heart beat faster. From the look of elation on his face, she could only presume that Frederick had good news to share. She held her breath, eager to hear.

"I told him that I knew where you were and I had spoken to you."

Sadie gasped. "You did?" For a moment, she feared that Frederick had told her father where she was. But she remembered what he had said to her about trusting people. Surely she could trust Frederick above all others.

He nodded. "*Ja*, I did."

"And what did he say?"

Frederick moved over to the table and sat down. "I didn't tell him where you were, Sadie. Just as I promised. But I shared with him that we had conversed."

She clutched her hands together and waited for Frederick to divulge the details of his meeting with her father.

"Jacob was close to tears to learn that you are safe, Sadie," Frederick continued. His expression softened as he spoke. "He was quite distressed and looked as if he truly has been suffering from your absence."

"Oh help," she whispered. It had never been her intention to inflict pain upon anyone, especially her father. "How sorry I am to hear that."

Frederick bowed his head. "I felt the same way, Sadie."

"And Rachel? Was she there when you spoke to him?"

"*Nee*, she wasn't." He leaned his elbow on the edge of the table, staring for a long moment into the fireplace. "At least not when I spoke to Jacob. She answered the door when I knocked and she looked none too pleased when I asked to speak with your *daed* in private."

That didn't surprise Sadie, but it *did* worry her. "I wonder why."

He shook his head. "I'm not certain," he confessed. "Mayhaps she thought something was amiss or that I was involved in your disappearance."

Sadie highly doubted that but remained silent on the matter, preferring to let Frederick continue his story.

"Anyway, when Jacob and I spoke, we were outside in the dairy barn. When I told your *daed* that I knew where you were and that you were, indeed, safe, he wept." Frederick paused, letting his words sink in. "He was overcome with joy and relief, Sadie, for I believe he suspected the worst."

She frowned. "The worst?"

Frederick lifted his hand. "I don't want to speculate what

he thought, but I can assure you any good opinion he may have held of John Rabor has been lost."

"Oh?"

Frederick exhaled slowly. "Apparently John never once looked for you and showed little concern about your well-being. Instead, he was more concerned about what people would think now that his intended bride had run away."

"'Intended bride' indeed!" she scoffed.

"My thoughts exactly."

Wanting to redirect Frederick to her most pressing concern, Sadie asked, "And what did you and my *daed* discuss?"

Frederick sobered for a minute, a dark cloud passing over his face. "I told him about your lack of feelings for John Rabor and how pressured you felt. How your step-mother insisting that you help him was wrong and how when John took you for a buggy ride, you were upset at his assertion that you should marry him." He lifted his eyes and looked directly into hers. "I explained to him that the way John treated you made you feel small, as well as how his expectation that you would marry him made you fearful that Rachel's hand had been behind all of this. And that you were uneasy about Rachel's reaction when she realized you would *never* marry such a man."

She felt a moment of panic. While nothing Frederick had told her father was untrue, it certainly wasn't flattering to Rachel. "Oh, I hope she didn't eavesdrop!"

Frederick shook his head. "*Nee*, she did not. I made certain of that, Sadie. She was inside the *haus*. Jacob and I spoke for almost half an hour in the dairy barn. There was no way for her to overhear our conversation."

Feeling comforted by his words, Sadie returned to the next most important thing. "So what did my *daed* say?"

Frederick hesitated, his eyes softening once again as he appeared to seek the right words to explain her father's response. "He told me that he never *intended* you to marry John Rabor, Sadie."

Sadie almost interrupted him. Hadn't her father been insistent that she take that buggy ride with John? How could her father make such a claim?

But Frederick read her mind and held up his hand to stop her from speaking. "Not at first, anyway. But Jacob confessed that Rachel was rather persuasive and finally convinced him that marrying John Rabor was in your best interest."

"She must have been very convincing," Sadie quipped.

Frederick chuckled. "I imagine so. Apparently, she insisted that marrying a widower was the perfect arrangement for you. That no one else in Echo Creek was interested in courting you."

Sadie caught her breath. How could her father have believed such a thing? And then it dawned on her that it was true, in a way. She *hadn't* found anyone in Echo Creek to court. And her father hadn't known about Frederick's interest in her. Perhaps courting in such secrecy was *not* such a good idea for Amish youth after all.

Frederick continued. "But Jacob understands now that Rachel manipulated him, trying to compare your situation to hers. He realizes now that your circumstances have nothing in common with what your stepmother's were when he married her. Most importantly, your *daed* knows that not only is John Rabor *not* the right husband for you, but that someone much better than that old widower seeks your hand."

She blushed. "And . . . and what did he say to that?"

"First and foremost, Sadie, he wants you to come home. And, of course, he wants you to be happy." The serious expression on his face faded, replaced with joy once more. "He's given his blessing, Sadie, for us to be married!"

Upon hearing his words, her happiness was so great, she almost felt like crying out in gleeful celebration. How could she have doubted her father? All she had needed to do was to talk to him. If she only had had faith in his love for her and his righteousness. Perhaps she, too, was partially responsible for creating this terrible situation she had found herself in?

However, behind her, there was a collective groan. She had forgotten that they were not alone, and from the sounds of it, Frederick's good news was not met with the same level of joy by the others in the room.

"But that means Sadie won't stay here." Ben's disappointment was immediately echoed by the other Grimm brothers, all of them except for David.

"Now, now, *bruders*!" Ever the pragmatic one, he positioned himself next to Sadie. He raised his hand to silence their grumblings "We knew that this arrangement with Sadie was temporary. We offered her safe haven, but we always knew it would not be permanent."

Stevie sniffled. "But I certainly hoped it might be." His voice sounded congested. "Her tea makes my allergies feel better."

"And my clothes smell so fresh after she washes them," Samuel chimed in.

For the first time, even Hank did not appear happy. "And her cookies! Who will make us cookies?"

David gave his brothers a look of reproach. "*Ach!* You all sound like children, not grown men! Regardless, those are not reasons for Sadie to stay here in the forest with us. She is young and has her whole life ahead of her. We should be thankful for the time we've had with her."

Frederick tapped his fingers against the table. "I agree with David. Sadie does have her life to live, and that life is not taking caring of you old *buwes*."

"Personally I can't wait until the house doesn't smell so"—Gideon looked around the room—"clean!"

Sadie couldn't help but laugh at the miserable scowl he wore. "Somehow I don't believe that, Gideon."

When the color rose to his cheeks, Sadie knew that she was correct: he hadn't meant it.

"Jacob is thrilled to have his *dochder* coming home." Frederick smiled. "We should be elated to learn that news, *ja*?"

Reluctantly, six heads nodded in unison. Only David abstained. "While I am pleased to learn of this, I do have one concern. What of Rachel? You said she looked none too pleased when you arrived. Surely she isn't happy her step*dochter* will be returning."

Frederick held up his hand as if to silence his eldest cousin. "Don't be so certain of that, David. When Jacob told her the news that Sadie would return, she appeared very relieved to me."

Sadie, however, wasn't convinced.

As if sensing her doubt, Frederick stood up and walked over to the counter where he had left his bag. Reaching inside, he withdrew a large covered pie pan. "I believe her, Sadie. Why, before she left, she approached me and begged me to give this chicken pot pie to you," he told her before she could form the words to say how she was feeling. "She insisted that I deliver it to you at once, as a token of her love for you and her desire for your quick return."

"A chicken pot pie?" That *was* Sadie's favorite dish; however, she eyed it suspiciously. Was Rachel trying to bribe Sadie into forgiving her?

Fredrick must have noticed her apprehension. Setting it on the table, he gave Sadie a look of gentle reproach. "Sadie, sometimes things aren't how they seem. She told me that she had feared your becoming an old *maedel* like she was when she married your *daed*. She didn't want you to miss out on having *bopplin* of your own. She knew you did not care for any young man in Echo Creek and, obviously, she knew nothing of our special friendship."

She wondered about Frederick's last statement. Hadn't Frederick gone to the house looking for her that one day?

The day when she had fallen into the stream? And Rachel had surely seen Frederick bring her home after the youth gathering. "I'm not so sure about that, Frederick."

"Well, regardless, I believe she's genuinely happy for you, for us," Frederick continued. "She commented that nothing was the same since you left and she couldn't wait for things to return to normal." He pointed to the pie. "She made this for you while Jacob and I talked in the barn. When we came inside, she made me promise to give it to you and to tell you that it was sent with much love."

Reluctantly, Sadie picked up the pie and lifted it so that she could smell the delicious aroma of the creamy mixture beneath the flaky crust.

The Grimm brothers stared at her as she held the pie, their faces bright and eager.

"Oh, a chicken pot pie!" Samuel said. "I haven't had one of those in years!"

"Might we eat it tonight?" Daniel asked as he licked his lips in anticipation.

Sadie sighed. God told his children to forgive their enemies. Perhaps she needed to trust Frederick and her father, and as part of that trust, she must forgive Rachel as well. After all, she would soon be married and leave her father's farm for good. Her interactions with Rachel would be limited, and Sadie didn't want her feelings toward her stepmother to come between Rachel and Jacob.

"I suppose I can heat it up, *ja*," she agreed. She looked at Frederick. "Will you stay for supper?"

But Frederick stood up, shaking his head. "Now, if you don't mind, I must hurry home. I need to speak to my parents and tell them the *gut* news. You can pack up your things this evening and I will fetch you tomorrow morning," Frederick said. "After I speak to my bishop, that is. And then we shall go speak to your bishop, in Echo Creek. But we shall visit him together."

She set down the pie and walked with him toward the

door. While she knew that it was only a matter of hours until she saw him again, it felt as if a lifetime would pass before then.

"Tomorrow shall never arrive soon enough," she whispered as she leaned against the doorframe, hoping that the Grimm brothers couldn't hear her.

Frederick reached out and brushed his thumb along her cheek. "Only days separate us from forever, Sadie. And then, as long as one of us breathes, we shall never leave the other's side."

He glanced over her shoulder before he bent down to brush his lips across her forehead, a chaste but tender kiss. And then he turned and hurried down the dirt path that led through the forest and toward the main road where he had tied his horse.

Behind her, Sadie could hear the clamoring of the brothers, eager for her to begin cooking the pie. But she couldn't tear her eyes from the place where Frederick had just disappeared. How was it possible that hours could feel like days and days feel like years? And yet she suspected that there would come a day in her life when she would look back on the joyous years she would spend with Frederick Keim and realize that, in reality, time spent with a loved one was only but a few seconds.

Chapter Twenty-Five

An hour after Frederick left, the room smelled delicious; the fresh scent of buttery pastry and the enticing smell of chicken filled every corner of the little house.

The Grimm brothers milled about the small room, eagerly awaiting the presentation of Rachel's famous chicken pot pie. Despite the fact that Sadie would be going home in the morning, their sadness had been replaced with joy when they had learned that she would soon be marrying Frederick.

And, once married, she had promised she would come visit twice a month to clean and do their laundry. It was a suggestion that was met with cheers from all seven of the brothers Grimm.

"Mayhaps you could bake us some bread each week, too," Hank said and laughed. "We'll be cousins by then, you know."

"And those cookies," Ben suggested, a blush covering his cheeks. "The chewy ones with oats and chocolate?"

Laughing, Sadie heartily agreed. "Of course. The cookies, too."

Sadie made her way over to the iron stove to check on the pie. She opened the oven door and peered inside. "Just a few more minutes," she announced as she took a knife and poked at the crust.

"Now, while we're waiting," Sadie said, "I have a going-away gift for each of you."

"A gift?" Ben's eyes widened.

"For us?" Hank grinned, his eyes alit with joy. "Oh, I love gifts!"

Gideon scowled at him. "When was the last time you had a gift?"

Hank gave him a sly look. "Whenever it was, I can assure you that I enjoyed it tremendously!"

"Bah!"

Sadie ignored their bickering and hurried over to her little cot in the back corner of the room. She dug under her blankets and withdrew an armful of quilts. Carefully, she carried them to the table. For a moment, she stood there and stared at each one of the brothers. Despite their short time spent together, Sadie felt as if they were, indeed, her own kin. She'd never had siblings, but if she had, she imagined that she would have felt as much love for them as she felt for the Grimm brothers.

"I can never repay you for your kindness in taking me in and keeping me safe." She gave them each a small smile, hoping she didn't get too emotional and start to cry. "You will never know the way your acceptance and care has warmed my heart. During a time of great turmoil in my life, you showed me that, even in the darkest part of the forest, a light shines bright."

Ben blushed, and Hank gave a little laugh.

"To thank you, I made each of you your own brand-new quilt." She set down the stack of quilts and held one up. The different colored squares, each pieced together by hand, created a lively pattern. In the center of each square was a piece of yarn, knotted to hold the backing in place.

"During the cold winter months, you will be wrapped

in these blankets, which were made with my appreciation as well as my love, and I hope you will think of me."

She had dreaded the thought of giving the Grimm brothers the quilts, afraid she might cry. While she was eager to return home and prepare for her wedding to Frederick, she would miss each and every one of the Grimm brothers, even grumpy Gideon.

For a moment, the brothers simply stared at the quilts, their eyes wide and their expressions blank. Sadie watched them, wondering at their reaction. Didn't they like the quilts?

And then, to her surprise, she saw Gideon turn his head, but not before he swiped at his eye, the quilt clutched in his hands.

David cleared his throat and looked at Sadie, his own eyes watery. "Sadie," he began. "That night when I found you, exhausted and asleep in a pile of leaves, you truly surprised me. And my *bruders* were just as surprised when I returned home, reporting that I had found a young woman in the woods. We carried you here in our arms." He extended his short arms and stared at them as if remembering that moment.

"But nothing surprised any of us more than the way you have accepted us for what we are: men," he continued. Several of his brothers nodded their heads. "You never once treated us any differently than people normally treat each other. Being smaller than other men has not been easy for any of us."

His words touched her heart. For a moment, she thought of Adam; the Amish community had not been kind to him, either. *What is it about the way a person looks on the outside that makes people judge the inside?* she thought.

It was a shame, too, because the Grimm brothers were some of the kindest Amish men she had ever known. They would have made excellent husbands and attentive fathers.

By judging them so severely, the world had missed out on knowing these wonderful men.

She felt humbled by David's words and wasn't certain how to respond. "I reckon I did what others *should* have done," she said at last. "It's not the size of the man, but the size of the heart in the man that counts."

Ben blushed.

David took a moment to wipe his eyeglasses on the edge of his shirt. When he put them back on the bridge of his nose, he met her gaze once more. "Thanks to you and your kindness, we are not only looking forward to welcoming you into our family, but we are looking forward to visiting you and Frederick in your new home."

Gideon spoke up. "I may or may not join them. I haven't made up my mind yet."

Sadie tried not to smile.

"To thank you for your attentiveness while you were here," David continued, "we, too, have a small gift for you. Just something for you to remember us by." He reached down, and from his brother Samuel's outstretched hand, he took a wooden figurine. He looked at it for a moment and then, with great pride in his eyes, he handed it over to her. "We all took turns carving this for you."

It was a small figurine of a bird.

"Your songs delighted us each morning and night," David said. "You will always be the 'little songbird' to us."

"*Our* little songbird," Stevie added, then sneezed twice.

"Didn't you take your allergy medicine?" Gideon snapped.

He shook his head. "Not yet." Another sneeze. "I'll look for the new bottle after supper."

Sadie turned the figurine over in her hands, inspecting it from every angle. Oh, how she would treasure this beautiful gift!

"I don't think I can ever tell you how very special this

is to me," she whispered, still studying the intricate carvings of the wooden figurine in her hands. "My time spent with you has been some of the happiest I can remember."

"Even when Gideon tracked mud everywhere?"

She laughed. "I could've done without that mess, but yes, I treasure that memory, too." She narrowed her eyes in a teasing way as she looked at Gideon. "Mayhaps you might remember to remove your boots before you enter the *haus*, *ja*?"

"Bah!" But hidden in his scowl was the hint of a smile.

A moment of silence fell among them. It was as though no one quite knew what to say next. Sadie took the opportunity to fetch the pie from the oven and set it down on the counter to cool a bit. She was suddenly famished and couldn't wait to dig in to the chicken pot pie.

"Now," Sadie said, changing the subject because she wasn't used to such sentimental displays of affection, "I suggest we bow our heads in prayer, then enjoy this savory pot pie before it gets cold, don't you think?"

No one argued with her as the Grimm brothers took their seats at the long wooden table. Sadie stood up and carried the pie from the counter to a trivet in the center of the table, where she dished a serving onto everyone's plate, saving herself for last.

David bowed his head for the silent prayer and Sadie said a special thank-you to God for having brought the Grimm brothers into her life. They were just one more of God's indescribable gifts.

When the prayer ended, the men began to eat while Sadie poked at the food with her spoon. She was feeling melancholy and didn't really have much of an appetite. In a way, she knew that a small part of her would miss living with the Grimm brothers. Each of the men had such a unique personality, and in some ways, they behaved more like naughty children than adults. Perhaps it was because they lived alone, deep in the woods, far removed from the rest of the Amish community.

Still, she found comfort in the fact that she would soon be their true cousin and thus would surely be seeing them often.

"It's *gut*!" Hank announced, a broad smile on his face as he chewed his first bite.

"Is it now?" Sadie lifted her fork and scooped up a large forkful. "I shouldn't be surprised. For all of Rachel's flaws, she has always been a *wunderbarr* cook."

She lifted the fork to her mouth and tasted it. She couldn't remember the last time Rachel had made a pot pie. As she savored the taste of the rich, creamy filling, Sadie wondered why. It was one of the best chicken pot pies she had ever tasted. The chicken was moist and the carrots so sweet they practically melted in her mouth, and the pastry was so flaky and golden brown; obviously it had been brushed with an egg wash.

"I have to agree with you," she said between bites. "It is *wunderbarr*."

"Mayhaps she'll make a few more of these pies for your wedding feast!" Samuel said before suppressing a yawn. "Although I'm so sleepy, I'm not certain I can finish it." He stared at his plate and sighed. "Perhaps I will save the rest for lunch tomorrow."

Gideon eyed him—and the leftovers on his plate. Clearly he was not pleased and let his thoughts be known. "Don't waste food, Samuel. Remember what Mother always told us!"

Hank laughed.

Apparently Samuel didn't need much encouragement to awaken and shovel another forkful of pie into his mouth. He could tell Gideon was ready to eat the rest of his food, and it was too good to give up, despite how tired he was.

When Sadie had finished her last bite and set her plate to the side, she felt a rumbling in her stomach. It twisted and turned in a way that made her realize something wasn't quite right. And her throat began to feel odd, as if she had eaten cotton. It was soon followed by a strange prickling sensation. Setting down her fork, she reached for her glass of water. As she started to take a sip, she felt her throat constrict. She swallowed, hoping that the cool water would quell the feeling of dryness that made it suddenly difficult to breathe, but that didn't help.

The itchiness she felt didn't go away.

She noticed that David was watching her, his eyes wide behind his glasses. "Sadie?"

She cleared her throat, not once but twice. It felt scratchy and tingly. The constriction made it difficult to breathe. Perhaps she, too, was suffering from allergies. She reached up and placed her hands around her neck, applying gentle pressure. Beneath her fingertips, she could feel her pulse. It quickened, throbbing as if her veins were also gasping for air.

If she didn't know better, she'd think she was having an allergic reaction. But Sadie knew that there were no apples in the cottage, and certainly nothing that they had eaten would have contained that forbidden fruit.

"Are you feeling okay?" Ben questioned, his eyes wide with concern. The other brothers were on their feet, crowding around the chair where she sat.

"You don't look so good," Ben whispered.

"That's a terrible thing to say to a woman!" Gideon scowled. "Even I know not to say such things to a woman!"

But even Samuel agreed with Ben. "Maybe she just needs a good night's rest. Too much excitement?"

Stevie added his own observation. "Her face. It's swelling."

Sadie started to drink the water, but she found that she

was so weak, she could hardly raise the glass to her lips. It fell from her hand, shattering on the floor.

David reached for her arm, just as she started to fall over. "Get her to bed!" Without hesitation, six more pairs of hands took hold of her and gently lifted her off the chair, then carried her over to the makeshift bed near the fireplace. Ben smoothed out the blankets and fluffed the pillow while the others laid her down on the heap of quilts.

"I told you she just needs to rest," Samuel said.

Gideon elbowed him. "Shush now!"

David sat on the edge of the bed next to Sadie and leaned over so that he could touch her forehead. "Sadie? What's happening?" He removed his hand. "You're clammy, and your face"—he hesitated—"well, it's swollen and it's covered in hives."

At that moment, Sadie knew. Oh, the extent of her stepmother's jealousy! "Apples," she managed to whisper through her parched lips. "She must have put apples in the chicken pot pie."

"Who?" Samuel asked in a hushed voice.

"Rachel."

"But you're allergic to apples," Dan said.

"Thanks for pointing out the obvious," Gideon whispered.

Ignoring the others, David took charge. "We need to get her allergy medicine!" He stared at Stevie. "Fetch whatever you have left!"

Sadie shut her eyes. She could barely breathe. Her throat was swollen shut and when she tried to swallow, hoping to get some air, it felt as if she had bits of broken glass in her throat. In all of her life, she had never felt this way. She'd had several allergic reactions, mostly as a child, before her parents knew about her allergy to apples. But nothing, not even the soup that Rachel had inadvertently given to her just two weeks before, had caused her to react in such a way.

Surely Rachel had done this on purpose and with the most sinister of intentions.

In the fog of her mind, she heard the shuffling of feet. Was that someone standing by the bedside?

It was Stevie.

Her eyes were so swollen, she could barely open them to see him by David, an empty bottle of allergy medicine in his hand. He tipped it to the side and stared at his older brother. "I . . . I don't have any more."

Inwardly, she groaned.

"Check the bag Frederick brought," David commanded as he snatched the empty bottle and flung it to the floor. "He said he brought more medicine for you!"

She heard the panic in the room as more than one of the brothers ran to the counter where Frederick had placed the bag that had contained the pie. Someone rustled through the bag, and then the room was silent.

"What—what's wrong?" she managed to ask through her closed throat.

David placed his hand upon her arm. "Sadie, it appears that Frederick forgot to leave the medicine. The bag," he said, "it's empty."

"No medicine?" Gideon cried out.

"He must have forgotten to leave it," David repeated to his brother.

"Then we must get her medicine!" Gideon shouted, his voice alarmed instead of merely cantankerous. "Who shall go to town?"

David's large, frightened eyes fell onto Sadie's face and he cringed. "It's too far away," he mumbled. "And, without a horse, we won't get there in time."

The Grimm brothers began to bicker among themselves, but Sadie couldn't make sense of their words. She began to feel light-headed. "I . . . I have to sleep," she mumbled, not even sure if she was being heard. All she knew was that she couldn't breathe, and sleep was all she wanted.

A darkness began to engulf her and she tried to wave her hand. Everything would be all right, she thought, if she could only sleep.

"I . . . must . . ." She didn't finish the sentence before her head touched the pillow, her prayer *kapp* fell from her head, and her eyes shut. Sadie fell into a slumber so deep, no one could wake her.

Chapter Twenty-Six

Sadie could barely move. She didn't have to open her eyes to know that the Grimm brothers stood around her bed, waiting for her to say something. With her breath coming in short waves, accompanied by a high-pitched wheezing, it was all she could do to focus on her breathing, let alone talk. Her tongue felt thick in her mouth and she could barely swallow.

In all her life, she had never had such a bad reaction. Of course, when her parents had first learned that she was allergic to apples, they had taken every precaution to help her avoid being exposed to them. Even when she went to school, the community had come together and none of the parents sent apples to school in their children's lunch pails. Occasionally she had accidentally ingested something with apples in it, but usually it was in such a small quantity that she'd had just a minor reaction. Nothing like what she was experiencing tonight.

Now, however, Sadie feared the worst.

Could her stepmother have been filled with such jealousy and hatred that she wanted her dead? Or had she hoped to teach Sadie a lesson for running away and refusing to marry John?

In either case, Sadie knew she would have to find it in herself to forgive Rachel. It was the only way she could enter God's kingdom. And without any medicine, she feared that she would enter his kingdom a lot sooner than she had expected.

"Hello? Where is everyone?"

The voice filtered through the house and Sadie heard a murmuring among the brothers. But she had a hard time making sense of what she was hearing. Surely it wasn't the doctor. David had said they lived too far away to fetch the doctor. Hadn't he?

She wasn't even certain if she remembered *that* correctly.

More voices floated through the room. But Sadie was floating, too, in and out of consciousness. For what felt like a long moment, she was no longer in the Grimm brothers' house but in a large field. She was sitting among golden grass, beneath the most beautiful blue sky. And near her were birds, rabbits, and deer. They seemed to be speaking, and for once, she could understand what they were saying.

They were singing, too.

And Sadie smiled.

She felt light and breezy, sitting in the midst of that field. Without a care in the world and among the gentlest of animals. God's creatures.

"Sadie."

The voice came from behind her. Sadie slowly turned her neck, expecting to see someone approaching.

"Sadie!"

This time, the voice was sharper and closer by her ear. "Drink this."

A floral scent hit her nostrils and she inhaled deeply. It smelled like the color purple. She liked the color purple.

A coldness filled her mouth and then moved down her throat. At first, she wasn't certain what the sensation was. But it wasn't long before she felt it again. This time, she realized that it wasn't just coldness that filled her mouth, but wetness as well.

She drifted back and forth, between hearing the voice and sitting in the field listening to the animals sing. She had no idea why, but she felt torn between the two. Such a difficult decision, she thought each time she started to come around for a moment.

"Get me a cold cloth," the voice said, and moments later, she felt something cool on her forehead, a dampness covering her eyes.

She returned to the field, drifting away as she watched the animals once again.

The next voice she heard was dearly familiar. A deeper voice that stole her away from the field.

"How much of the antihistamine did you give her?" the voice asked.

"Double the recommended dose."

A pause before a third voice said, "Let me give her the adrenaline." Within seconds, she felt a pinch in her arm and, slowly, she drifted back to the field.

Then, all at once, the song ended, and the animals surrounded her. Sadie smiled at them, lifting her hand to let a bluebird rest upon her little finger. She thanked them for the song, but told them she had to leave now. Gently she flicked her hand upward and the bird fluttered away, slowly fading before her eyes.

She looked down at the other animals. Without moving their limbs, they began to disappear too.

"Goodbye," she called out, raising her hand to wave at them. "Until next time." But, for some reason, she knew that there would be no next time.

Her eyes fluttered open and it took her a moment to focus. Where was she? Over her head were rough rafters and wide plank boards. She blinked, focusing her eyes on them.

She wasn't at home. And this didn't look like the heaven she had always imagined, of that she was sure.

"Sadie!"

Slowly, she turned her head, her eyes focusing on the figure seated beside her. Frederick. She tried to smile, but it was hard to move her muscles.

"Don't move," he said quickly, pressing his hand on her shoulder so that she remained still. "Just rest."

"Wh-what happened?"

"Shh." Frederick stared down at her, his hazel eyes scanning her face.

Then, slowly, everything began to come back to her. Frederick's arrival from Echo Creek. The wonderful news that her father had approved their marriage. The gift of Rachel's chicken pot pie. The little songbird figurine. The tightening of her throat.

Sadie reached for his hand and, upon finding it, squeezed it with whatever strength she had left. "Apples. Rachel put apples in the pie."

Frederick took a deep breath. "We know, Sadie."

The enormity of the situation hit her. "I—I could've died," she whispered. Without medicine, that surely would have been the outcome.

"But you didn't, dear Sadie." Frederick held her hand tightly. "You will be fine, thanks be to God."

"How . . . ?" She shut her eyes as she tried to remember. "There was no medicine. David told me so. You hadn't left it."

Frederick's voice caught. "I know, Sadie. I was so overjoyed about my conversation with your *daed* that I forgot it." He clutched her hand, squeezing it. "When I unsaddled my horse, I discovered the medicine in my saddle bag. Part of me thought about waiting until morning to bring it to Stevie. I told myself he would be fine for just one night. But then a little voice in my head told me to turn around." He leaned his cheek against her hand. "Or perhaps it was me, selfishly wanting to see you again."

He pulled her hand up and pressed the back of it to his lips.

David appeared beside Frederick, his eyes wide, with dark circles beneath them. "Truly God must have spoken to our cousin, Sadie. Without that medicine, you would have left us for God's kingdom, for sure and certain."

For a moment, Sadie digested what David had just said. From the way they both looked so disheveled and worried, she knew how serious her situation had been. Truly she must have approached death. And yet, she had felt such peace, sitting in that field, surrounded by all the animals. Was it possible that she had been dreaming, her body's defense mechanism while she fought to live? Or had she truly been approaching heaven, the animals waiting to take her to God's kingdom?

"Thank God that I returned," Frederick whispered. "To think of what might have happened if I had not."

While it was true that without the medicine she might have left them, Sadie suspected that it was God who hadn't called her home. It wasn't her time to leave yet. But, after today, Sadie knew that, when her time did come, she would fear nothing, for God's kingdom was everything she had imagined.

Suddenly, it dawned on her that she was not in heaven, but on earth. And while she was here, she knew that there was something she did fear. Or, rather, someone: Rachel.

"Frederick!"

He clutched her hand tighter. "I'm here."

"Surely I cannot return to my *daed*'s *haus* now! What if she tries to poison me again? And my *daed* mustn't find out what Rachel did to me. It would ruin their marriage. Promise me that you won't tell him."

And then she heard it. Her father's voice.

"I'm afraid we already know."

Once again, Sadie tried to sit up. She felt warm hands upon her back as someone assisted her. She glanced to her right and saw that the bishop was seated to her left. And her father stood next to him.

"Daed!"

Jacob moved forward, kneeling by the side of the mattress. He reached for her hand and clutched it close to his heart. "Sadie," he said in a voice that cracked with emotion. "I came as soon as Samuel Grimm arrived at the *haus* and told me what had happened. I am so terribly sorry." He lowered his eyes. "I was afraid that we were going to lose you."

Sadie pressed her lips together, willing herself not to cry.

"I cannot believe Rachel did this." His eyes narrowed. "And yet I have no choice but to accept the truth. She must be completely mad. How could I not have seen it?"

The guilt that clung to her father broke Sadie's heart. But she had no words to console him.

"I believed her," Jacob murmured. "I believed that she was truly remorseful over what she had done. And yet, I know that I am not guiltless."

"Do not blame yourself," Sadie said, hoping to console him.

But Jacob didn't seem to hear her words. "Why, I never should've listened to her, Sadie. To think that I allowed her to convince me you'd be a good match for John Rabor." He shut his eyes and shook his head. "What a fool I was to listen to her!"

"Daed—"

He held up his hand, determined to continue. "*Nee*, Sadie, let me finish, for my shame is great."

She pressed her lips together and nodded. In all her

life, she had never seen her father look so forlorn and distressed.

"What I did was wrong," Jacob admitted. "There is no excuse, Sadie. In fact, I can't quite understand how it happened at all. Perhaps I just wanted peace in the *haus*. Perhaps I just needed Rachel to be at peace. Perhaps I just gave in because it was easier to do so. But I'm ashamed to admit that I was willing to condone your marrying a man who was ill-suited to you." He laughed, but there was no joy in it. "Completely ill-suited. I don't know how I ever thought otherwise. And when you ran away, I was distraught, knowing that my actions had played a part in your flight. I saw the error of my ways. That I had not listened to my own flesh and blood, but to a woman I realize now I know not. How ever can you forgive me?"

Sadie squeezed his hand. "You are forgiven, Daed."

He met her gaze. "You're far too generous, Sadie Whitaker. I fear that I am not deserving of your forgiveness."

Behind him, the bishop cleared his throat, and Sadie looked at him. "As for Rachel," he said in a solemn voice as he stroked his long beard, "you've nothing to fear, Sadie. You can return home safely, for she will not be a threat to you any longer."

Her eyes traveled from the bishop's face to her father's.

Jacob moistened his lips, the color draining from his cheeks. "Until you are married, she will be under the Meidung."

Sadie gasped. "Shunned?"

She had heard of people being shunned, but had never known anyone who actually *was* banned. Once shunned, Rachel would not be able to share a meal with others, worship with others, or even converse with members of their community, let alone members of neighboring communities. She would, in fact, be banished from all forms of Amish life until the bishop deemed otherwise.

Her father continued. "She will stay with the bishop and his *fraa*. Dorothy will provide spiritual guidance to Rachel until she confesses her sins to the church."

"*Will* she confess?" Sadie asked. She couldn't imagine the strength it would take to confess to having poisoned another person. Even harder to imagine was how Sadie could ever trust her stepmother again. She knew that, through prayer and her faith, she would eventually find a way to forgive Rachel, but could she truly forget? Could anyone?

The bishop raised a brow. "Rachel *is* willing to confess, *ja*. However, I have instructed her that the Meidung shall stay in effect until she has redeemed herself in the eyes of God."

Stunned, Sadie sank back into the pillows.

Lifting his chin, the bishop clenched his teeth, the muscle in his jaw tightening. "And that could be quite a while," he said tersely. "I'll not have her confess just so she can return to the *gut* favor of our community." His eyes softened as he returned his attention to Sadie. "As for you, Sadie, I will have you come home to Jacob's *haus* as soon as you are well enough to travel." He gestured toward Frederick. "I leave that decision in the hands of your future husband."

Frederick straightened his shoulders. "I'll make certain she is well tended to here at my cousins' *haus*."

The bishop nodded his approval. "Dorothy will come with some soup and to sit with her. I'll send her as soon as I return to Echo Creek." He leveled his gaze at Sadie. "I'm of the opinion that it's better to have another woman stay with you until you can travel. The way the Amish grapevine has been spreading like the weed of sin that it is, I won't risk having your reputation soiled by these most unusual of circumstances."

Sadie blushed and averted her eyes.

"In the meantime," he said as he set his straw hat upon his head and started to walk toward the door, "I must prepare my sermon for tomorrow's worship as well as prepare to announce the wedding banns for the two of you." He paused and looked at Frederick. "A week from next Tuesday, you say?"

Sadie's eyes widened.

"*Ja*, that's right." Frederick reached out and placed his hand on Sadie's arm. "And, unless Sadie objects, the wedding will be held at my parents' farm. My *maem* insists. Without her stepmother there to assist her, it would be too much of a burden for Sadie to prepare the *haus*." He smiled down at Sadie. "Besides, she is eager to meet her new *dochder*, who will be living with us in just nine days' time."

Nine days? Sadie could hardly believe it. "I've so much to do," she murmured, more for herself than for anyone else to hear.

But Frederick had heard her. "You've only one thing to do, Sadie Whitaker. And that's to rest. You leave the preparations for the wedding to my *maem*."

Obediently, she shut her eyes. She *was* tired and felt the need to sleep. Her body had fought a valiant battle and, apparently, won. Sleep would help her heal and would also help the time pass so that nine days would become eight and eight would become seven. While she was eager to return to her father's house, she was even more eager for the day she would join Frederick at his parents' farm as his wife.

Chapter Twenty-Seven

While every bride cherishes her wedding day, Sadie was struck by how different *her* wedding was from Belle's, the last wedding she had attended.

For starters, as Frederick had told her and the bishop, his mother had insisted that the wedding be held at their house. Sadie suspected that Frederick had made the suggestion, and for that she *was* grateful. With all the harsh memories still fresh in her mind, it would have been much too difficult to host the wedding at her father's house, despite the Amish tradition of the bride's family hosting the ceremony and reception.

When the big day arrived, Sadie was so nervous, she could hardly focus on the sermon. Instead, she kept searching the crowd of men across the room, seeking Frederick out in the sea of hats. Once she spotted him, each time her eyes met his, she found that he, too, was watching her.

It was with a giddy sort of happiness that she finally stood up and walked to the front of the room once the bishop beckoned them forward to exchange their sacred vows.

And then, afterward, Frederick never left her side. Without doubt, he was the most attentive groom she had ever witnessed. And how fortunate that he was all hers!

When they sat at the corner table to enjoy their first meal as husband and wife and greet the many guests who approached them to give their blessings, Frederick reached beneath the table to hold her hand. The touch of his warm fingers laced through hers sent goose bumps up her arms and made her heart flutter. He caressed her hand while remaining considerate of all the people who approached the table to congratulate them.

Oh, how joyously happy Sadie Whitaker Keim was!

For hours their family and friends gathered together, the older people leaving in the midafternoon so that the younger ones could enjoy even more food and desserts before singing well into the evening. For Sadie, time passed far too quickly, although she found herself eager for the nighttime—she hadn't spent one moment alone with Frederick all day.

By the time the last guest left, it was nearing ten o'clock. Frederick's parents had already retired for the night and now Sadie stood alone in the center of the large living room, staring at the remains of what had been the happiest, and perhaps the longest, day of her life.

The room was empty of furniture with the exception of several pine benches that needed to be put away. Someone had pushed them to the side of the room near the staircase. But the floor was dirty and the counter was covered with dishes and plates, thankfully mostly already washed.

A door opened and shut. Sadie moved away from the sitting area and peered around the corner into the kitchen. Unlike her father's small farmhouse, the Keims' home was a bit more modern, with walls that folded and unfolded to accommodate large gatherings. Frederick had told her it was similar in style to the old houses lived in by the Amish in Lancaster County, Pennsylvania. However, because the house was old and had been retrofitted, when the walls were tucked away, the opening was not one large rectangular room. Instead, it was L-shaped.

Now, hidden by the corner of the wall, Sadie watched as Frederick removed his hat and set it on the counter. For a moment, he stood there, his hands on the Formica counter as he stared out the window into the darkness.

She wondered what he was thinking. Was he reflecting on the day as she had been just moments before he entered the house? Or was he thinking about the future and how different their lives would be now that they were married?

Quietly, Sadie slipped into the large kitchen and padded across the floor.

He turned as she neared.

"There's my Sadie," he said with a smile.

"And there's my Frederick," she teased back.

When she stopped and stood before him, he reached out his hand and brushed his finger along the side of her cheek. She shut her eyes and pressed her face against his touch.

"Tired?"

She nodded. She had awoken at five o'clock in the morning to help prepare for the day, although she wasn't certain she had slept a wink the night before. She was too focused on the fact that, never again, would she call her father's house her home. And she also couldn't stop thinking about her father being alone without Rachel. Who would cook for him? Clean for him?

Of course, the bishop would eventually lift the Meidung from Rachel. What would happen then? Was it possible for her father to welcome Rachel back after what she had tried to do to his daughter? He'd have to do that, for she was his wife and the bishop would most likely counsel them. But could he ever really trust her again?

Her thoughts wandered until Frederick brought her back to the present.

"I imagine you *are* tired," Frederick said, his voice barely heard in the quiet of the room. He glanced around.

"I reckon the rest of this mess can wait for us until the morning."

Sadie took a deep breath and surveyed the scene. The benches needed their legs folded and to be carried outside so that they could be put away in the church wagon. And the plates and glasses needed to be stored. Sadie also knew that she would help his mother wash all the floors before Frederick and his father moved the regular furniture back into the rooms and unfolded the walls so the living area was once again separated from the large kitchen.

Still, it wasn't an overwhelming amount of work. It would free up their time in the afternoon to assess what work they needed to do in order to move into the smaller *dawdihaus* next door. And that was something Sadie was excited to do.

"It's not too much of a mess," Sadie said quietly. "The women were awful kind to stay and wash all of those dishes. I've seen kitchens left in a lot worse shape after a wedding celebration."

Frederick gave a small laugh. "That's one way to look at it."

She stared up at him, her adoring eyes meeting his. "Overall, I'd say that it was a perfect day, wouldn't you?"

"Indeed I would."

"And your cousins came." She had almost expected the Grimm brothers to back out of attending the celebration. She knew how uncomfortable they were with being watched by strangers. However, true to their promise, they had come to both the worship service and the celebration afterward. And true to *her* promise, Sadie sent them home with boxes filled with all of their favorite sweets.

At the mention of his cousins, Frederick snapped his fingers. "I almost forgot something." He motioned for her to stay put and then he hurried over to his mother's pantry.

When he returned, he held a plain brown box. "I asked them to make this. A small wedding gift from me to you."

Embarrassed, Sadie hesitated before reaching out to take the package from his hand. It was wrapped in plain brown paper but had a piece of red string around it that was tied in a bow on top.

"It's heavy," she commented as she took it from him.

"Open it."

Carefully, she carried the box over to one of the long pine benches near the staircase and sat down. Placing the box on her lap, she carefully removed the string and unwrapped the paper, then lifted the top of the box and set it on the bench beside her. When she looked into the box, there was a piece of cloth covering something.

"What is it?" she asked.

Frederick chuckled, then took a seat beside her. He carefully removed the cloth and reached inside. For a moment, he struggled before lifting out a round piece of wood. It was easy to see that it was a cross section of a tree trunk, no more than two inches thick. On the one side it was unfinished and dry to the touch. But when Frederick turned it around, Sadie gasped.

Carved into the front was a beautiful scene. Trees lined the edge of a pond, their branches dipping toward the water. A rock jutted out along the water's edge, and upon that rock sat a little bird, its beak lifted just enough so that it was clear the bird was singing. Just behind the bird, higher on the bank, was a beautiful deer, a six-point buck, which appeared to be standing guard over the little songbird.

She hadn't expected a wedding gift from him.

"I . . . I have nothing to give in return."

He put his finger under her chin and tilted her head, so that he was peering down into her face. "Oh, Sadie, don't you know? You've given me the best gift."

She blinked. "I have?"

He gave a soft, gentle laugh. "*Ja*, you have, Sadie. You've given me *you*."

She felt the heat rise to her cheeks.

"And I vow to you that I will be the very best of husbands, loving my *fraa* as God loves us." He leaned down and gently brushed his lips against her forehead. "I will forever be your loving and loyal husband, Sadie Keim."

She shut her eyes, enjoying the feel of his soft lips as he kissed her. When she pressed her cheek against his shoulder, his arms tightened as he held her in a warm embrace. With a satisfied sigh, Sadie whispered, "And I will be your obedient and loving *fraa*, Frederick Keim."

For a long moment, they stood like that, holding each other in the middle of the kitchen. She inhaled the strong, musky scent of her husband and knew that she would never forget this beautiful moment. God had guided her through some difficult and challenging times. But she had never lost faith in his love for her. Time had quickly proven that he rewarded the faithful with goodness and joy.

Epilogue

Standing on the edge of the field, Sadie leaned against the fence and stared at the herd of cows as they grazed on the green grass. In the distance, she could make out the team of four Belgian mules pulling the cutter through the hay that grew in the back fields.

She squinted and lifted her hand to her brow to shield the sun, trying to see whether the man driving the team was Frederick or if it was one of the younger men who worked the farm alongside him.

So many things had happened since their wedding last autumn.

Right after the holidays, Frederick's father had agreed to allocate 100 acres for Frederick to begin his educational farming program. Within thirty days, word had spread, and more men applied to work the farm than Frederick could possibly accept.

Together, they had mulled over the applications and prayed. They were both saddened by the realization that they needed to turn some of the men away. But they were pleased that Frederick's idea had proven valuable to the young people and the community.

Four men had been selected from the many applicants to help with growing corn, cutting and baling hay, and tending to the small herd of dairy cows that Frederick bought from Sadie's father. Already he was making money and so were the young men who worked alongside him.

Sadie turned away from the cows and began to walk back to the small house where she lived with Frederick. It was only a *dawdihaus*, a two-bedroom structure right next to the main farmhouse, where Frederick's parents still lived with their two teenaged daughters.

Years before, Frederick's grandparents had lived in the *dawdihaus*. And, in two or three years, Frederick and Sadie would move into the larger house and *his* parents would live in the *dawdihaus*. One day, many years down the road, Sadie and Frederick would do the same: relinquish the larger house to one of their children and return to the smaller house. It seemed this was the circle of life on an Amish farm, and Sadie was grateful to be part of it.

But, for now, Sadie didn't mind living in the smaller house. It was warm and cozy, and it was where they'd welcome their first child this autumn.

As she passed the dairy barn, she heard her husband call for her.

Smiling, she stopped walking and waited for him to catch up. "I thought you'd be supervising the hay cutting."

Frederick shook his head. "*Nee*, Sadie. Those young men know what they're doing by now. What is this? Our third cutting of the season? Why, if we don't get our first frost early, we're bound to have at least two more cuttings this year!"

"Can you imagine?" Five hay cuttings would be a true blessing. They'd have more than enough hay to feed the cows and horses for the winter, plus some to sell to other farmers who needed extra for their own livestock.

Frederick gave her a warm smile. "There's a lot of things

I never could've imagined, Sadie Keim. Why, last year at this time, we hadn't even met yet! And now, ten months later, just look at us." He opened his arms and gestured around them. "We've our own little *haus*, our own little farm, and soon, our own little family."

Sadie let her hands caress her round belly. As if on cue, the baby rolled, its foot pressing against her hand. "If this *boppli* doesn't stop growing, I'm not so certain about the little part."

He laughed and leaned over to press his lips against her forehead.

"Speaking of little"—his mouth twitched as if trying to suppress his mirth—"you do remember that my cousins are coming to supper tonight, *ja*?"

"Frederick Keim!"

"Aw, you know I mean it with love."

Still, she gave him a teasing look of chastisement. "Of course, I remember. And I have a big"—she emphasized the word "big," which made him laugh once more—"meal for them. Plus, I invited your parents and *schwesters*. The more the merrier, don't you think?"

"The more the merrier, indeed," he agreed. "But remember that my favorite part of the day is spending time alone with you."

She blushed at his compliment.

"Now," he said, his tone changing from one of adoration to seriousness, "before the workday is finished, we have some business things to discuss."

"Oh? And what would that be?"

Frederick put his arm around her expanding waist and guided her toward the house. "Seems to me that your idea is taking off, Sadie Keim."

Startled, she looked at him. "What idea is that?"

"The one about raising the milk prices and marketing

our dairy products as healthier for people. Why, even your *daed* stopped by earlier to tell me that he's on board, too."

Sadie gasped. "My *daed*?"

"*Ja*, the one and only."

Sadie could hardly believe that her father had agreed. She wondered what Rachel thought of it.

Sadie still remembered hearing about how Rachel had knelt before the members of her former church district, sharing her confession. Ella had shared the details of the moment when Rachel, always so prideful of her appearance, burst into tears before every baptized member of Echo Creek.

While Sadie had been thankful that she had not witnessed that event, she did believe that Rachel was truly sorry for her actions, and she had forgiven her stepmother. It seemed that God, too, forgave her as, less than three months later, Sadie had learned that Rachel was, at last, pregnant.

Surely facing her flaws had redeemed Rachel, not just in the eyes of God and the community, but in her own heart and soul.

For that, Sadie was truly happy.

"And there's more!" Frederick gave Sadie a broad smile. Sadie could hardly wait to hear. "Do tell me!"

"Your dear friend Belle's husband is on board, too, and Ella's husband has agreed to not only carry the products in Troyers' General Store but his *daed* agreed to help with distribution to other stores." Frederick laughed and gave her a gentle squeeze. "It seems that the Little Songbird Dairy Products Company is off to a good start."

As they ascended the steps to their small house, a cow called out from the nearby pasture. Sadie glanced over her shoulder at it, not surprised to see the cow standing near the fence as it chewed its cud. Behind the pasture, birds flew across the growing hay toward the numerous birdhouses that lined the back field. And far in the distance she caught sight of a buck with a large rack upon its head as it stood atop the hill, gazing into the distance at a small herd of does that grazed nearby on the edge of the wooded area that they had designated a "No Hunting" zone.

A good start indeed, she thought as she followed Frederick into the house.

Recipes

Sadie's Bread

Ingredients

- ¼ ounce active dry yeast
- 2¼ cups warm water
- 3 tablespoons sugar
- 1 tablespoon salt
- 2 tablespoons vegetable oil
- 6 cups all-purpose flour

Instructions

Preheat oven to 375°F.

Dissolve yeast in warm water.

In a separate bowl, mix the sugar, salt, oil, and half of the flour. Add the dissolved yeast mixture and mix. Slowly, stir in remaining flour to form a soft dough

Turn onto a floured surface; knead until smooth and elastic, 8–10 minutes. Place in a bowl greased with oil, turning once to grease the top. Cover and let rise in a warm place until doubled in size. Punch dough down.

Turn onto a lightly floured surface; divide dough in half. Shape each into a loaf. Place in two greased 9x5 loaf pans. Cover and let rise until doubled, about 30–45 minutes.

Bake for 30–35 minutes or until bread is golden brown and sounds hollow when tapped. Remove both pans from oven and place on wire racks to cool.

Yield: 8–10 slices per loaf.

Root Vegetable and Apple Soup

Ingredients

    1 acorn squash
    2 butternut squash
    3 apples
    4 yellow onions
    4 tablespoons butter
    2 teaspoons salt
    ½ teaspoon black pepper
    2 cups water
    2 cups apple juice

Instructions

Separately peel and chop the acorn squash, butternut squash, apples, and onions.

Melt the butter in a large stock pan and add the onions. Cook uncovered over medium heat until the onions are translucent.

Add the squash, apples, salt, pepper, and water to the pot. Cook over low heat for 30–40 minutes, until the squash and apples soften.

Mash the vegetables until it becomes a soft puree. Add the apple juice. Add more water, salt, and pepper as needed.

Yield: 6–8 servings.

Simple Pie Crust

Ingredients

   1¼ cups all-purpose flour
   ¼ teaspoon salt
   ⅓ cup shortening
   4 to 5 tablespoons cold water

Instructions

In a bowl, combine flour and salt; cut in the shortening until crumbly. Gradually add water, tossing with a fork until a ball forms. Roll out pastry to fit a 9-inch or 10-inch pie plate. Transfer pastry to pie plate. Trim pastry to ½ inch beyond edge of pie plate; flute edges. Fill or bake shell according to recipe directions.

Yield: One 9-inch unbaked pastry shell.

Pumpkin Pie

Ingredients

   3 large eggs
   1 cup canned pumpkin
   1 cup evaporated milk

½ cup sugar
¼ cup maple syrup
1 teaspoon ground cinnamon
½ teaspoon salt
½ teaspoon ground nutmeg
½ teaspoon maple flavoring
½ teaspoon vanilla extract
1 unbaked pie shell

Instructions

Preheat oven to 400°F.

In a large bowl, beat the first 10 ingredients until smooth; pour into pie shell. Cover edge loosely with foil.

Bake for 10 minutes. Reduce heat to 350°; bake 40–45 minutes longer or until a knife inserted in the center comes out clean. Remove foil. Cool on a wire rack.

If decorative cutouts are desired, roll additional pastry to ⅛-inch thickness; cut out with 1-inch to 1½-inch leaf-shaped cookie cutters. With a sharp knife, score leaf veins on cutouts.

Place on an ungreased baking sheet. Bake at 400°F for 6–8 minutes or until golden brown. Remove to a wire rack to cool. Arrange around edge of pie. Garnish with whipped cream if desired.

Yield: 8 servings.

Chicken Pot Pie

Ingredients

2 cups diced potatoes
1 cup diced carrots
1 cup butter, cubed
1 cup chopped yellow onion
1 cup all-purpose flour
1 teaspoon salt
1 teaspoon dried thyme
Pepper to taste
2 cups chicken broth
1½ cups milk
3 cups cubed cooked chicken
1 cup peas
1 cup corn
2 unbaked pie shells (one for the bottom of the pie,
   one to cover it)

Instructions

Preheat oven to 425°F.

Bring a large saucepan of water to a boil. Cook potatoes
and carrots for no more than 10 minutes, until tender.

In a large skillet, heat butter over medium-high heat. Add
onion; cook and stir until tender. Stir in flour and season-
ings until blended. Gradually stir in broth and milk. Bring
to a boil, stirring constantly; cook and stir 2 minutes or
until thickened. Stir in chicken, peas, corn, and potato
mixture; remove from heat.

Unroll a pastry sheet into each of two 9-inch pie plates; trim even with rims. Add chicken mixture. Unroll remaining pastry; place over filling. Trim, seal and flute edges. Cut slits in tops.

Bake 35–40 minutes or until crust is lightly browned. Let stand 15 minutes before cutting.

Freezing option: Cover and freeze unbaked pies.
To use, remove from freezer 30 minutes before baking (do not thaw). Preheat oven to 425°F. Place pies on baking sheets; cover edges loosely with foil. Bake 30 minutes. Reduce oven setting to 350°F; bake 70–80 minutes longer or until crust is golden brown and a thermometer inserted in center reads 165°F.

Yield: 2 pot pies (8 servings each).

Chewy Oatmeal Cookies

Ingredients

> 1 cup butter, softened
> 1 cup sugar
> 1 cup packed brown sugar
> 2 large eggs
> 1 tablespoon molasses
> 2 teaspoons vanilla extract
> 2 cups flour
> 2 cups oats
> 1½ teaspoons baking soda
> 1 teaspoon ground cinnamon

½ teaspoon salt
1 cup chopped pecans
1 cup chocolate chips

Instructions

Preheat oven to 350°F.

In a large bowl, cream butter and sugars until light and
fluffy. Add the eggs, molasses, and vanilla; beat well.

Combine the flour, oats, baking soda, cinnamon, and salt;
gradually add to creamed mixture and mix well. Stir in
the pecans and chocolate chips. Drop by tablespoonfuls
2 inches apart onto greased baking sheets.

Bake for 9–10 minutes or until lightly browned. Cool on
pans for 2 minutes before removing to wire racks.

Yield: About 5 dozen.

*Don't miss any of the books in Sarah Price's
Amish Fairytale series!*

BELLE
An Amish Retelling of Beauty and the Beast

*In author Sarah Price's fresh and inspirational
retelling of a beloved classic, a dutiful young
Amish woman agrees to marry a notorious recluse
for her family's sake—but the consequences are
more than either bargained for . . .*

To most townsfolk, he's known simply as The Beast.
Annabelle Beiler has little interest in gossip, but she's
heard about Adam Hershberger's scars and his gruff,
solitary ways. Though he sounds like a character from
one of Belle's treasured books, the man is real and,
it turns out, just as unreasonable as the rumors claim.
When a buggy accident wipes out the last of her daed's
money, forcing him to sell their farm, Adam buys it.
Then he offers Belle a deal—marry him,
and her family can keep their home.

Everyone is shocked by Belle's decision, but she's
determined to be a good *fraa*, cleaning Adam's run-
down house and tending the overgrown garden.
Breaking through her new husband's icy reserve will
be another matter. Belle's courage and strength are
abundant, but it will take true faith to guide Adam
back to the heart of his Amish community—
and to the loving marriage they both deserve.

ELLA
An Amish Retelling of Cinderella

In Sarah Price's heartwarming Amish version of this best-loved fairytale, a hardworking, overlooked young woman is rewarded in unexpected ways . . .

"Be kind and have faith." Ella Troyer strives to abide by her mother's final words, although life in the small Amish town of Echo Creek isn't always easy. Her new stepmother, Linda, treats her coldly, and her two stepsisters, Drusilla and Anna, delight in gossip and laziness. After her father's death, Ella's stepsisters are free to attend youth singings while Ella stays at home to manage the household chores, rarely seeing another soul. Until one day, while running an errand, she has a chance meeting with a young Amish man from a nearby town.

Drusilla and Anna are full of admiration for charming, affluent newcomer Johannes Wagler, and Linda hopes to ensnare him as a husband for one of her girls—while keeping Ella out of the way. As for Hannes, he longs to catch another glimpse of the mysterious young woman who can sing so sweetly and bake the most delicious pie he's ever sampled. Now, with a little help from some unlikely sources, Ella dares to hope she might find her heart's dearest wishes—for love, family, and a home of her own—coming true at last . . .